THE PALACE OF GLASS

VOLUME III IN
THE FORBIDDEN LIBRARY

DJANGO WEXLER

KATHY DAWSON BOOKS

KATHY DAWSON BOOKS
PENGUIN YOUNG READERS GROUP
An imprint of Penguin Random House LLC
375 Hudson Street
New York, NY 10014

Text copyright © 2016 by Django Wexler.
Illustrations copyright © 2016 by Alexander Jansson.

Printed in the United States of America
978-0-8037-3978-9

1 3 5 7 9 10 8 6 4 2

Design by Jasmin Rubero
Text set in Lomba

This one is for *your* cat!

CONTENTS

THE PALACE
OF GLASS

PROLOGUE

IN HER NIGHTMARES, ALICE looked into the magic mirror and watched the steamship burn all over again.

Her father had been on that ship, the *Gideon*, rushing to South America for reasons she still didn't understand. When his ship had sunk with no survivors, Uncle Geryon had taken her in, giving her a place to live at his Pittsburgh estate with its fantastic library. When she'd fallen *inside* a book, it was Geryon who'd explained that this made her a Reader, like him, able to wield magic. To summon fantastic creatures out of books, to use their powers and even take on their forms. He'd introduced her to Ending the labyrinthine: a creature with the form of a great black cat who could manipulate space and distance and control the endless labyrinth of his library.

It was Geryon who'd saved her life, when she might have died fighting one of those creatures. And it was Geryon who'd sent her to the fortress of the Reader Esau-of-the-Waters, where she'd fought the labyrinthine Torment and his mad apprentice. Deep in the maze-demon's sanctum, she'd found the magic mirror and called up a vision of what had happened to her father.

And it was Geryon she'd seen in the mirror, Geryon who'd let the *Gideon* burn.

He'd been lying to her all along, claiming to know nothing about her father's fate, when he'd been responsible for his death.

When she woke from the latest nightmare, she lay in her small bed, beside the pair of stuffed rabbits she'd rescued from her former life, and shouted her rage into her pillow. She thumped the mattress, imagining it was the old Reader's face.

He can't get away with it. He won't get away with it.

Alice would have her revenge.

CHAPTER ONE
THE SIEGE

T HE DISTANT BUZZING GREW louder and louder.

"Isaac!" Alice shouted. "They're coming over the wall!"

"You have to keep them back!" he called. "If they get to the flower, this is all for nothing!"

That's *not very helpful.* Alice bit back a caustic remark. She could hear Isaac's summoned creatures fighting, the sleep-inducing song of the Siren and the *whoosh* of the salamander spitting flames, and she guessed he had his own problems.

They were in a little courtyard on an alien world, surrounded by a crumbling stone wall. Overhead, three suns, each touching the edge of the next like beads on a string, descended slowly through a violet sky. In the center of the yard was a squat stone hut that protected an ancient stone well.

In that well there was a flower, a huge white-and-purple thing, which would—Alice had been told—soon produce a crop of fruit. Geryon had instructed her in no uncertain terms to wait until the flower opened and then bring those fruits back to him. He had somehow *not* mentioned that an army of angry insects were intent on getting it for themselves.

The first of the enemy came over the wall: stick-thin legs hauling a bloated yellow-and-black body across the jagged rock. It looked like a wasp, with a segmented torso, gossamer-thin wings, and six legs, but as big as a good-sized dog. Its compound eyes, glittering like mirrors, were the size of Alice's clenched fist. A stinger like a butcher knife jutted from its hindquarters, and wide jaws held two pairs of long fangs.

The creatures were, she and Isaac had discovered, smarter than they looked.

Alice grabbed the Swarm thread and started calling swarmers into existence. As each one—an apple-sized ball of black fur with beady eyes and a long, sharp beak—dropped from nothingness to perch on her hand with a *quirk,* she tossed it up to the top of the wall. The swarmers scrabbled for purchase when they landed, hopping agilely from rock to rock, manning the ramparts of the fortress like a defending army.

The wasps could fly, but not higher than the level of Alice's head, so they needed to climb to get over the wall. That gave the swarmers a chance to attack, beaks slashing at the eyes and legs of the wasp-things. The first enemy to gain the top of the wall lost its grip and fell back under the blows of several swarmers, and the second had one eye punctured with a gush of black ichor. Alice stood in the courtyard below, the commanding general directing her forces.

The wasps were nothing if not single-minded. They ignored the swarmers, pushing the little creatures aside. One wasp, trailing a broken leg, lurched over the wall and flopped into the air like someone falling into a pool, the noise from its wings rising to a fast drone. It came at Alice, fangs bared, drifting through the air with the stately grace of a blimp.

Alice left the swarmers to fend for themselves and grabbed her club. It was a piece of wood about the length of a baseball bat, spreading to a wide paddle at the end. A flyswatter, Alice thought, for very large flies.

She wrapped Spike's thread around her, giving her the

dinosaur's strength, and her body was suddenly as light as a feather. She swung the swatter at the oncoming wasp, the end whistling through the air, and hit it so hard that its broken body splattered against the wall in a splash of goo. The next one got the same, and the next, while the swarmers sliced and poked at the flanks of still more as they came on.

Behind her, she caught a glimpse of Isaac fighting beside his own creatures, guarding the single gateway into the courtyard. The Siren, a barely visible wisp of a ghost-woman, held the gate, her hypnotic song keeping a good dozen wasps asleep at her feet. The iceling was nearby, a slim figure all in white like a statue made of packed snow. She directed bursts of icy air at the wasps as they tried to climb over the walls on that side, driving them back and shredding their wings with tiny splinters of flying ice.

Isaac himself attacked anything that got through. The salamander's fire jetted from his palms, producing a hose-like roar, and any wasp caught in it blackened and withered. Isaac's long, battered gray coat flapped around him as he moved, scorched here and there by stray sparks. Little grass fires burned merrily all around him.

Three wasps came at Alice at once, coordinating their attack to strike from all sides. She mashed the first one

into paste, and dodged the second as it swiped at her with its stinger, but the third darted in and sank its teeth into her side. Alice gave a yelp and bashed it on the head with her elbow, Spike's strength smashing its chitinous hide with a *crunch*. As it fell away, she ducked the third wasp again and fell back, toward the stone hut.

She released the swarmers and wrapped the Swarm thread around herself, imbuing her skin with the little creatures' rubbery toughness. Thus reinforced, she met the next wave of wasps without flinching, sweeping left and right with her swatter as they slashed and bit at her. Her clothes were ripped and torn, but the skin underneath was too tough for fangs or stingers, and the smashed bodies of her assailants piled up at her feet.

One of them landed on her back, gripping her with all six legs, fangs desperately trying to close on her neck. Alice spun, hand stretched over her shoulder, but couldn't get a grip on it.

"Hold still!" Isaac said.

She stopped, and a moment later felt a wash of heat as a precisely targeted burst of flame blew the creature into crispy bits. Alice turned, looking for a fresh target, but there were no more wasps in the air. She could see a few of them retreating the way they had come, over the wall.

"Looks like they've had enough for the moment," Isaac said. He patted his coat where it was smoldering, then came over to Alice. "Are you all right?"

"I'm fine." Alice shook some of the gunk off the end of her swatter.

Isaac frowned. "No, you're bleeding!"

Alice looked down. There was a red stain on her ruined shirt where the wasp had bit her, and now that her adrenaline was fading, the wound started to hurt. She winced and peeled her shirt up to have a look.

"It's not deep," she said, poking the cut gingerly. "I'll be okay."

"We ought to wash it out and bandage it," Isaac said. "As long as we're waiting for them to come back."

"I said I'll be—" She stopped when she saw his expression and sighed. Isaac could be very stubborn. "All right. There's water inside."

They had to push their way into the stone hut through a spray of wide green leaves that blocked the doorway. Inside, the flower sat on the side of the well, as big around as a car tire, several petals at its center still tightly furled.

They went to the opposite rim of the well. The water was only a few feet down, close enough that Alice could reach down with an empty canteen and hold it below the surface, watching the bubbles blub up until it was full. She sat down on the soft mulch of dead leaves, with her back to Isaac, and grit her teeth as he let a little water trickle across the wound.

When he peeled the bloodied fabric of her shirt away from the skin, Alice couldn't help letting out a little hiss of pain. Isaac flinched.

"Sorry," he said.

"I'm *fine*," Alice said. "Just get it over with."

"I'll try to be careful."

To distract herself, Alice nodded toward the huge flower. "Did your master tell you why he wants this thing?"

"No," Isaac said, pouring cold water from the canteen over the stinging cut. "Just that I wasn't to touch the flower until it opened, and that I should bring him four of the fruits inside. What about Geryon?"

"The same."

"And . . ." Isaac hesitated. "Are you still . . . working on what you talked about before?"

"Am I still going to get Geryon for killing my father, you mean?" Alice snapped.

Isaac winced, as though speaking the words aloud made them more real. "Yeah."

"Of course," Alice said. "Were you hoping I would give up?"

"No!" Isaac said. "I just—I worry about you."

Alice closed her eyes. The anger that had been born three months ago in Esau's fortress, when she'd watched the *Gideon* sink in Torment's magic mirror, had lodged like a hot coal behind her breastbone. It could be banked and quiescent, or flare to sudden, painful life, but it was always *there*, as impossible to ignore as a broken tooth. Now it burned bright, and her chest felt tight and hot.

"He has to pay for what he did," she said. "And I'm the only one who can make him. If I give up, he'll just *get away with it.*"

"I know!" Isaac said. He sounded miserable. "I know. You think I don't hate Anaxomander for what he did to my brother? But . . ."

"But what?"

"What can you actually *do*?" Isaac said. "Geryon's too strong to fight."

"I'm not just going to attack him," Alice said, anger flaring a little hotter. "Ending is helping me learn Writing, so I can craft my own magical books. She says that's where a Reader gets her true power."

In truth, it was something Alice had worried about

herself, alone in her bedroom at night. Writing was all well and good, but it went so *slowly*. No spell she'd tried to Write had ever worked properly, although she thought she was finally getting close. More to the point, even if she mastered the rudiments of it, she couldn't see how that would help her make Geryon answer for his crimes. *He's been building his power for thousands of years. How can I catch up?*

"Ending." Isaac's thoughts had gone in a different direction. "Do you trust her?"

"Why shouldn't I?"

"She's a labyrinthine," Isaac said. "Who knows why they do anything? Torment tried to kill us all."

"You don't have to remind me," Alice said, a little more harshly than she'd intended. "But Ending has always helped me."

"That doesn't mean she always will."

The Dragon had warned Alice against Ending as well, before it had gone to sleep. She shook her head. "What else am I supposed to do? She's the only ally I've got."

There was a pause.

"Against Geryon, I mean," Alice said. "I'm sorry. I know you're on my side too. But—"

"It's all right." Isaac stood up, dug in one of his coat's

many pockets, and handed her a roll of clean white bandage. "Here."

"Thank you." Alice stood as well. She tried to catch his eye, but he avoided her gaze. "I shouldn't have—"

"I said it's fine," Isaac said, a little too quickly. "I understand. I'll go check on the walls."

Before she could answer, he left, sliding out between the leafy branches. Alice pulled her shirt up and wound the bandage around her midsection a few times, then tied a knot to hold it in place.

What's he so sensitive for, anyway? she thought as she got out her knife to cut the rest of the roll free. *It's not as though he volunteered to help. All he ever tells me is "be careful."* Anger pulsed, hot and bright, and her lip twisted. Isaac had been the first other apprentice she'd met, her first real friend; they'd fought the Dragon and survived the terrors of Esau's fortress together. *But he still thinks he needs to protect me.*

"Alice!" Isaac's voice came from outside. At the same time, she felt a surge of alarm from the tree-sprite, who was still on guard in the maple tree.

"Be right there!" she shouted back, sheathing the knife. "Are they coming?"

"I think so," Isaac said. "But you'd better get out here."

CHAPTER TWO
THE CENTURY FRUIT

WHAT *IS* THAT THING?" Isaac said.

"It looks like a daddy longlegs," Alice said.

"With about a hundred wasps riding it," Isaac said.

They stood atop the stone wall, looking toward the three setting suns. Here and there, a wasp was visible in the grass, but they were all still, watching the progress of the gargantuan spider. Eight long, multi-jointed legs the size of steel girders supported a gray oval body, flecked with tiny black spots like hundreds of eyes. As Isaac had said, dozens of wasps were clinging to the bottom of the thing, which was considerably taller than the courtyard walls. It moved slowly but inexorably, and every footfall shook the rocks like distant thunder.

"If that many get inside the walls, we're not going to be able to keep them away from the flower," Isaac said. His earlier peevishness, Alice was glad to see, had been forgotten in the face of this new threat.

"Yeah," Alice said. "I think we have to try and stop it before it gets here."

"How? All we can reach are its feet. You don't have anything that can fly, do you?"

Alice shook her head, then looked at him speculatively. "Not exactly. But I might have an idea . . ."

It took a few moments to explain the plan, and a few more for Isaac to admit that he didn't have anything better. They slithered down from the wall into the grass outside the courtyard, Alice dragging her flyswatter behind her.

"Can't you clean that thing off, at least?" Isaac said. "It's covered in wasp goo."

"We're both covered in wasp goo," Alice said. "Get on with it."

Isaac sighed and thrust his hands in his pockets. He closed his eyes, and his form began to change. He grew slimmer, and color drained out of him, like he was becoming a black-and-white sketch of himself. Finally his features softened and changed, and instead of a boy standing in front of Alice, it was the snowy figure of the iceling.

"Here," Alice said, setting the flyswatter down.

"I can't help but feel this is a bit undignified," he said, his voice like a winter wind.

"You sound like Ashes," Alice said. "Hurry up. Some of those wasps are taking an interest."

Isaac squatted on the wide end of the flyswatter, hugging his knees, and flurries of ice and snow sprang up around him. The lines of his body blurred, melting into one another, rounding off the edges and filling in the gaps with snow. In a few seconds he had become, essentially, a snowball. Alice tried hard to stifle a giggle.

"I heard that," Isaac said, his wind-voice whistling from nowhere.

"Sorry."

"Just don't miss."

Alice nodded, called on Spike's strength, and lifted the flyswatter, careful not to tip Isaac off. She hefted it, feeling the weight of his snow-body, and turned to face the oncoming spider-thing. A loud drone nearby indicated that several wasps were getting close, but she focused on the length of wood in her hands.

Here goes nothing.

She ran forward a few steps, picking up momentum,

and swung the flyswatter over her shoulder with all of Spike's strength, like a lacrosse player chucking a ball into a net. Isaac soared into the air, gleaming in the light of the three setting suns, and Alice held her breath as he started to descend. She couldn't help an excited shout when the snowball impacted squarely on the side of the lumbering behemoth, a good thirty feet above the ground, smashing against it in a spray of snow.

The snow shifted, briefly flickering through the shape of a boy in a long, tattered coat before changing again into something long and lizard-like. The salamander was a brilliant, glowing crimson, red-hot claws digging into the side of the giant daddy longlegs, mouth gaping wide to spew liquid fire over the wasps that clung to the huge beast.

Then Alice's attention was drawn by more immediate problems. Half a dozen wasps were closing in on her, and she wrapped herself in the Swarm again just in time to let a stinger glance off her side. The wasps clustered in, buzzing furiously, and for a few minutes she had to devote her full attention to the fight, dodging and swinging and smashing the vicious insects into goo.

She looked up again as she fought her way clear. One of the spider's legs, as thick as a telephone pole, had been severed near the base, and it crashed to the ground in a cloud of dust. Isaac, still a salamander, went to work on the next leg. The wasps tried to rush him, but when they got close, he raised his head and breathed a cloud of fire, sending them falling away engulfed in flames.

The second leg went just as the insects tried again. This time, one of them dodged the billowing flames and got a grip on Isaac's back. He bucked, trying to dislodge it, but it clung tenaciously. The spider groaned, six remaining legs splayed, but it had lost its balance. It started to tip, falling with the slow inevitability of a great tree coming down.

Oh, no. Isaac, fully occupied with the wasp, didn't notice the collapse of the spider until it was too late. His claws scrabbled at its hide but couldn't hold on, and he started to slip.

Alice moved fast. She hurled her flyswatter aside, splattering one last wasp, and pulled the Swarm thread around her. Her body dissolved into hundreds of tiny, rubbery swarmers, bouncing through the grass. A kaleidoscope of images whirled around her, the world as seen through hundreds of beady little eyes, but Alice was used to this by now. She kept herself together in a single pack, racing over the ground toward the collapsing spider, trying to gauge the distance.

Isaac lost his grip and fell. He was shifting back into

a boy, but he didn't have time for another transformation. He didn't have anything like the Swarm, Alice knew, something to toughen his body or soften the landing. She pushed herself, tiny legs blurring, flowing around roots and rocks like a stream.

She got her tiny bodies underneath him just before he hit the ground. Isaac landed heavily on the swarmers and *bounced* back into the air, arms windmilling wildly, before landing again in the dirt a few feet away. Alice let the Swarm thread go, drawing herself back together, and found herself sitting in the grass. Her boots stood back by the wall where she'd left them. Try as she might, her transformations always left her footwear behind.

"Are you okay?" she said, hurrying over to Isaac in her socks. But he was already sitting up, rubbing his head.

"I think so." He winced, and gingerly touched the top of his skull. "I'm going to have quite a bump, though."

"Next time," Alice said, "I'll make sure to bind some sort of pillow-monster."

Behind them, the mammoth spider hit the ground in a spray of dirt and grass.

The wasps had evidently decided they'd met their match, because they didn't bother the two apprentices on their way back to the wall. Alice retrieved her boots as they went.

In the central hut, the huge flower had only one petal still closed, curled tightly at its very center.

"Thanks," Isaac said. "Did I say thanks?"

"Several times," Alice said.

"Sorry."

"Look," Alice said. "It's opening."

The last petal quivered, and with a slow sigh unrolled itself. The sweet scent of the flower filled the room. In the center of the mass of white-and-purple petals, six purple fruits, each about the size of an apple, hung from a long, drooping stem.

"That's it?" Isaac said. "That's what we came for?"

"Looks like it." Alice frowned. "There are supposed to be eight."

"That's what my master told me." Isaac reached in, carefully, and tapped one of the fruits with his finger. "Maybe it's not a good batch or something."

"There's three for each of us, anyway," Alice said. She grabbed one of the fruits and tugged. It came free of the stem with hardly any effort. "That'll have to be enough for Geryon."

Isaac nodded, and collected his own fruits, stuffing

them deep into the pockets of his coat. The flower was already wilting by the time they'd stripped the plant bare, purple leaves shriveling into brown gunk.

"I guess that's it," Isaac said.

"I guess." Alice held the three fruits awkwardly in one hand. "Where's your portal-book?"

"That way." Isaac pointed.

"Mine is this way," Alice said. "So. I'll see you some other time."

"Yeah."

There was a moment of awkward silence.

"I really am sorry I snapped at you," Alice said.

"You told me already," Isaac said.

"I—" Alice shook her head, not sure what to say. When she was with Isaac, her anger at Geryon seemed a little more distant, but the prospect of going back made it flare up again.

"I get it," Isaac said. "Just—"

"Be careful?" Alice finished for him.

"Yeah." He shifted uncomfortably. "There's something else. I shouldn't tell you this."

"What is it?"

"I overheard my master talking to some of his servants. He's calling a conference of all the Readers. I think they want to get to the bottom of what happened with Esau and Torment."

"Do you think they have a way to find out?" Alice said.

Alice, Isaac, and the other apprentices had been assigned by their masters to investigate the murder of the Reader Esau. When she'd returned, she'd mostly told Geryon the truth: Esau had been killed by his apprentice, Jacob, at the urging of the mad labyrinthine Torment, whom she and her fellow apprentices had defeated. She'd left out the fact that they'd only survived with help from the Dragon—a creature she'd bound from a prison-book that even Geryon couldn't control—and of course what she'd discovered at the end, in the magic mirror hidden in Torment's storeroom. *If Geryon finds out I know he killed my father, who knows what he'd do to me.*

"I don't know. But you should ask Ending." Isaac sighed. "I still don't know if we can trust a labyrinthine, but you're right. She's the best ally we have, and you're the one who's in the most danger. I worry about you."

Alice smiled, and her heart gave a little flip-flop, like a landed fish. "Thanks."

"I'd better go." He was blushing, just a little, as he turned away.

◈

Geryon's study faded into view around her, the portal-book on one of his side tables snapping itself shut. Geryon was waiting for her in his ancient, fraying chair. His desk was a mess, as always, covered with scraps of paper and bowls of the concoctions he used for Writing and binding his books.

"Welcome back, Alice," he said. "Your mission was a success, I trust?"

Alice was suddenly aware of what a state she was in. Her clothes hung ragged and torn, and her skin and hair were liberally smeared with dirt, blood, and wasp goo.

"Yes, sir," Alice said.

Geryon himself wore the same ratty, stained robe he always did. With his flyaway hair and fantastic, out-of-control sideburns, he cut an almost comical figure, if you ignored the cold, hard set of his eyes. Alice forced herself to meet his gaze, and not to flinch. She couldn't believe she'd ever thought of trusting this man. Disgust and hatred burned furiously inside her, and she had to fight to keep her expression neutral. His words scraped across her ears, and every moment that she had to pretend to be calm felt like holding back the tide.

If I summoned Spike, right now, he could charge across the room and put a horn through that nasty old man's chest.

She pictured Geryon pinned to the wall, like a butterfly mounted in an insect collection.

It wouldn't work, of course. Geryon hadn't gotten to be as old as he was by being careless. He'd have defenses, and his own summoned creatures to back him. In a head-on fight, she was still no match for him. *Patience.*

"You retrieved the century fruit?"

Alice held out one of the purple globes, and Geryon took it, his face betraying, for once, a hint of eagerness. He held it up to the lamp on his desk, admiring the smooth, unblemished skin.

"Ah, perfect. The very peak of ripeness. Exquisite."

"What is it good for?"

Geryon was pleased enough that he didn't mind this impertinence. "Many things. Elixirs of longevity, or protections against certain poisons. Crushed into ink, it makes an excellent medium for some types of spells."

He pressed his thumbnail against the skin of the fruit until it broke, then delicately peeled back a thin strip. Inside was a mass of little round seeds, translucent and faintly pink. Geryon worked one loose and held it between thumb and forefinger.

"But mostly," he murmured, "it's the taste."

He popped the seed into his mouth, and Alice heard it

crunch between his teeth. For a moment, his face went slack, and he let out a long, satisfied breath.

"They ripen only once every hundred years, you know," he went on, setting the fruit on his desk.

"Those wasp things certainly wanted them badly," Alice said.

Geryon chuckled without humor. "I daresay. They've been feeding that flower for a hundred years. Without the fruit, their queen will starve, and the rest of the colony will die with her."

Alice thought about the blind desperation with which the wasps had hurled themselves against her and Isaac. Her throat went thick.

Her master misinterpreted her expression. "Don't fret about it. Herd-wasps are useless creatures anyway. Not worth the trouble of binding. And there are plenty of other colonies out there." He leaned forward. "Now. The rest of the fruit?"

She handed over the two remaining globes. Geryon frowned.

"I instructed you to bring four," he said, voice taking on a hard edge.

"I'm sorry, sir," Alice said. "There were only six there, so Isaac and I thought—"

"You *thought*?" Geryon's lip twisted. "I *instructed* you to bring me four century fruit."

"Anaxomander told Isaac the same thing," Alice said. "There weren't enough."

"Then you should have taken what you needed by force," Geryon snapped.

"Isaac fought the wasps just as much as I did," Alice said, a sick feeling growing in her stomach to go with the hot anger in her chest. "It wouldn't be fair."

"*Fair* is not my concern." Geryon's face had gone cold. "You are entirely too friendly with this Isaac. I believe I will tell his master that any further joint ventures will have to be suspended until the two of you can correct your attitude." He put the two century fruits down and gave an irritated sigh. "I was going to let you taste this, as a reward for a job well done, but now I see I have been spoiling you. I will have to devise an appropriate punishment."

"Yes, sir," Alice grated. "I'm sorry, sir."

"Go. Do not come back until I call for you."

I could throw a swarmer at him, right in the eye—

"Yes, sir," Alice said, slipping out of the study.

Chapter Three
WRITING LESSONS

ALICE SAT ON THE dusty stone floor, eyes closed, cocooned in the warm, stale smell of Geryon's library. In her inner vision, swarming letters of liquid blue fire hovered tantalizingly on the edge of comprehensibility. There were hints and suggestions of meaning, brushing past her like moths in the dark. And if she could only line them up in the right order, if *this* piece would fit *here*, it would all suddenly become obvious ...

"Don't push too hard." Ending's voice was a thoughtful purr. "You cannot force clarity, or insight. If it will not link, find a way around."

It's so close, though. The last gap in the web she'd been constructing all afternoon obstinately remained unfilled. Her fingers twitched against the leather cover of the book by her side, and in her mind she saw a well of twisting blue-and-green fragments, circling endlessly like water around a drain. She teased them out, delicately, feeling them squirm and wriggle against her mental grip as if they were alive. She saw one that might fit *there,* and the end of it would link the other piece, which fit *here* . . .

Her father had once brought her a jigsaw puzzle with a picture of three kittens sleeping. Alice had put it together in one afternoon, but she kept it intact on her bedroom table for a week, unable to think of anything else to do with the thing. She'd decided it was a fairly pointless amusement, and had never asked for another. Now she wished she had, for the practice; *this* was like doing a jigsaw puzzle without the picture on the box, with pieces that twisted and *fought* when you tried to put them down.

The last link snapped into place, and the whole structure shivered. Alice released her mental grasp, tentatively, and saw the lines of azure flame tremble like trees in a strong wind. After a moment, they settled down, and the structure held. *It held!*

Alice opened her eyes. She was sitting in a dark corner of the library, in between two tall piles of books. A hurricane lamp burned by her left knee, throwing long shadows. Across from her, Ending lay in the gloom, her cat-slitted yellow eyes glowing with interest.

Between them were three thick pieces of parchment. When Alice had started, they'd been blank. Now they were covered with words, the same almost-but-not-quite-comprehensible script she'd seen in her mind, printed neatly in ink instead of written in blue fire. She could feel the meaning inside them, not random and undirected like the scraps she'd found in the books but tuned, harnessed, humming with power. Just glancing at them almost brought the magic forth, and she hurriedly looked away and started folding the sheets over, hiding the words from view.

"I did it," Alice said. The fatigue of a long day's work melted away in her excitement. "It held!"

"It certainly seems so," Ending rumbled. She yawned, and lantern light gleamed on her ivory fangs. "We'll have to test it, of course."

Excitement changed to frustration, all at once. The thing she'd constructed was a sort of trap for magical creatures, a set of wards that created a barrier that would contract until anything inside it was securely restrained. Ending had told her that creating this kind of magical trap was one of the simplest uses of Writing.

Simple or not, it had taken her a long time to get this far. Ending could only advise, never help her directly—the labyrinthine was a creature of magic, not a Reader, so for all her vast knowledge she could not see the scraps of magic and lines of meaning in books as Alice did. She could only explain things in general terms, leaving Alice to puzzle out the exact methods by herself through laborious guess-and-check.

If Geryon would teach me, things would be so much easier. Of course, if Geryon had been willing to teach her Writing, things might have been very different.

Ending said the creation of new books was one of the old Readers' most closely guarded secrets, the source of their power, and that learning it would help Alice undermine her master. But Alice's patience was fraying. The hot spark of anger in her chest wanted *action*, the sooner the better.

And now Ending wants to test the wards. A long series of tests, no doubt, and revisions to the spell, and then more tests and more revision. It made her want to scream.

"You should be proud," Ending said, as if sensing her mood. "You have come a long way in a very short time, without the instruction of a Reader to show you the path."

"It still doesn't *help*." Alice waved dismissively at the

wards. "Geryon's not going to fall for a trap like this, is he? How does this get us any closer to what we want?"

"One step at a time," Ending said. "Geryon will not teach you Writing because he knows with that knowledge you might threaten him. By learning what he does not wish you to know, you will see the limits of his power. One day—"

"One day," Alice said, and groaned. "You don't know what it's like. He calls me into his office, and I have to do what he says and act like I don't know *anything*. And all I can think about is what I'll do when I get my hands on him . . ."

"I understand," Ending said, voice low and dangerous. "Believe me, Alice, I understand. But I am a great deal older than you, and I have learned the virtues of patience. We will have our opportunity, sooner or later."

Alice had heard it all before. Privately, she thought that someone as paranoid as Geryon was not likely to grant them a perfect opportunity to take advantage of him. If they wanted a chance, they would have to *make* one. *No percentage in hanging about.* Her father's phrase made something in her chest twinge weakly, and she gritted her teeth.

"All right," she said. "How do we test the wards?"

"Later, I'm afraid," Ending said. "For now you had best return to your duties. I can sense that Mr. Wurms has begun to fret about your absence. We can experiment with your creation tomorrow."

Alice got to her feet, her legs complaining of so long spent in a single position. With a brief mental gesture, second nature now, she pulled on a thread at the back of her mind and brought swarmers tumbling into the world with a chorus of tiny *pops*. The little creatures scurried around for a moment, then organized themselves at her mental command, picking the books off their piles and carrying them, three or four swarmers to each. From Alice's height, it looked like the books had sprouted tiny black legs, following behind her like a line of literary ducklings.

Ashes was waiting for her as she walked back through the narrow aisles, perched atop the shelves and looking down with haughty yellow eyes. He was a small gray cat—a half-cat, he would insist, as a son of the labyrinthine Ending—who had been Alice's guide when she'd first snuck into the library. He walked beside her atop the bookcases, padding from shelf to shelf, his swishing tail raising waves of dust in his wake.

"Any luck?" he said.

"I got the spell to work," Alice said. "Ending says it needs testing."

"Fantastic." The cat stepped daintily across a narrow gap between shelves. "In another two hundred years, you might make something of yourself."

Alice had learned to shrug off Ashes' needling, which meant little more than that he was in a good mood. "I suppose *you* trained long and hard to do . . . whatever it is you do around here." She shot him a smirk.

"Training is for those not graced with natural talent, as all half-cats obviously are. And I'll have you know that my siblings and I are a vital part of the defenses of the library."

"Defenses against rodents, you mean."

"Can you see Master Geryon out here chasing the little terrors down himself?"

Alice chuckled, and Ashes hopped to the ground beside her, circling her ankles.

"Well?" the cat said. "Are we going to walk all the way there?"

"You're going to get fat if you keep being so lazy."

"You say that like it's a bad thing. For cats, being fat just means that you're winning."

Alice grinned and reached out for the strange, slippery

fabric of the labyrinth. Searching the library for scraps of magical power that had ripened in the vast collection since the last time she'd come through was still one of her primary duties, whenever Geryon didn't have a more important errand for her. It had grown much easier, however, since her return from Esau's fortress. Not only had her ability to sense the magic from a distance grown as her own power had expanded, but the Dragon's labyrinthine abilities also let her step across the library in moments. Ending's power over her own labyrinth was superior, obviously, but Alice could twist space as she liked as long as the labyrinthine didn't stop her. It was one way she managed to fit in her lessons in Writing while still finding enough magic to satisfy Mr. Wurms.

It was also a power Geryon knew nothing about. She'd kept it secret when she'd come back from Esau's, in spite of a few probing questions from her master about how, exactly, she'd defeated Torment. The more he didn't know, she reasoned, the easier he would be to fool.

She gripped the fabric in her mind, folding it over just around the next corner, so that *here* became *there*. Ashes stepped ahead of her through the gap—he seemed to be able to sense the fabric as well, presumably as a result of his half-labyrinthine ancestry. Alice rounded the corner and passed into familiar territory, an aisle between two tight-packed shelves that led to Mr. Wurms' table.

They found him sitting at his table, as always. He looked like an older man in a black suit, with a high, shiny forehead and thick spectacles, but Alice knew now that he wasn't really human. Like Mr. Black, the big, surly groundskeeper, he was a magical creature in Geryon's employ—not something the Reader had pulled out of a prison-book, the way Alice could summon the Swarm or Spike, but an intelligent being who'd agreed to serve.

He looked up at her approach, a cloud of dust rising from his clothes at the slight motion. Mr. Wurms spent most of his time filling thick leather volumes with tiny, precise script, only his fingers moving. When he saw Alice, he made an effort to smile, showing a mouth full of rotting teeth.

The first time she'd come to the library, Alice had been afraid of Mr. Wurms. There was a *hunger* about him, and his eyes, huge and blurry behind his spectacles, bored into hers in a way that made her uncomfortable. Now, though, Alice realized he was deliberately avoiding her gaze and his long, thin fingers twitched nervously.

He's afraid, she thought. *He's afraid of me.*

"Ms. Creighton," Mr. Wurms said in his rasping,

German-accented voice. "Have you had a good day's hunting?"

"Fair," Alice said. The swarmers rushed past her, stacking the books beside the table. Controlling so many of the little creatures was always a challenge, especially on a complex task, and Alice felt a touch of pride when they finished the pile without a single book toppling.

"Good, good." Mr. Wurms set his pen down and closed his ledger with a *thump*. Alice was taken aback. She wasn't sure she'd ever seen him stop writing. "Our presence has been requested at the house this afternoon. The master wishes to speak to everyone." He looked up at where Ashes sat atop the bookcases. "Including you, rat-catcher."

"I'd like to see *you* catch a rat, mister scribbler," Ashes said. "Tell you what, we'll see how long your precious books last if my brothers and sisters quit keeping the vermin down."

"Did he say what he wanted?" Alice said, ignoring the cat.

"No," Mr. Wurms said. "Most unusual."

He pushed his chair back from the table and stood up, joints *cracking* and *crunching* like someone chewing a mouthful of popcorn. He was much taller than Alice would have guessed, his legs long and stick-thin. More dust puffed off his jacket, filling the air with haze.

"Well," he said, glancing down at Alice with another sickly smile. "Shall we be off?"

CHAPTER FOUR
HOUSESITTING

SINCE ALICE'S LABYRINTHINE ABILITIES were a secret from everyone but Ending and Ashes, she had to walk all the way to the entrance of the library beside Mr. Wurms. She pulled open the bronze door and stepped outside into a world of cold and brilliant white.

The new year had come and gone, as unremarked as Christmas. Somewhere out in the world beyond, 1932 was getting started, but Alice felt as far away from that world as if she lived on the moon. *This* was her home now, among the books and the portals, and only these brief passages between them reminded her that there was a world beyond the infinite shelves of the library. And in any case, celebrating a holiday here would feel *wrong*, and only make her miss her father more than she already did.

It had started snowing in November and hadn't stopped. The forests that surrounded the estate on all sides were robed in white, skeletal trees piled thick with snow. The lawn between the house and the library was buried under at least two feet of the stuff, fine, dry powder that rose in great swirling pale gusts when the wind blew. A path, kept clear by the efforts of Mr. Black, led from the library to the kitchen door.

Ashes hopped up to his customary position on Alice's shoulder, staring at the snow with an exaggerated shudder. "Nasty stuff," he muttered. "Gets in your fur, and then when it melts you're just miserable."

"I don't mind it," Alice said. Today, the wind was blessedly absent, and the sky was a clear, crystalline blue.

"That's because you haven't *got* proper fur," Ashes growled. "It ought to be done away with."

"We can ask Geryon to get you a nice warm coat."

He gave her a withering look, and Alice smirked. She put one hand on Ashes' back to steady him and sprinted ahead of Mr. Wurms. The kitchen door was open, and she slipped gratefully into the warmth.

Mr. Black was waiting for her, a hulking, gigantic figure in coveralls and a dirty cap. His dark curly hair met his beard and mustache to form a thick black mane, from which his eyes peered out, tiny and suspicious. He grunted what might have been a greeting and turned away.

Alice understood, now, why Mr. Black had never liked her. Before she'd arrived, he'd been the chief among Geryon's servants, but as a magical creature, he would always be inferior in status to a Reader, no matter how young. In the past, he hadn't been shy about expressing his distaste, but since Alice had kept her mouth shut on the matter of Mr. Black's selling information to Esau, the big groundskeeper had treated her with a modicum of respect. Mostly this meant avoiding her whenever he could and speaking in monosyllables when he couldn't.

Now, seeing how he also wouldn't meet her eyes, Alice wondered if he was afraid of her too. With her threads coiling at the back of her mind, she certainly was no longer afraid of *him*; he might be big and tough, but he wasn't as strong as Spike or as indestructible as the Swarm.

"Alice," he muttered. He didn't call her "girl" anymore, either. "And the furball. I thought you were banned from the house after that business with the slippers."

"I am here," Ashes said primly, "at the master's invitation, on Mother's behalf."

41

Mr. Black grunted again and glanced at the door, where Mr. Wurms was just entering. "Come on, then. He's waiting."

The two armchairs in Geryon's study had been pushed aside, so Alice and the others had to line up in front of him, like troops being reviewed by a general.

Emma was already there, standing straight-backed, with every indication that she would be willing to do so until she collapsed from exhaustion. She was a skinny, freckled girl, taller than Alice, with a painfully blank expression. Unlike Mr. Wurms and Mr. Black, she was human, and had once been an ordinary girl with the Reader talent, just like Alice. She'd either refused to become Geryon's apprentice, or failed the old Reader somehow—Alice had never discovered which—and Geryon had *removed* the talent from her. The procedure had left Emma more like a robot than a human, mindlessly following instructions without any will of her own. The thought that this could have happened to her often figured in Alice's nightmares.

Geryon gave Alice a long look as she fell in beside Emma. It had only been a few days since the business with the century fruit, and the promised punishment had yet to materialize. *Is that what this is? But then what are the others doing here?*

"Alice," he said. "Gentlemen. I've called you here to inform you that I will be leaving the Library for a time."

Alice blinked and stood up a little straighter. Geryon hardly *ever* left the estate and never for more than a few hours. It was his fortress, his place of power. All the old Readers were so afraid of one another, in the murderous, twisting games they played, that they'd practically made themselves prisoners within their own defenses.

"I am leaving tomorrow morning, and I will be gone *precisely* one week. I have left an ample supply of power for the house wards until then. While I am not expecting trouble, should there be any difficulties, you should all take shelter in the library." He looked from Mr. Black to Mr. Wurms, and then to Alice, locking eyes with her for a moment. "Ending will be more than adequate to protect you, I'm sure."

Mr. Wurms nodded, and Mr. Black said, "Yes, master."

"Alice, the estate is in your charge until I return." Geryon's eyes flicked to the two non-humans, then to Ashes. "My apprentice is to be obeyed as though she were myself. Is that understood?"

Alice was sure she could hear Mr. Black grinding his teeth, but he nodded again.

Ashes cleared his throat. "When you say obeyed," he began, "do you mean—"

"I mean *obeyed*," Geryon said, a touch of rumbling thunder entering his voice. "Please inform your mother, as well."

"Yes, sir," the cat said, flattening himself against Alice's shoulder. His tail flipped back and forth.

"There should not be a great deal to do," Geryon said, returning his attention to Alice. "I expect to see you on my return, with a full report. Is that understood?"

"Yes, sir," Alice said, working hard to control her voice. "Good luck on your trip, sir."

"Thank you." He gave a brief, humorless smile. "That's all."

Mr. Black stomped back to his basement and Mr. Wurms returned to the library. Emma stood quietly in the main hall, with the blank look she got while waiting for instructions. Alice and Ashes went to the dining room, where the house's invisible servants prepared a meal of sausages swimming in gravy beside a mountain of mashed potatoes for Alice, and flakes of something that was probably tuna for the cat. Ashes ate with every sign of enjoyment, but Alice worked her way through the food mechanically, lost in thought.

Is this the meeting Isaac mentioned? To investigate what happened at Esau's fortress? If so, it could be serious trouble. *If Geryon somehow realizes I can use the Dragon's power, or that Ending has been helping me, who knows what he'll do?* She was worried for the labyrinthine, but more worried for herself. *Without her, I'll never find a way to get to Geryon.*

"I'm going to bed," she announced, letting her fork fall with a clatter.

"Don't mind me," Ashes called after her as she left the room. "I'll just struggle home through snowdrifts taller than my head. All in a day's work for a half-cat!"

Alice's hands were covered in blood, slimy and slick with the stuff. It squelched between her fingers, dripped down her forearms, and pattered to the ground like warm, salty rain.

She was in the forest, among the silent, snow-shrouded trees, beside a stream running fast and cold between icy banks. Her father was there, in his neat suit and his traveling hat, looking down at her gory hands with wide eyes. Alice looked up at him and felt her heart sink.

It's all right, she wanted to say. *It's not my blood. It'll wash right off.* But she couldn't speak, as if the winter chill had frozen her tongue in her mouth.

Instead, she knelt beside the stream and plunged her hands into it. It was deeper than it looked, deep enough that she couldn't touch the bottom, and for a moment she felt herself teetering on the edge of an unknowable abyss. The water was bitterly cold, and her skin went numb almost at once, but she bore with the chill and the pain, watching the blood stream off her in puffs and gouts.

Finally, she turned around, raising her hands for her father's inspection. *See?* she wanted to say. *All clean.*

But her hands weren't clean. Brilliant crimson drops still tumbled from her fingers and splashed silently into the snow.

Furious, and a little scared, she put her hands back into the stream. Her fingers started to hurt, spikes of pain shooting up her arms and into her shoulders. She kept them there until her hands felt like useless clubs, until it felt like her skin would shatter into icy fragments when she moved. She didn't care. Blood kept washing off, swirling eddies of it floating downstream.

At last, when she couldn't bear the pain a moment longer, she lifted her hands. Her fingers wouldn't move, and she could barely lift her arms. Her skin was still coated in slick blood, steaming in the cold air.

She looked at her father, and found his eyes had shifted away from her. Following his gaze, she saw that the stream had changed. The cold, clear water had thickened and shaded through pink and into red; a river of blood washed off her hands and flowed through the pure white landscape like a wandering knife-cut.

Alice looked from the stream to her hands, then desperately back up at her father.

It's not my fault! It's not!

He didn't look angry. He'd never looked angry, not with her. Just that little frown, the frown that broke her heart, that said he'd expected better. He shook his head, slowly, then touched the brim of his cap and turned away.

Wait! Alice struggled to her feet and ran after him, blood pattering and steaming beside her. *Wait, wait, please wait!* Her strides stretched, snow swallowing her feet, and something twisted beneath her. Suddenly she was falling—

—into a hard, narrow bed, moonlight painting a familiar pattern across the wall of her room near the top of Geryon's house.

She was breathing hard, heart slamming against her ribs. It was *cold*; she'd kicked the sheets and the blanket to the floor, and knocked her pillow aside. Her nightshirt was damp with sweat.

The same dream. She'd had the dream, or something like it, every few nights since she'd come back from Esau's fortress. It made her want to yell in frustration.

I know, all right? Father wouldn't want her to take revenge for his sake. She *knew* that, but the hot beast that roared inside her wouldn't let her rest. *What else am I supposed to do? Be his nice little apprentice, until ... what? Until I'm grown up and I can get away from here?*

She couldn't live like that. *Father would understand,* she wanted to shout at the dream. *He* would *understand.*

Or if he wouldn't—well, he was dead, and it didn't matter anymore.

Alice got up and stalked across the room, through the long-eared shadows thrown by the pair of stuffed rabbits in the window that were all she had left of her father's house. Anger seethed and roiled inside her, and for a moment she felt like if she didn't yell she might explode. She stopped, breathing hard, and swallowed the feeling. *I can't afford to show it. Not yet.*

Someday, though.

Little by little, her breathing calmed, and her heartbeat slowed. Alice picked up the sheets and blankets, remade the bed, and adjusted her pillow. She climbed back into the narrow bed, staring at the shadows of the rabbits for a moment, then closed her eyes.

Someday Geryon would understand just how badly he'd hurt her.

The next morning, Ashes was waiting outside her door.

"Geryon's off on his trip," the cat said, slinking into her room and winding himself around Alice's ankles. "Mother says she's got something important she wants to talk to you about."

"What is it?"

"Who knows?" Ashes yawned, showing his tiny white teeth. "Nobody tells me anything. But she said to bring a coat."

CHAPTER FIVE

MAKING YOUR OWN CHANCES

F OR ONCE, ALICE DIDN'T have to sneak off to meet
Ending. She simply announced to Mr. Wurms that she
was on Geryon's business, and the scholar accepted it
with a grumble.

The whole estate felt different with the master
away, as though a sound she'd never noticed had suddenly stopped. Everything still *worked*—the servants
brought her breakfast and cleaned her room while she
was out—but there was a feeling of living on borrowed
time. Geryon's power suffused the Library, keeping its
magic running day and night. Without that wellspring

50

of energy, everything was winding down, and sooner or later it would stop.

Alice had taken Ending's advice and dressed warm, in a fur-lined leather jacket, leather gloves, and thick trousers. It had been over eight months since she'd left her father's house, and many of the clothes she'd arrived with were either worn out or too small now. Fortunately, new additions to her wardrobe regularly materialized in the hallway outside her room. It was related to the invisible servants, she assumed—she couldn't imagine Geryon picking out clothes for a thirteen-year-old girl—but however the process worked, it had thoughtfully provided warmer garb as the days had grown cold.

Once she passed through the bronze door of the library, the air became warm and slightly stuffy, and she folded her coat over her arm. She chose a direction at random, and the first corner she turned brought her face-to-face with Ending.

"I hope you slept well." Ending's voice was a deep rumble.

"Well enough," Alice said irritably. Remnants of the dream still clung to her, like a spiderweb she couldn't quite brush off. "You heard about Geryon, I assume?"

"Of course. I felt him leave last night." Ending bared

her teeth. "He told me I am to obey you in his stead."

Alice smiled weakly, then shook her head. "Listen. Isaac told me something, while we were fighting the wasps. He overheard Anaxomander planning a conference of the old Readers, to investigate what happened at Esau's fortress. What if Geryon finds out what really happened?"

"A conference." Ending's eyes narrowed. "The death of one of their own is the only thing that could stir the old Readers from their complacency."

"They could find the magic mirror, couldn't they?"

"Without power, the memories would have faded by now. But if they question Torment himself . . ." Ending's tail flicked. "He was half-mad to begin with, and being dispersed and bound will not have improved matters. There's no way to know what he might tell them."

"So what are we going to *do*?"

Light glinted on long ivory fangs as Ending bared her teeth. "Strike first."

Alice blinked. "Strike?"

"Geryon's absence has given us a rare chance. I do not know if you are ready, but I think we must take the opportunity. It may not come again."

Alice felt her pulse quicken. "What opportunity?"

"You asked if your ward would be any use against

Geryon, and I said it would not. He would see any such primitive trap well in advance, and in any case his power is sufficient to break it. But there *is* a trap subtle enough to catch even Geryon, and strong enough to hold him. It is a weapon, crafted by one Reader to use against another. Its maker is dead now, and I believe the others have forgotten that it exists. But I remember." Ending's tail lashed. "It has been held beyond my reach. But if you can retrieve it . . ."

"We could trap Geryon?"

Ending nodded. "And keep him there until he agrees to our terms. But you must leave at once. Seven days may not be enough time, and if Geryon returns before you do, his suspicions will be aroused."

"I'm ready," Alice said. "Just tell me what I need to do."

After a little more thought, Alice decided she wasn't *quite* ready. With her experience in Esau's fortress still painfully strong in her memory, she resolved to be more prepared this time. She didn't have a proper pack, but a little work with knots transformed a pair of sheets into an acceptable alternative. She filled them with food she thought would travel well, a few canteens of water, and an extra shirt and set of underthings.

In addition to her supplies, she took her camping knife, three of the magic acorns charged with life-energy that had proven so useful in Esau's fortress, and the thick sheets of parchment on which she'd Written her first ward. All this made for quite a bundle, and she shifted it experimentally across her back as she went out the kitchen door again and back into the library, sweating in her leather coat in spite of the cool air.

Ending met her just inside the door, amid a swarm of smaller cats that were her children and grandchildren. The labyrinthine looked Alice over.

"Good," she said. "You will need this, as well."

Another cat, a white-and-black one Alice hadn't seen before, padded up to her with something in its mouth. It was a pocket watch, dangling from a delicate silver chain. The cat set it down, yawned, and wandered off.

"What is it?" Alice said, picking the thing up. It was intricately carved, the cover inscribed with an hourglass surrounded by tiny gears and levers.

"Essentially what it appears to be," Ending said. "Keeping track of time in other worlds can be a tricky business. This will tell you how long it has been here in the library."

Alice found the catch and clicked the cover open. In addition to the usual hour, minute, and second hands, a long, thin needle was just below the seven. *Days*, she realized. *Seven days until Geryon returns.*

"You must be back before it reaches zero," Ending said. "Or I will not be able to protect you from Geryon's wrath."

"I will," Alice said, snapping the watch shut and putting it in her innermost pocket.

"Let's go," Ending said.

Alice fell into step alongside Ending, who hugged the bookshelves and managed to stay in their shadow. Brief flickers of light threw silver highlights across her dark fur.

"I will not pretend," Ending said, after a moment, "that this journey will not be dangerous. I warned you our path would be difficult."

"I know," Alice said.

"I'm taking you to a portal-book that leads to a village of fire-sprites. They can be vicious creatures, but they have an agreement with Geryon. You should be able to secure their aid."

"All right."

"Elsewhere in their world is a wild portal, a rift between worlds not yet bound by a Reader's touch. The fire-sprites can show you the way there. What we need is on the other side."

"What exactly am I looking for?"

"A book, of course," Ending said. "The trap is in a book called *The Infinite Prison*. It is in a place called the Palace of Glass, somewhere beyond the wild portal."

Alice was beginning to wish she'd brought a notebook. "And I just have to find this book and bring it back?"

Ending nodded, then looked up at her. Alice had been getting better at reading the labyrinthine's moods in the set of her huge eyes, and now she thought the cat looked uncertain.

"The Palace of Glass is a dangerous place," Ending said. "It is said that anyone who goes there is driven mad, if they manage to return at all."

"I'll be all right," Alice said, forcing a smile. "Ashes always says I'm half-mad already."

"You must be careful."

They'd come to the back of the library, where clusters of shelves hid the portal- and prison-books. Passing among them, Alice smelled mowed grass, hot metal, and baking bread, and heard the roar of a crowd and strange, alien music.

Ending stopped. "This is where you'll find the book that will take you to the fire-sprites. You will probably want to remove your shoes and socks."

An octagon of empty bookshelves stood in front of them. The cracks between them glowed red, and even from here, Alice could feel the heat rolling over her in great waves that ruffled her hair. She dropped her pack and shrugged off her coat, folding it over one arm, and knelt to untie her shoes.

"You're sure I'm going to need the coat?" she said. But when she straightened up, the labyrinthine's yellow eyes were nowhere to be seen. *Typical.*

Alice picked up her pack again and pushed forward, edging gingerly into the crack between two of the shelves. It looked far too tight for her to squeeze all the way through, but somehow never quite narrowed enough to stop her, as though she were shrinking or the bookshelves were growing. She pushed through and emerged onto a wide, flat expanse of jagged black rock.

Her first breath was like being punched in the chest—the air was *hot,* and reeked of sulfur. She stumbled backward a step and felt a sharp pain in her bare foot. She'd cut it on a shard of black glass, one of thousands that littered the ground. She looked at the shoes in her hand and rolled her eyes. *Is this Ending's idea of a joke?*

Alice pulled on the silver Swarm thread at the back of her mind, wrapping it tightly around herself. Her skin toughened, becoming thick and rubbery, and when she stepped forward again, she felt the glass fragments *crunch* underfoot. The cut still hurt, but it wasn't bleeding badly, and Alice set her jaw and made her way forward.

At first she wasn't sure what she was looking at. The backs of the bookshelves were vast, dark monoliths now, soaring into the distance overhead. Black rock mounded into a small hill just ahead. On the other side of the hill, something glowed red-hot.

It wasn't until the surface of the glowing stuff shifted that Alice understood. The glow came from a lake of *lava* that filled the other half of the cluster, the hill of black rock pushing out above it like a promontory over the sea. With every step Alice took forward, the heat increased, as though she were climbing into an oven. At the top of the hill, she could see a boulder of the black glass—*obsidian,* her mind supplied—and atop that boulder, she was certain, there would be a book.

The ground underneath her was getting hot. Alice suddenly understood Ending's warning; the rubber soles of her shoes surely would have melted by now. Breathing was getting difficult. There was smoke coming off the lava, evil blue-gray stuff that smelled noxious.

When she reached the base of the little hill, Alice took a deep breath and held it, running the last few yards to the boulder. There was a book there, as she'd thought, a fat volume bound in black, cracking leather. Even with the Swarm's toughness, the scorching ground was painful, and she hopped from foot to foot while she flipped the cover open. The magical text crawled under her eyes for a moment, and then Alice read,

She found herself in a dark space, blessedly cool . . .

She found herself in a dark space, blessedly cool compared to the hellish scene she'd left. This was a relief—she'd been expecting something even *worse*—and she took a few moments just to breathe and let her feet cool against what felt like gritty rock. The air was still tinged with the scent of sulfur, but without that choking, nasty smoke. After a while, Alice began to realize it was not merely comfortable but actually chilly, and she fumbled her shoes and socks back on.

Letting go of the Swarm, she called on the devilfish, summoning a ghostly green glow around her hands. She was in a roughly circular tunnel, which stretched into darkness in one direction and dead-ended behind her in a chaotic jumble of fallen rock. Set among the tumbled stones was a portal-book, identical to the one she'd just opened.

Only one way to go, then. Alice took a moment to shrug into her coat. *No percentage in hanging about.*

She set off down the tunnel at a brisk walk, hand held aloft to light her way. For all that it was almost perfectly circular, it didn't feel like a man-made space. The passage twisted and turned, apparently at random, though the general trend seemed to be downward. There were no forks or side passages. Alice, feeling with her new senses, couldn't find the strange, slippery fabric that would have meant she was in a labyrinth.

Just because it's not a labyrinth doesn't mean it's not dangerous, of course. Ending had said the fire-sprites had some sort of agreement with Geryon, but hadn't given her much else to go on. *First I need to find them. Getting their help comes after—*

The sound, a grinding, crunching noise like someone chewing a mouthful of ice, gave her a split second of warning. Something shifted off to her left, and she turned her head in time to see a whole section of the rock wall come apart, dust billowing toward her in a cloud that stung her eyes. Alice backpedaled, one hand coming up to protect her face, and at the same time she instinctively wrapped the Swarm thread around herself, just before something big and heavy came through the still-swirling dust and slammed into her with the force of a boulder.

Alice was lifted off her feet and smashed against the opposite wall in a collision that would have shattered the bones of a normal girl. In this case, it was the wall that gave way, rock cracking behind her with a rumbling clatter, and she was suddenly falling. A moment later, she and her assailant landed hard and skidded across the stony ground.

That, Alice thought, *is* quite *enough of that.*

There was still too much dust in the air to get a clear look at her attacker, but she could feel the thing, sitting on top of her with the weight of a pile of rocks. The Swarm kept her from being squished, but it didn't make it any easier to breathe, and she was beginning to feel light-headed. She yanked Spike's thread around her as well, feeling the dinosaur's strength in her limbs. She gathered her legs under the thing and kicked out with both feet, sending it tumbling through the air to slam against another wall in an explosion of rock shards.

Breathing hard, Alice got up. She'd let the devilfish thread slip away in the confusion, but the chamber was

lit by a dull red glow that seemed to be coming from her opponent. Amid the billows of dust, she caught sight of a big, dog-like form, shoulders level with her chest. Instead of fur, the thing had lumpy, bulbous black stuff that looked more like rock than skin. It had two heads, side by side on a thick, stumpy neck. The glow came from each mouth and each set of eyes, as though the creature were lit by internal fires.

It had righted itself by the time she got to her feet, and

emitted a low, threatening growl like two stones scraping together. Alice stood her ground, spread her feet a little wider, and waited.

She expected it to charge again, going for her throat like the wolves she'd fought in Torment's palace. Instead, it came forward in quick dashes, pulling up short each time for another round of growling. The light inside it got steadily brighter. Alice worked out what was happening just in time to dive sideways as one glowing mouth opened wide to unleash a torrent of flames, lapping over the ground where she'd been standing.

The second head tracked her, preparing to do the same. Alice could see keeping her distance was not going to work. She pulled harder on the Swarm thread, triggering the transformation, and in mid-roll she disintegrated into a mass of tumbling, bouncing swarmers. Confused, the creature backed up a step before breathing another sheet of fire in her direction. The swarmers charged, slipping beneath the flames, *quirking* as stray sparks settled in their thick fur. They ran past the fire-creature, around and behind it, and melted together again into a very cross Alice.

"That," she said, aloud this time, "is *enough!*"

She grabbed the thing's back legs and lifted. It was

heavy, but Spike's strength was prodigious. Alice pivoted on one bare foot like a shot-putter, hoisting the rocky creature into the air. She spun in a half circle, building up momentum, then let go. The thing flew across the room and smashed into a wall with a clatter like colliding billiard balls, sliding to the ground amid a new cloud of dust.

Alice waited, panting, to see if it would get up again. The red glow flickered, then grew brighter again, and she saw the dim outline of the dog-thing climbing back to its feet. She frowned.

"You don't know when to give up, do you?" Alice stalked forward, rock chill against her bare feet—transforming, as always, had left her shoes behind—and raised her hands. "Come on. Let's get this over with—"

"No!"

Alice stopped in surprise. Another figure, this one humanoid and close to her own size, had appeared from nowhere and put itself between her and the dog-thing. It held a long, black spear, tipped with a dangerous-looking glass shard, which it leveled directly at Alice's throat.

"No!" the thing said again. "Leave him alone, *Reader*!"

CHAPTER SIX
FLICKER

ALICE PULLED UP SHORT and called on the devil-fish for more light. The dust was clearing, giving her a better look at the person standing opposite her.

He was slim and pale-skinned, wearing only a pair of ragged shorts. Though he had long hair and fine, androgynous features, Alice decided she thought he was a boy. If he'd been human, she would have guessed he was close to her own age. His eyes shone a deep red from within, but it was the brilliance of his hair that held her attention.

To say that it *glowed* wasn't doing it justice. It shone like liquid fire. It wasn't a solid red, but a shifting mass of color, crimson and orange and yellow, swirling and flickering around one another in a never-ending dance.

It lit up the tunnel just as real fire would have, the light rising and falling, clashing with the cold green glow of the devilfish.

He was breathing hard, letting out little puffs of steam, and his hands were tight on the shaft of his shaking spear.

"I'm not going to hurt you," she said. He ought to be able to understand her. Geryon had explained that the magic of Readers allowed them to communicate with practically anything.

"You were hurting Ishi." The spear-point wavered a little.

"Ishi? That's your . . . pet?" Alice said. The boy—a fire-sprite, surely—nodded. "It attacked me. I didn't mean to hurt it."

"He . . . didn't know it was you." The spear dropped a fraction. "You're not supposed to be up here. No one is. When we heard something moving around, we thought . . ."

The fire-sprite chewed his lower lip, trying to look down at the dog-thing and up at Alice at the same time. Alice let her hands fall.

"I'm not going to hurt you," she repeated. "Why don't you put the spear down and see if Ishi is all right?"

With one last, suspicious glance at Alice, the boy turned

away, kneeling beside the dog-thing. The tough, rocky creature was already on its feet, and the fire-sprite patted its two heads. Alice went to retrieve her boots, which were lying where she'd changed into the Swarm. The flames had singed them a little, but she was pleased to see they were mostly intact. The same could not be said for her pack, which had torn open in the fall and spilled food everywhere. She managed to tie it all up again with a few more knots and gathered everything that hadn't been ruined.

When she turned back to the fire-sprite, the boy was on his feet again, staring at Alice but not actually pointing his spear at her. She supposed that counted as an improvement.

"Ishi's all right," he said, "luckily for you."

"I'm glad I didn't hurt him," Alice said. "I'm Alice. What's your name?"

"Flicker." The boy peered at her. "You're not the Reader who usually comes, are you? Geryon."

Alice couldn't see how anyone could think that she and Geryon were the least bit similar, but she let this pass. "No. I'm his apprentice."

"Oh." Flicker's expression darkened again. "You should have sent a message ahead. Nobody ever comes up here anymore. You could've gotten lost."

"I'm sorry," Alice said. "I'm glad I ran into you, then."

"I'm not," Flicker said, and sighed. "With all this noise, there's no chance of catching the bluechill now. I had better take you back to see Pyros. Come on."

Flicker led her at a quick pace, padding barefoot through the cold, rocky tunnels. However much Flicker's hair *looked* like fire, it certainly didn't shed any warmth. Ishi stayed by his side, keeping well away from Alice, which felt a bit unfair. *He attacked me first, after all.* They entered an area where the passages showed definite signs of being adapted for habitation—the curved floors had been flattened, and there were arched doorways leading to chambers on either side. It all looked disused, though, and a thick layer of black dust covered everything. Here and there rocks had fallen from the ceiling and lay scattered on the floor. Every passage sloped down, as though they were descending into the heart of the world.

Her guide seemed determined to be uncommunicative. He directed her with grunts and gestures, as though he begrudged every word. If she was going to secure the firesprites' help, Alice decided, it was up to her to begin the conversation.

"Ishi is your pet?" she asked again.

Flicker looked over his shoulder, his expression pained. Since he'd decided she wasn't about to attack him, a kind of arrogant disdain had replaced his fear, as though he could hardly be bothered to talk to her. Alice could have understood a little irritation—after all, she was the intruder here—but this seemed uncalled for. *He could at least be polite.*

"He's my friend," the fire-sprite said, after a pause long enough to be insulting. "I wouldn't expect you to understand."

Alice wanted to argue but decided to let it pass. Instead she said, "If this area is abandoned, what were the two of you doing here?"

"Tracking the bluechill." He slammed the butt of his spear on the ground irritably. "We would have found it too, if you hadn't gotten in the way."

"I'm sorry," Alice said. "I expect you'll get another chance to catch it."

Flicker pulled up short and rounded on her, his red eyes blazing a bright hue. Yellow streaks flickered and danced in his mesmerizing, ever-shifting hair, as if responding to his emotions. His voice had a strange undertone, a crackling like the roar of a distant fire.

"The bluechill is a *monster*," he said. "It killed three

69

people last night and hurt a lot more. I *expect* I'll get another chance to catch it, yes, the next time it gets hungry. Assuming it doesn't pick me for dinner."

Ishi growled, picking up on Flicker's mood.

"I'm sorry," Alice said. "I didn't know—"

"Why should you?" Flicker snapped. "You're a Reader. You're just here to collect your precious tribute."

"I'm not—"

But the fire-sprite had already turned away, stomping around a corner with the dog-thing at his heels. Alice followed hurriedly, and they entered another long, downward-sloping corridor. The air grew perceptibly warmer as they went along, and at the far end a metal door was set into the rock. Another fire-sprite, tall and broad-shouldered, stood beside it with a black spear in his hand.

"I lost the bluechill," Flicker said, by way of introduction. "But I found the Reader. Pyros will want to see her."

"He wants to see you too," the guard said, staring openly at Alice.

Flicker muttered something under his breath, a sound like the sharp pop of a log on the hearth. "Come on, then, Reader. This way."

"My name is Alice," said Alice. "Not Reader."

Flicker didn't respond, and the guard dragged the door open with a creaking of old hinges. Alice followed the boy through, into the village of the fire-sprites.

While she'd encountered any number of beasts and monsters in her travels through the library and its books, Alice hadn't met many intelligent magical creatures, and hadn't had much opportunity to see the way they lived. There had been the needle-elves who'd nearly devoured her and Isaac, but she'd been too focused on getting herself out alive to really pay much attention.

Here, she felt like a tourist, wandering through a strange country and gawking at the native customs. The arched doorways here were covered by cloth or beaded curtains, and stone and glass tools were stacked neatly in corners. Confections of black glass hung from the walls, teased out into thin strings and elaborately interwoven and braided. They were beautiful, especially in the shifting light from Flicker's hair. Alice wasn't sure if they were decorative or had some more practical function.

Fire-sprites were everywhere, in the corridor or visible through doorways. Most were larger than Flicker, the size of human adults, and though they all had the same long, liquid-fire hair, Alice did not see any women among them. *I wonder if they live separately.* She'd heard of places on Earth where things were done that way.

There were children too, running and playing in a way that was not too dissimilar from human children, although once or twice Alice saw them kicking around tiny balls of fire as humans might toss a beanbag. They stopped their games as soon as they saw Alice and stared in wonder. The adults watched her too, but there was less awe and more anger in their glowing eyes. She could understand the curiosity—after all, with her leather coat and her dull, flame-less hair, she was probably just as odd to them as they were to her—but she wondered about the rage. She thought about asking Flicker, but before she got the chance, a little fire-sprite emerged from a doorway and wrapped him in a hug.

"Flicker! Are you okay?"

Flicker hugged the newcomer back and ran a hand through his hair affectionately. "I'm all right."

"I was so worried." The other fire-sprite pulled away slightly. He was shorter and thinner than Flicker, with a blue tint to his hair at the edges. "Pyros was very angry with you."

"I'll handle Pyros."

"Did you find the bluechill?" the smaller sprite said excitedly. "Did you kill it?"

Flicker shook his head. "I ran into this instead." He hooked a thumb at Alice. "I need to take her to Pyros."

The fire-sprite looked at Alice and blinked in confusion. "The Reader?"

"It's not the same one," Flicker said. "The old one was taller, and had hair on his face, remember?"

"This one must be a runt, then." The smaller sprite came up close, goggle-eyed, like someone peering into an aquarium.

"Actinia!" Flicker barked. "Stay out of her way."

"It's all right," Alice said. "My name is Alice. It's good to meet you." She offered her hand to shake.

Actinia gave a squeak like a teakettle and jumped backward. Then, hesitantly, he mimicked her gesture. Flicker's hand shot out and caught his wrist before they touched.

"Remember what your spark told you about Readers," he said, his voice low and dangerous. "Where can I find Pyros?"

"In the banquet hall," Actinia said, tearing his eyes away from Alice. "With the people who were hurt this morning."

"Then we'd better not keep him waiting." Flicker jerked his head to indicate Alice should follow. "Come on."

"I wasn't going to hurt him," she said as they left Actinia behind and passed through a beaded curtain.

"He's too curious for his own good," Flicker muttered. "In here."

A short corridor passed through another curtain and opened up into a high-vaulted cavern taller than any of the tunnels they'd come through. Huge slabs of polished rock were set out in rows, like tables for a feast, and smaller boulders might have served as chairs. A hundred fire-sprites could have dined there comfortably, but now there were only half a dozen, clustered around the tables nearest the door.

On those tables, Alice saw, a number of other fire-sprites were laid out. Smoke rose from them, little trails from their mouths and larger plumes from other places on their bodies. The closest one was missing his arm above the elbow, and smoke gushed from where it ought to have been.

They're bleeding, Alice realized, with a sudden sick feeling in her stomach. Her throat went thick.

"Pyros!" Flicker said.

The fire-sprites on their feet were gathered around one slab, their backs to Alice. One sprite, thin and frail compared to the rest, pointed a finger and said, "Try it again!"

Another one did something that produced a flare of orange light. The smoke stopped for a moment, then redoubled, accompanied by a fierce hiss like a bucket dumped on hot coals.

"Stop," the thin sprite said. "It's no good. He is with the Heartfire now."

All the sprites murmured something Alice couldn't catch, including Flicker. She saw him make an intricate gesture above his bare chest, ending with his fist against his heart.

"Pyros," Flicker said, more subdued now but still insistent.

The thin fire-sprite looked up. His hair, even longer than the others', wavered between a snowy white and ash gray, with only a small corona of bright flame reaching down to his ears. His face didn't have the lines a human's would, but something about the set of his dull red eyes gave Alice the impression of immense age.

"Flicker," the old sprite said with a sigh of relief like the creak of a forge bellows. "You're all right. And—" His eyes found Alice, and he ducked his head in a half bow, long white hair falling around him like a curtain. "Reader. I'm sorry. I didn't see you."

The other sprites turned to her at this, naked hostility

on their faces. One by one, they bent as Pyros had, but Alice felt herself shrinking under the glare of all those red eyes.

"It's all right," she said. "You don't have to do that."

"She's not the same one as last time," Flicker said. "She's a kindling of his, or something—"

"An apprentice," Pyros said, straightening to look Alice over. "Bitumen, can you see to Glare's arm? I must have words with the Reader in private, and I fear I am near exhaustion in any case."

He looked at the largest of the other sprites, standing close behind his shoulder. After a moment, the big man grunted, and Pyros gestured toward another curtained doorway leading off from the big room.

"If you would, Reader?" Pyros' eyes found Flicker, who had begun to edge to the rear. "And Flicker, I would appreciate it if you would join us."

Without waiting for an answer, the old man turned away. Flicker slunk after him, shoulders hunched. Alice followed. She couldn't help but glance at the table they'd all been gathered around, steeling herself for the sight of something gruesome, but there was nothing there but a pile of flaky gray ash.

Chapter Seven
AN OFFER OF AID

Pyros LED THEM TO a room with a few stone chairs and two of the elaborate glass sculptures. There were also a great many long stone cylinders, about as thick as Alice's arm, leaning in bundles against the walls or stacked in the corners. They were covered in intricate inscriptions, and Alice wondered if they served the fire-sprites in place of books. She hadn't seen any paper since she'd gotten here, or indeed anything that might have come from a plant; everything the sprites used for clothing or furnishing was made from leather, glass, or stone.

As soon as the beaded curtain had fallen closed behind them, Pyros spun on his heel, looking furious. Alice grabbed the Swarm thread at once, ready to defend herself, but the old man was advancing on Flicker, one bony hand coming up to slap the boy hard across the face. Flicker's hair pulsed a wild blue-white for a moment.

"You have been accused of many things," Pyros said, "but never, until now, of being an *utter fool*. What were you thinking?"

"That we have a better chance of finding the bluechill if someone looks for it," Flicker spat back. The impression of Pyros' hand was livid on his cheek. "That I'd rather *do* something than cower and hide."

"And what were you planning to do if you found it?"

"I had Ishi with me," Flicker said, sullen defiance in his voice. "And my spear."

"A hound and a boy with a spear against a monster out of legend," Pyros said. "I'm sure that would have been a fight to remember."

"Then I'd be dead," Flicker said. "So what? At this rate, we'll all be dead sooner or later. Better than just *waiting* here." His eyes, glowing bright, went to Alice. "Better than running to the *Readers* for help."

Pyros slashed a hand in the air. "Enough. Be silent." He turned to Alice. "I am sorry for that. Flicker is young, and like all youth, inclined to foolishness."

"It's all right," Alice said. "If he hadn't been there, I'd have had a hard time finding my way here."

She left out the part where Ishi had attacked her. Flicker watched her, eyes narrowed, trying to figure out what sort of game she was playing.

"A happy accident, then," Pyros said. "For both of you."

He turned and walked to one of the stone seats, limping a little, and waved Alice to another. She sat, shifting uncomfortably on the hard, cold rock.

"I am afraid I don't have much to offer in terms of hospitality," Pyros said. "In the past, Readers have told me that our food and drink does not agree with them. But I hope I can make you feel welcome here, nonetheless. We are honored to receive an apprentice of the great Master Geryon."

"Thank you," Alice said.

"And we are deeply grateful that he is willing to aid us in our time of need." Pyros bent his head again. "Please tell your master we appreciate his acting so quickly on our request."

Need? Alice thought quickly. Ending hadn't said anything about a request. *But better for everyone if they think I'm here on Geryon's business.*

"Yes," she said, making things up as she went along.

"The master appreciates your . . . your *loyalty*. I am here to help you however I can." She hesitated, then added, "Afterward, there may be some small matters in which you can help me, as well."

"Of course," Pyros said. "Anything we can do."

"What?" Flicker said, breaking his silence. "You can't mean that. You *know* what she wants. The agreement—"

"I said *enough*," Pyros spat, and bowed again toward Alice. "My apologies. We *are* grateful, I assure you."

"What exactly is the problem?" Alice said. "Flicker said something about a monster."

"A bluechill," Pyros said. "A terror my people thought we had left behind long ago, when we first came to this world. It must have come through the wild gate."

"It attacked your village?"

"Several times. We tried to kill it, but—"

"It can burrow through the rock," Flicker broke in. "Break from one tunnel into another, faster than we can follow. It came in through a wall and took two boys away before anyone else could get there."

Pyros glared at Flicker but nodded. "He is, unfortunately, correct. The bluechill feeds on heat and flame, and the village stands out like a beacon. It will eat until there is nothing left. And it is growing bolder. At first it would strike and flee, but now it confronts us without fear. A dozen men attempted to stop it, this last time. You have seen the results." Pyros sighed, a sound like a burned log collapsing in a hearth. "We would not trouble Master Geryon in the ordinary course of events. But I judged that, by the time of our next tribute, there would be no one left to pay."

"All right," Alice said. "So you want me to get rid of this thing."

"With a Reader's power, surely even a bluechill would be no match for you," Pyros said.

"A kindling Reader," Flicker said contemptuously. "This is a bad idea, Pyros. If the bluechill kills her, Geryon will be angry—"

"How many times must I tell you to be silent?" Pyros waved his hand. "Go and tell Actinia and Verid that you're alive. They'll be worried."

"I saw Actinia already," Flicker said, but he wasted no time slinking out through the curtain, with one last glare at Alice.

"Again," Pyros said. "I must apologize. He is young, and angry, and has no spark to guide him."

"Spark?" Alice said.

"The one who kindled him. His . . . father, I think you

would say? Mother? Though I understand it is different for Readers." Pyros shrugged. "I have never been to your world, I'm afraid."

"Oh." Alice felt a touch of fellowship for the boy. "I hope you won't punish him too badly."

Pyros shook his head. "He must learn not to be so reckless. But that is not your affair."

She nodded. "Can you predict when the bluechill will attack?"

"Not with any certainty. It is clever, for a beast. But it has been coming more frequently. It will be back, in no more than a few days. When it invades the village, you can confront it."

Alice could feel the watch ticking away in her pocket. *I can't wait around for a few days. But they're not likely to help while that monster is out there.* She thought of the smoking, agonized sprites, and the table spread with ash.

"Wouldn't it be better to fight it in a place where nobody else will get hurt?" Alice said, improvising. "Can we lure it somewhere? If it likes flame, maybe we could make a big fire."

"That might work," Pyros said thoughtfully. "It can sense heat from a long way off. But if you hurt it, it will flee through the rock. You will need to trap it somehow."

"I think I can manage that," Alice said. "We should start as soon as we can, before it comes back here."

"I agree. I will have material for the fire fetched." Pyros got to his feet. "You will need a guide. If you do not object, I will assign Flicker."

"Him?" Alice frowned. "He seems to hate me."

"He needs to learn to work with Readers, whatever his feelings," Pyros said. "And he owes me a penance for disobedience. You will find he is quite a clever boy, when he wants to be, and he has explored farther than anyone else." The old man hesitated. "Just . . . make sure that he is careful."

"I'll do my best," Alice said.

As they walked through the endless, meandering tunnels, Flicker told Alice, grudgingly, about his world. The boy seemed caught between his dislike of her and pride in his knowledge, and eventually he couldn't resist showing off.

"At the bottom of the world is the Heartfire, where the rock is so hot, it glows and runs like water. All these tunnels"—he waved a hand at the winding corridor they were walking through—"were formed by the Heartfire in the old days. They wind around and on top of each other, like a bucket of worms, all the way up to the surface."

"What's on the surface?" Alice said. She was fascinated. While she'd explored through quite a number of portal-books in her errands for Geryon, this was the first time she'd felt a real sense of being on another world.

"Nothing," Flicker said. "It's just cold and dark. I've been up there," he added with a touch of pride. "Nobody else from the village has done that."

"Is that where the bluechill comes from?"

Flicker nodded. "The wild gate is up there, somewhere. The bluechill comes from the other side. We used to live there, until—" He glanced at Alice, stopped, and shook his head sharply.

"Until what?"

"Never mind," Flicker said abruptly. "This is what we're looking for." He pointed ahead, where the corridor flared outward into a wider, taller space.

Alice held her glowing hand high to augment the light from Flicker's hair. The same lava that had made the tunnels had also created a natural amphitheater, a large, roughly circular room, dished at the bottom. Or perhaps not entirely natural—there were at least three doorways leading off into other passages that looked like they'd been shaped by intelligent hands.

"Did your people used to live here?" Alice said.

"When the Heartfire was warmer, and there were more of us," Flicker said, and scowled. "That was a long time ago."

He stalked to the center of the room, shrugging off the bulky ceramic pot he had strapped to his back. Alice carried one too, and she set it down next to Flicker as he removed the leather plug and poured a thin, translucent liquid into the round depression.

"Do you need help?" Alice said.

"You handle the killing, Reader. That's what you're good for, isn't it? Leave the fire to me."

He stared intently at the oily stuff. Alice wasn't sure what it was made of, but she'd gathered—from the shouted argument between Pyros and Flicker—that it was precious to the fire-sprites. The amount the two of them carried represented weeks of labor on the part of the villagers, and Flicker had been opposed to wasting it on a Reader's schemes.

Alice looked around for good places to set up her wards. Each of the three squares of parchment was folded over, to prevent her from Reading it before she was ready, and they needed to be set up at the points of a triangle around whatever she wanted to capture. She laid one of them on top of a fallen stone at the far end of the room, and wedged the second into a long, vertical crack running down the opposite wall. The last she took with her, back to where they'd come in, and set it on a boulder.

Flicker was emptying the second pot of fire-oil into the pool. Tiny wisps of white vapor rose from the surface of the stuff, as though it were impatient to burst into flame. When the pot was empty, Flicker got to his feet and looked over at her.

"Now what?"

"Light it, and get over here, as fast as you can." They'd guessed it would take the bluechill at least a few minutes to sense the heat and arrive, but Alice didn't want to risk Flicker's being caught in the ward when she activated it.

Flicker raised a hand, and a tiny flame burst into being above it, burning merrily in midair. He held it out over the pool, then hesitated.

"If this doesn't work," he said, "we're dead. You know that, right? We don't have a chance of hiding from the bluechill up here."

"It'll work," Alice said, then hesitated herself. *I never did test the ward, after all.* "If something goes wrong, though, just stay clear. I'll handle it."

"Believe me, I intend to." Flicker tipped his hand

over, letting the little fire fall. The fire-oil ignited with a *whoomph* and a burst of flame that raced across the surface of the pool. Tongues of fire rose up, a tall, steady blaze, licking close around Flicker. The fire-sprite's hair whipped in the draft from the flame, spreading around him like a halo and dancing with shifting colors.

"Quick!" Alice said, crouched against the boulder. Flicker gave the bonfire a last, longing look and jogged across the room to squat beside her. Heat rolled off him in waves.

They waited for a while, listening to the steady crackle of the bonfire. Whatever the fire-oil was, it burned remarkably evenly, producing tall, hot flame without much smoke. Alice could feel the warmth all the way across the room.

"How big is the bluechill?" Alice whispered.

"I've never seen it," Flicker said slowly. "But the men in the village said it was as tall as the corridors."

Another pause. Alice stared into the hypnotic shifting of the flames.

"Pyros told me about your . . . spark," Alice said carefully. "I'm sorry."

Flicker snorted. "Don't pretend you understand me, Reader. Or that you care."

Alice was about to protest that she *did* understand, when the boy raised a hand for silence. A moment later she heard a grinding sound, quiet at first but quickly growing louder. Flicker turned his head in a half circle, then pointed to one of the arched doorways.

"There," he said. "It's coming."

Chapter Eight

THE BLUECHILL

Alice squinted. In the tunnel on the other side of the room, something *was* moving. It looked like a constellation of fireflies, lights that twisted and slid weirdly, and it took her a moment to understand what she was seeing.

Ice. The bluechill looked as though it were made entirely of ice, great curved blocks of the stuff, twisting and reflecting the glow of the bonfire like a fun-house mirror. The reflected pinpricks shifted and slid across its slick surface as it moved, letting her get a better sense of the shape of the thing. It reminded Alice of a scorpion, a triangular body with three multi-jointed legs on each side. It had no claws, but a long, curving tail arched above it, three spear-like points gleaming at its tip. At the front, where its head should be, there was a chaotic jumble of crystalline shapes, spikes, and feathery fronds, like a hundred snowflakes grown huge and mashed together.

Its body was a single, polished crystal of ice, light sliding across its curves, and its limbs were chunks of ice linked one to the next like beads on a string. The spikes on its tail were the tips of icicles, dagger-sharp. It moved with a disturbing fluidity, legs rising and falling in perfect unison, like they were powered by clockwork. Each shift of its body brought a grinding, squeaking noise.

It *was* big enough to scrape the corridor ceiling, nearly the size of a car, each leg as long as Alice was tall. Her heart started to beat faster. *If the ward doesn't work . . .*

"Well, Reader?" Flicker whispered. "What are you waiting for?"

The bluechill stuck its ragged, chaotic snout into the flame. Alice would have expected the finer filigrees of ice to melt instantly in the heat, but instead it was the fire that diminished, flames swirling around the bluechill's protruding crystals like they were caught in a strong wind. Where the fire touched the creature, it vanished, drawn inside that glassy skin.

It really does eat the flame. The bluechill took another step forward, deeper into the bonfire. *Perfect.*

Alice turned to the ward she'd left on the boulder, unfolded the parchment, and Read the words she'd Written there.

It wasn't quite like going through a portal-book—there was no feeling of dislocation, only a *twist* somewhere in her mind as the magic took hold. Lines of milky-white energy shot out from each of the three parchments, joining up with one another and stretching upward to form a triangular wall of light. Then, following the instructions she'd Written into the magic, the barrier began to shrink, glowing brighter as it contracted toward the bonfire and the bluechill at its center.

For a few moments, the creature didn't notice what was happening, basking in the pool of oil as the fire guttered and waned. Then the bluechill looked up and seemed to notice something was wrong. It stepped free of the pool, legs moving surprisingly delicately for such a large beast, and approached one of the walls of light. One leg came up, scratching at the barrier with a sound like a knife pulled across glass.

Alice felt the scrape, not as pain but as a chilly sensation at the back of her mind. The energy to create and maintain the barrier came from her, just as it did when she summoned her creatures. The harder the bluechill pushed against the wards, the harder they had to push back to keep it contained. She gritted her teeth as the creature threw itself into the wall, slamming against raw magic with a burst of light and a crackle of sparks. The milky-white walls grew thicker as the barrier contracted, only a few dozen yards wide now, corralling the icy thing into the remains of the bonfire.

"Is it working?" Flicker asked, shouting over the sound of another scintillating discharge.

"I think so!" Alice said, but she wasn't certain. She was starting to feel light-headed, power flowing out of her like blood from a wound. *This can't be how it's supposed to work.* She ought to be able to maintain the wards with energy to spare, but her heart was hammering as though she'd just finished a sprint, and Flicker's voice was distant through a rising hum in her ears.

The barrier was only a little bigger than the bluechill now. The trap was almost finished. *Just a little more.* Alice clenched her fists.

The ice-thing screamed, a high, keening sound like shivering crystal. It reared up on its back legs and came down heavily on the barrier, slamming its three-spiked tail forward at the same time. The impact drove Alice to her knees, her vision going gray for a moment. She tasted blood in her mouth, and realized she'd bitten her tongue. *Just a little more . . .*

Something behind her gave a weird ripping sound, like a wire *twanging* under high tension, and then broke with a *snap* like a gunshot. It was followed by a spitting, crackling shower of sparks, which lit up the darkened room and fell all around Alice like tiny fireworks. She turned to look at the ward she'd laid on the boulder, but only for a moment. The magical script was glowing brighter than the sun at midday, and Alice had to slap her hands over her eyes. She could see the bones of her fingers, outlined against the orange flesh, and her vision was full of purple and green afterimages.

Then, with another *twang* and crackle of sparks, the light show ended as suddenly as it had begun. Alice gasped with relief as the power stopped flowing out of her, though she was still breathing hard and shivery with fatigue. She lowered her hands to see thick black smoke pouring up out of the ruined ward, pooling under the ceiling.

"Reader!" Flicker said.

Alice turned. The barrier was fading, the last few scraps of white light disappearing as she watched. Behind them, the bluechill stretched itself out, legs kicking through the extinguished pool of oil, then turned slowly until it faced in their direction.

Just once, Alice thought as it gave that keening crystal cry of rage, *it would be nice if something went according to plan.*

Alice wrapped the Swarm thread around herself and pulled on Spike's thread in a single, practiced mental motion.

"Find somewhere to hide!" Alice shouted to Flicker. "I'll draw it away."

She couldn't tell if the fire-sprite heard her. The bluechill thundered toward them, rippling legs a blur as it went into a sprint, the sound of ice on ice rising to a tortured shriek. Alice tensed, then threw herself sideways with all of Spike's strength, tucking into a tight ball and rolling like a swarmer until she bounced off the wall and popped back to her feet.

She'd expected the creature to follow the motion, but instead it went straight for the boulder where she'd laid the ward, shoving the weird collection of feathery icicles at the still-smoking parchment.

The heat, Alice realized belatedly. When the ward had broken, the writing had briefly glowed white-hot. For the bluechill, that heat was food. *It won't last long, though, compared to the bonfire—* *Oh, no.* The creature backed away from the boulder, moving slowly, and turned directly away from Alice. *Flicker.*

She'd miscalculated badly. In Esau's fortress, she'd saved her friends by drawing Torment's attention. But as the Dragon had told her, that had worked because Torment was half *wolf,* with a full set of lupine instincts. The bluechill, icy and alien, was operating on an entirely different set of priorities. Compared to the blazing fire-sprite, Alice wasn't certain her own fleshy body was even visible.

She could see the glow of Flicker's hair halfway around the room as he picked his way through the rock. The bluechill zeroed in on him, ignoring Alice entirely. Its legs once again became a blur, startlingly fast for such a large creature.

"Flicker!"

She was running, the dinosaur's strength in her legs turning each stride into a leap, but it wasn't going to be fast enough. Flicker braced himself, spear in both hands, but the point slid off the bluechill's icy shell as it closed in. The fire-sprite spun away just as the tip of the monster's tail came down, stinger slashing through the space where he'd been. He slipped into a narrow gap between a boulder and the wall, ducking under another sting. It was too tight a spot for the bluechill to enter, but it could still lash out with its tail, and there was no way Flicker could get past it to escape.

Alice let go of the Swarm thread and pulled on Spike's, harder than she ever had before. The transformation came over her in mid-stride, a moment of nauseating uncertainty as her body thickened and expanded into the dinosaur's stumpy, four-legged form. She stumbled, briefly, but managed to maintain her momentum, picking up speed as she broke into a gallop.

Being Spike was, Alice imagined, like driving a motorcar. The dinosaur could build up a solid head of steam, but he wasn't agile, and turning could be a serious problem. But the bluechill was dead ahead, and too occupied with Flicker to notice her. Spike was heavier than he looked, giving him the momentum of a cannonball, and his head was crowned with four vicious horns. She aimed these right at the center of the bluechill's body and let the dinosaur's instincts take over.

Alice-as-Spike slammed into the bluechill, lifting it off the ground and smashing it against the wall of the chamber. The noise was terrific, a grinding, crunching cacophony of ice and the snorting, grunting breath of the dinosaur. The impact hurt less than Alice had expected—Spike's body was built for this sort of thing, with a thick skull and muscular neck. One of her horns had skidded on the icy surface and snapped off, but the other three had punched into the bluechill's body, sending a web of cracks through the ice. The monster gave another shriek, legs flailing.

When Alice tried to back away, however, she found

that her horns were stuck. Before she could shake herself free, the bluechill recovered itself, and reached around to grab hold of her. Icy claws dug into Spike's tough, pebbly hide, drawing blood while they scrabbled for purchase. The thing's arching tail stabbed down, punching into the thick plating along Alice's back. It hurt, but only for a moment; then her flesh went numb, as though the bluechill had injected the essence of cold into her veins. Alice tossed her head, trying to break free, and the stinger struck again and again.

She realized that if she didn't do something, she was going to *die*. After facing down a labyrinthine, she'd been overconfident here on Flicker's world. The bluechill terrified the fire-sprites, but she'd taken it for granted that she could handle it. Now she could feel the venom spreading through her body, chilling Spike's tough flesh as it reached for her heart. *Do something!*

Alice let go of Spike's thread, letting the transformation slip away. The bluechill lurched as she returned to her real body, smaller and lighter than Spike's, spread-eagled and clinging to her opponent. The poison was still in her, spreading faster now that she was only a girl, and Alice felt as though she'd been tossed into a pond in mid-winter. Her teeth began to chatter.

She dug in her pouch for her acorns. Her fingers were stiff and shaking, but she managed to extract one, and with all the strength she had left she rammed it into one of the holes Spike's horns had left in the bluechill's hide. A moment later, the bluechill righted itself, and Alice slumped to the stone, curled up against the cold as the monster turned away from her and toward Flicker's hiding spot.

Grow, Alice urged the acorn. *Grow as fast as you can.*

The ice-creature paused. Alice could see something spreading *inside* the bluechill's translucent carapace, a dark network worming through the cracks Spike had left, pressing through the ice with the strength that sends a tree root burrowing through concrete.

The bluechill screeched, body flexing as it tried to contain the vegetable invader. Then, all at once, it exploded, with a *crack* like the shattering of a mountain. Fragments of ice blew across the room and *pinged* off the walls, raining down around Alice like a strange, dense snow.

Alice closed her eyes, knees pressed against her chest. Her whole body shuddered with the cold, but she couldn't feel it anymore, as though it were a far-off thing that didn't really concern her. She'd wrapped herself in the Swarm thread, hoping their toughness extended to poisons, but it didn't seem to have helped. Each breath felt like it was going to freeze in her throat.

Her heartbeat roared in her ears, and she could barely make out Flicker's voice. "Reader? What happened?"

Alice tried to force words out, but it was no use. Her jaw was clenched so tight, it felt like her teeth would crack.

"Are you all right?" Flicker said. "Reader? Alice?"

Then the fire-sprite's voice vanished entirely into a cold, dark void.

CHAPTER NINE
PYROS

ARE YOU SURE?"

"I'm sure. Humans aren't like us."

"My grandspark always swore the cure for bluechill venom was to soak in oil and then let it burn off. Drives out the cold, he said."

"I told you, it doesn't work that way for humans."

"We could at least try to get her to eat something."

"I'm giving her water."

"How is *that* supposed to help? She needs flame, the hotter the better!"

"For the last time, Actinia, you can't set humans on fire! It never helps."

"I think she's waking up!"

Alice opened her eyes. She lay on a stone bench, padded with a lumpy strip of leather. Pyros stood on one side of her, the blazing colors from the crown of his head reaching only a few inches down the long, ashy gray of his hair. Actinia, his flame tinged with blue, waited by her feet. A fire crackled and spat in a stone bowl by her side, hot enough to make sweat stand out on her brow; her skin had gone red, but the memory of deep chill made her want to huddle closer to the flame.

"Can you hear me?" Pyros said. "Are you all right?"

"And do you think setting you on fire would help?" Actinia said.

The old fire-sprite glared. Alice took a deep breath, coughed, and found her voice.

"I . . . think I'm all right." She felt surprisingly free of pain, though her palms were stinging. When she lifted her hands, she found she'd clenched her fingers so tightly, her fingernails had dug bloody half-moons into her skin. "And setting me on fire won't help, I'm afraid."

Actinia sighed, and Pyros scowled at him.

"I could use some food," Alice said. Remembering that the fire-sprites likely had nothing she could safely eat, she added, "There should be some in my pack."

"Go and get the Reader's things," Pyros told the boy. "And another pitcher of water."

Actinia made a face, but he turned and left the room, the beaded curtain clattering behind him. Pyros settled himself onto a stone beside Alice, moving with an old man's caution.

"Is Flicker all right?" she said.

The fire-sprite nodded. "He was the one who brought you back here, with a bit of help from Ishi." Pyros paused. "He told me you killed the bluechill."

"It came close to killing us both," Alice said. "My wards didn't hold it. I had to . . . improvise."

Alice sat up cautiously, feeling herself for injuries. There still wasn't much pain, but she felt a strange tickle at the back of her mind. When she reached for her threads, it took real effort to grasp them.

Power, she thought. She'd exhausted herself, not physically but magically—something in the ward had gone badly wrong, and it had siphoned off far more of her energy than it had been supposed to. The last time she'd felt like this had been in Esau's fortress, after hours of fighting, and then the depletion in her magic had been matched by her aching muscles. She'd need to rest before her powers would come easily again.

"Regardless," Pyros said, watching her closely, "my people owe you a great debt. In truth I did not expect assistance from Geryon at all, let alone so promptly. Your master . . . surprises me."

"My master is away," Alice admitted. "I came here of my own accord." It was not *quite* a lie—she *had* come here on her own, just not to answer any request from the fire-sprites. *But if he wants to believe that, all the better.*

"Ah. I thought as much." Pyros cocked his head. "In the past, Geryon has seemed interested in our tribute, and little else."

Alice said nothing. She felt as though the sprite were sounding her out, testing the extent of her loyalty to Geryon, and she wasn't sure how far she could trust him. After a moment's pause, he sat back, white hair rippling.

"Well," he said. "We are saved, and that is all that matters. They are feasting already, down in the hall, and drinking toasts to you and young Flicker."

"I'm glad you'll be safe," Alice said.

"You said you had something to request of us," Pyros said. "Might I know what?"

He looked worried. Alice frowned. "Is something wrong?"

"If it is additional tribute you seek, some of my people

may react . . . poorly." Pyros schooled his face to a smooth mask. "Of course, we are obligated to you and Master Geryon, and I will arrange it as best I can, but—"

"I don't understand," Alice said. "What sort of tribute?"

She'd wondered about that since he'd first mentioned it. She couldn't imagine what Geryon could possibly want from the fire-sprites—certainly gold or gems, or even intricately carved glass, held no appeal for the old Reader.

Pyros cleared his throat with a crackle. "By the terms of our agreement with Master Geryon, he grants us permission to live here, safe from other Readers. In return, we provide him one of our own, every two years, as tribute."

"One of your own?" Alice blinked. "You mean one of your *people*?"

Pyros nodded. "To be written into a prison-book. I understand he trades the books to the other Readers. Our . . . services . . . are quite valuable."

Alice just stared.

Ending had warned her, months ago. *Geryon is a Reader. His magic is based on cruelty and death.* She'd known that the creatures in the prison-books had to come from *somewhere*, and although he'd only asked her to fight mindless beasts, she knew there were intelligent beings in his collection. Since returning from Esau's, however, she'd been too wrapped up in her revenge to worry about them.

He keeps them here as a . . . a commodity. *Like Father's business might warehouse bricks or pork bellies.* Better than that. The sprites had children; properly tended, they would yield fruit forever, like a well-kept garden.

"It is not such a bad arrangement," Pyros said. "Some of the other Readers would demand more, or simply imprison us all. And Geryon allows us to select who the tribute is, so we can spare the young."

"Why don't you leave?" Alice said, forgetting herself for a moment. "There must be somewhere else you can go."

"Not anymore," Pyros said, smiling sadly. "Once we roamed across a dozen worlds, moving through the wild gates as we pleased, slipping to your world and back again to find our sustenance. This was before my time, of course, in the days of my grandspark's grandspark. I am not *that* old. But now we have no choice but to huddle close to the Heartfire."

"What happened?"

"You did. Humans. Readers." Pyros shrugged. "The wild gates are closed, bound into books. Those that remain lead farther away from your world, to realms where we cannot live. The power that once flowed freely is caged now, locked away between covers and inside libraries. We do what we must to survive."

Alice shook her head, trying to take it all in. After a moment, she remembered the original question. "It's not tribute," she said. "Nothing like that. I need your help here, in your world."

"What can we possibly do to help a Reader who can defeat a bluechill?"

"I need to find the Palace of Glass," Alice said. "Beyond the wild gate."

Pyros froze, dull red eyes locked on hers. Alice stared back, until his glowing gaze left flickering spots on her vision.

"I did not think Master Geryon knew about the Palace of Glass," he said.

"I don't know if he does." Alice lowered her voice, as though her master might be listening. "I'm not doing this for him. I need to find it for my own sake."

"It is a dangerous place," Pyros said.

"I can take care of myself," Alice said.

"Not dangerous for you. The Palace is a *prison*. There are things buried there that must never be released. Even when we lived beyond the wild gate, my people knew better than to venture there."

Alice felt a chill, despite the fire. "I'm not going to release anything."

"Then what do you hope to accomplish in such a place?"

"That's my own business," she said. Her anger flared a little. *This is what I need to do to beat Geryon. I don't have to justify myself.* "All I need is for one of you to guide me there."

"Even that is a great deal. Those who venture so far from the village rarely return. But . . ." Pyros shook his head and sighed. "I suppose a Reader must know what she's doing."

Actinia returned, bearing Alice's torn, makeshift pack. Alice rooted around until she came up with some hard crackers, which she dipped in the jug of water. The sprite watched in fascination as Alice chewed and swallowed.

"And you enjoy that?" Actinia said. "It doesn't hurt?"

Drinking water probably did look odd, Alice thought, to a creature made of flames. She nodded, her mouth full of cracker. She hadn't realized how hungry she was.

"Actinia," Pyros said quietly, "please go down the hall

and ask Flicker to join us. Then you are dismissed. Join the feast."

"I can't stay?" Actinia said. "I wanted to talk to the Reader."

"Go. Now."

The young sprite left again. Pyros looked after him fondly.

"He doesn't seem to hate me as much as Flicker does," Alice said, opening a tin of ham.

"He is . . ." Pyros paused, waving a hand vaguely. "It is difficult to explain, to a human. You have two sparks, yes? A 'mother' and a 'father'?"

Alice nodded, tearing apart strips of meat and sucking the juices from her fingers.

"But when you are first kindled, you are . . . blank."

"Blank?"

"You have no memories. No thoughts." Pyros shook his head. "It is difficult. I do not know very much about humans."

"You mean when we're babies?" Alice said. "I don't suppose babies remember much, no."

"It is not that way for us. Each spark passes memories on to his kindling. A fraction of himself, something

109

he chooses to preserve. The new kindling knows these things from the very beginning, as part of his being. Some memories have been passed down since before the time of the Readers."

Alice had an image of a line of candles, each one lit from the next, passing the flame on and on. She nodded hesitantly.

"Each line, each lineage has its own notion of what to pass on," Pyros said. "Practical things, skills and knowledge. Treasured memories and joys. Grudges. Some let the oldest memories fade, and others keep that flame bright. Flicker's spark gave him some of our oldest memories, from the days when our people roamed free. It makes him . . . quick to anger."

"What about Actinia?" Alice said, fascinated.

"He is my grandkindling," Pyros said. "His spark and I agreed that it was time to let go of the old days. To accept the way things are. He remembers nothing but this world, the tunnels between the surface and the Heartfire. He does not carry the hatred of his ancestors on his shoulders." Pyros sighed. "Though I fear he may learn it soon enough."

Alice tried to imagine what it would be like, to be born with memories from hundreds or thousands of years ago, but her mind rebelled. She shook her head. Though they might be human-shaped, there were aspects to the fire-sprites that were as alien to her as the bluechill or the Swarm.

The bead curtain clattered, and Flicker appeared. His pale skin was slightly flushed, and his hair was brighter than normal, sparks of brilliant white floating across the strands. He was smiling, but his grin faded at the sight of Alice.

"You wanted to see me?" he said.

"I did." Pyros pushed himself to his feet, shaking out his long white hair. "We should leave the Reader to her rest."

Flicker glanced at Alice, then looked away. "You're going to be all right?"

"I think so," Alice said. "They told me you brought me back. Thank you."

"I couldn't let you die," Flicker said with a scowl. "Geryon would be angry if he found out. But don't think it means anything—"

"Flicker," Pyros said from the door.

The boy nodded to Alice, then followed his elder out through the curtain. Alice lay back on the lumpy leather blanket and closed her eyes.

Maybe we're not so different. Human parents taught their children what they believed, after all. What things were right and which were wrong. Stories about what had happened in the past. *It's the same thing, isn't it?*

Right and wrong. She closed her eyes. Sleep was not hard to find, but her father's sad, disappointed face was waiting.

CHAPTER TEN
TO THE SURFACE

Actinia woke Alice the next morning, carrying a pot of water with the extreme caution of a factory worker handling a vat of toxic waste. Alice drank gratefully, a process which the young fire-sprite watched in fascination, and then ate breakfast from among her supplies. She clicked open the silver pocket watch and tracked the second hand as it made its smooth circuit. *Six days and a few hours to go.*

While she was rooting through the torn bedsheet she'd tied into a pack, Actinia hesitantly spoke up.

"I got you this too." The boy held out a leather bundle. "I saw that your pack was torn, and we had an old one."

Alice took the bundle and unfolded it. It was a proper backpack, all stitched from leather with thick, tough thread. The clasp was made of black glass, worked into the shape of a tiny flame.

"Thank you," she said. The bedsheet wouldn't have lasted much longer.

"I heard you were going on a journey," Actinia said, eyes fixed firmly on his feet. "And you saved us from the blue-chill, so I thought . . . my spark said you could have it."

"Please give him my thanks as well," Alice said, repacking her things. She got off the stone slab and stretched, feeling surprisingly well. Her boots were at the foot of the bed—Flicker must have brought them—along with three slightly scorched-looking squares of parchment. *The wards.* Alice picked them up, frowning as she felt for the magic within them. It was still there, but broken, incomplete, like a snapped thread.

Actinia escorted her down a short corridor to the great hall. She'd last seen it being used as a makeshift surgery. Now it was quiet, though the tables and a certain amount of mess attested to a party having ended not long before, and the air was thick with the scent of smoke.

Pyros was waiting, with Flicker. The old man looked

grave, and the boy bore his usual angry scowl. They both got to their feet as Alice and Actinia entered.

"Reader," Flicker said curtly.

Pyros frowned and ran one hand through his hair. He looked uncertain.

"I have decided," he said, "that Flicker will accompany you as far as the Palace of Glass. It is quite possible you have saved us from annihilation, and we can offer no less."

"Flicker?" Alice looked from one of them to the other. "*He's* coming with me?"

Flicker's scowl deepened. "I'm not good enough for you, Reader?"

"Flicker has the most complete memories of the surface and the other side of the gate," Pyros said. "He may not be the greatest of our warriors, but he knows where you need to go and the difficulties you may encounter."

"I . . ." Alice paused. What she wanted to say was, *I thought Flicker hated Readers.* The boy noticed her hesitation and crossed his arms.

"It wasn't my idea," Flicker said, glaring. "But Pyros is the elder here. Unless you'd rather have someone else?"

"No," Alice said. "I'd be happy to have you along. I was

just . . . surprised. I know it's dangerous. I'll do everything I can to keep us safe."

"Do you have any further preparations to make?" Pyros said, over a fresh scowl from Flicker. Alice shook her head, and the old man went on, "Then I suggest you go as soon as possible."

"No percentage in hanging about," Alice agreed with a touch of melancholy.

Flicker, equipped with a glass-tipped spear and a pack of his own, hugged Actinia tight for a long time. Alice waited while Pyros whispered a few final words in the boy's ear. Behind the elder, a few other fire-sprites were watching. Their expressions were not pleasant.

Tribute. She *wasn't* taking Flicker away to lock him in a prison-book, but from the sprites' point of view it looked the same. She wanted to promise them she'd bring him back, but how could she? *No wonder Pyros wanted us to get moving quickly.*

With good-byes completed, Flicker opened the single door that led back out into the tunnels beyond the village. Alice followed and let it crash closed behind her.

A grinding, crackling sound filled the air as soon as they'd rounded the first bend. Flicker stopped and waited, and a moment later Ishi bounded into view, stumpy rock-tail wagging and both heads drooling flame. The fire-sprite bent and rubbed the dog-thing affectionately.

"Is he coming with us?" Alice said, giving the creature an appraising look.

"Ishi?" Flicker shook his head. "He couldn't survive on the surface. I can eat anything that will burn, more or less, but he needs molten rock." He looked at the dog-thing and added, "That's why there's even fewer of them left than there are of us."

"Oh."

"Take care of everyone, Ishi." Flicker rubbed the dog-thing's muzzles, then pointed the way they had come. Ishi gave a double bark, like a pair of rocks cracking, and trotted off. Flicker gestured and said, "Come on. It's this way."

They walked in silence for a while, winding through tunnel after tunnel, always tending slightly upward. Sometimes the tubes connected of their own accord, joining up like tributaries to a river, but more often doorways had been cut between them by long-ago sprites. Here and there, rock-falls had blocked the path, and they had to backtrack and work around, but Flicker's confidence never wavered.

"Is this all in your memories?" Alice said. "The ones you got from your . . . spark?"

Flicker looked back at her, glowing eyes unreadable. "Pyros told you about that?"

"A little."

The boy shrugged. "Some of them. I've done a lot of exploring on my own too. I told you I'm the only person in our village to have been to the surface."

"What's it like?"

"Nothing special. Cold. Dark."

They walked on for a few heartbeats. The light from Flicker's hair was bright enough to see by, so Alice hadn't invoked the devilfish, but the slow churn of the colors made the shadows bend weirdly.

"I remember your world," Flicker said abruptly. "Almost none of the others can, but I do. It's so . . . bright."

"Sometimes," Alice said.

"And strange. Full of things to eat, but also so *wet*. I remember *rain*." He shivered. "I don't know how my ancestors stood it."

"Does water really hurt you?" Alice said.

Flicker looked back at her again. "Not *hurt*, exactly. Just . . it's . . . urgh. Disgusting. Does it rain very often?"

"It depends where you are," Alice said. "Where I live, it

rains all the time, in the summer. In the winter, it snows."

"What's *snow*?"

Apparently that hadn't been included in Flicker's inherited memories. Alice grinned, thinking of Ashes and his opinion on the subject. "It's a bit like . . . fluffy ice, I suppose? It falls from the sky like rain and builds up in mounds. I think you would hate it."

"I think you're right." Flicker smiled for a moment, then replaced it with a scowl as soon as he realized what he was doing. He gestured to a larger doorway up ahead. "This is what we're looking for. It's the quickest way to the surface, but it's a little bit of a climb." He raised an eyebrow. "I assume a Reader can handle it?"

"I can handle it," Alice said, all too aware of the ticking in her pocket. She tested her threads and found them near to hand. She didn't think she was quite back to full strength, but she felt recovered enough for a little exertion.

Flicker led the way into a large tunnel, different from the others. It was rougher, wider, and went upward at close to a forty-five-degree angle, like the eaves of a house. The slope was strewn with bits of rock and glass. Flicker picked his way forward, moving from boulder to boulder and scrambling over the smooth patches. Alice took a deep breath, called on Spike's strength, and followed.

It went on for longer than she'd expected, but she realized she had no idea how deep underground they were. The first hint that they were approaching the top was a change in the air. The tunnels had a faint sulfurous smell that Alice had stopped noticing, but the new breeze carried a different taste. It was cold and dry, and smelled of ice.

There wasn't much light, though. Alice guessed it was night, then wondered if there *were* days and nights here. *Assumptions. I can't make too many assumptions.*

"Almost there," Flicker said, pausing in the lee of a large boulder for a rest. He was breathing hard, the fire in his hair pulsing raggedly. He looked at Alice with a little more respect. With the dinosaur's borrowed strength, she'd strolled up the steep slope as easily as walking a garden path. "A bit more, and we'll be out."

"Then what?"

"Then we try and find the gate."

"Try?" Alice raised an eyebrow of her own. "I thought you remembered where it was."

"I remember where it was hundreds of years ago. The gate won't have moved, and I can guess where to go by looking at the mountains, but it's not exact." He shrugged. "We'll find it. The question is what happens when we get there."

"Why? What's at the gate?"

"I don't know. Didn't I just say no one had been there for hundreds of years? But *something* will be using it." Flicker sighed. "Whatever it is, I'm sure you'll be able to kill it. Come on."

Flicker pushed off the boulder and started climbing again. After a short scramble up a narrow rock shelf, the slope leveled out a bit, and they could walk more comfortably. Ahead, Alice could see a narrow band of darkness, rapidly expanding as they moved toward it.

Oh, she thought. *So they* do *have day and night here . . .*

Between one step and the next, she'd emerged from under the overhang of the cave roof and into the open. Her eyes went to the sky, and stayed put while her mouth hung loose and her thought trailed off in wonder.

It was a perfect dark night, darker than even Geryon's estate, miles from the lights of Pittsburgh. There was no moon, and the stars were ablaze, rank on rank of them, glittering across the heavens like diamond dust spilled on black velvet. But it wasn't their clarity or number that made Alice stop in her tracks. They were *moving*.

Not the slow, night-long rotation of stars on Earth, the imperceptible rise and set of constellations. Here the brilliant pinpricks crawled visibly across the sky, making a great, stately circular sweep around a point halfway between the overhead and the horizon. It felt like looking into a giant whirlpool, a huge, endlessly spinning vortex, and for a moment Alice felt a queasy vertigo, as though she were going to fall *up* and drown in the void.

Then her perspective shifted. The stars didn't move, they'd taught her that in her lessons. The *world* did, spinning on its axis. She'd never *felt* it spinning before, but she did now, watching the steady procession of the heavens. Her stomach flip-flopped, and she forced herself to look at the ground before she threw up.

"It used to take me like that, sometimes," Flicker said, coming up beside her. He glanced up at the stars, unconcerned. "I thought you humans lived out in the open, though."

"It's not being in the open," Alice said, keeping her breath slow and regular. "The stars here are ... wrong."

"Really?" Flicker looked at the sky again. "What are they supposed to be doing?"

Apparently Flicker's memories of Earth weren't *that* extensive. Alice shook her head, steeled herself, and looked around. The wheeling stars tugged at her gaze, but as long as she didn't stare upward, she didn't get the sick *falling* sensation in the balls of her feet. She swallowed.

"It's . . . hard to explain," she said. "How long until dawn?"

Flicker shook his head. "I remember that. When the sun comes up, right? We don't have it here. I told you, it's just cold and dark." He gestured with his spear. "Do you need to rest? Otherwise we should keep moving."

CHAPTER ELEVEN
THE FROZEN FORTRESS

*N*O SUN, *AND NO* moon. It was no wonder the fire-sprites never came up to the surface.

The landscape was bleak and unwelcoming. They'd come up out of a crack in the ground at the base of a range of hills stretching off in both directions. Facing the other way, a row of jagged mountain peaks were visible only as blots against the stars, reminding Alice uncomfortably of the bowl of mountains surrounding Esau's fortress. In between was a dusty plain, scattered with a few rocks and the occasional glint of a frozen-over stream.

Not dust, she realized as they started walking. *Ash.* The stuff was pale gray and as light as powder, puffing around their feet when they moved and leaving a clear trail of footprints behind them. Here and there, wind tugged it up into tiny ash-devils, gray whirlwinds that danced around them like playful spirits.

Flicker led the way with confidence, sighting down his spear at the distant shapes of the mountains to get his bearings. His long, glowing hair was a beacon, throwing red and yellow light all around them, like a pool of life amid a gray, dead emptiness.

After a while, to break the silence as much as anything else, she said, "Why *do* you come up here, if there's nothing to see?"

"It must look stupid to you," Flicker said. "You can walk through a book into any world you like, and I have to scrape and crawl to get *here*." He waved a hand at the bleak landscape. "It wasn't always like this."

"You . . . remember?"

Flicker's lip twisted. "That's right. My spark made sure of it. I look out at this and I remember a time when the Heartfire was so strong, rivers of molten rock ran across the land, and my people lived under the stars."

"What happened?"

"Every year, it gets a little weaker, a little cooler. Every year we move down a little farther. Every year there are fewer of us. Eventually, there'll be nothing left but ash. I used to think there might be something else to find if we looked up instead of down."

"Does Pyros know about this?" Alice said.

"Of course. Everyone knows. But they'd rather not think about it. Pyros says we can trust the *Readers* to help us."

"A Reader *could* help you," Alice said cautiously. "If you could use the portal-book, you could find a new home."

"And what would we have to pay for it?" Flicker waved again at the dead world. "My spark told me that it was the Readers who caused all of this in the first place! That the Heartfire began to weaken when they locked away the portals in their books and their libraries."

"Do you believe that?"

"I have no idea. But I know what happened to my spark. Your precious master wrote him into a prison-book, and traded him to some other Reader like a pretty stone."

Oh. Alice fell into silence. Pyros had said that Flicker's spark was gone, and she'd wondered if he'd been killed by the bluechill or another monster. *But Geryon took him.* In spite of the sprite's vicious tone, she felt a sudden kinship with Flicker. *Does Geryon haunt his nightmares too?*

Flicker was clearly fuming, his hair brighter than normal and laced with yellow and white. Alice waited a few minutes, trudging carefully across the monotonous landscape, before she spoke again.

"Not every Reader is like Geryon."

"Oh no?" Flicker turned on his heel, eyes blazing like twin stars. "And I suppose you're going to tell me that *you're* one of the good ones?"

"I . . ." The image of her father's sad, disappointed face flashed through her mind, and she willed it away. "I *try* to be. I've never trapped anyone in a prison-book."

"You've used prison-books, though. You've bound creatures."

"Only animals. Beasts. Not people." *Except the tree-sprite. But I refused to kill it! And the Dragon. But that's different!*

"That makes it better? You'd take someone like Ishi and trap him in a prison forever, just for your own power, and it's better because he doesn't *understand*?" Flicker squared off against her, as though about to throw a punch, and his eyes were so bright, Alice couldn't look directly at them. "I helped you, Reader, because we're *better* than you. And I'm helping you now because Pyros says I have to. But none of that means I have to like you or forget what you are. You're the one who chose to pursue power at the cost of other people's lives, so *stop making excuses.*"

Flicker shook his head, a wave of blue-white sliding through his hair. "I'm wasting my time, aren't I?" he said, turning away. "Come on. We've still got a ways to go."

Alice didn't move. Anger squeezed her lungs and wrapped itself around her heart. For a fleeting moment, she fought down an overpowering urge to pull on her threads, to summon monsters into the world and blot this impudent sprite out of existence. It was, she imagined, how Geryon must feel, how all the old Readers must feel; utterly secure in the knowledge that everyone and everything around them existed only on their sufferance, because they chose not to wield their immense power. Their cruelty was the cruelty of elephants to insects—a casual indifference, until a bite began to itch, and then obliteration with a flick of the trunk.

And behind the anger, hiding in its shadow, a darker feeling she didn't want to acknowledge. *Guilt.*

Alice forced herself to take a deep breath. *I'm not like them. I'm* not.

"I didn't choose this," she said. "I don't mean to make excuses, but it's the truth. Geryon killed my father and brought me to live with him. Once he knew I had the talent to be a Reader, he told me I could be his apprentice or have my mind erased."

Flicker cocked his head. "Then why serve him? *You* can use the portal-books. You could go to any world you like."

"He might follow me," Alice said, but it didn't sound convincing. Because Flicker was right, as far as it went. She probably *could* lose herself somewhere in the infinite worlds of the library, especially if Ending was willing to keep her secrets. But that wasn't good enough. "And . . ."

His burning eyes were steady on hers. "And what?"

"And he has to pay for what he did. There's no one to make sure he does but me."

Flicker stared. Alice rubbed her face with her sleeve and sucked in a great lungful of the cold air.

"That's why I'm here," she said. "Why I'm going to the Palace of Glass."

"You never got Pyros' call for help, then."

She shook her head.

"Then why risk your life for us at all?"

"I didn't think you'd be willing to help, with the blue-chill out there," Alice said.

"We wouldn't have had any choice, if you'd demanded it in Geryon's name."

"I . . ." Alice hesitated for a moment, then finally shrugged. "I don't know. It seemed fair."

Flicker regarded her for a moment longer, then turned away again. "Come on," he repeated. "Still a ways to go."

Eventually they came to a hill with a fast-flowing river wrapped around one side of it. Flicker led Alice to the top, and from there she was able to see quite a long way. The river flowed toward a stone wall about fifteen feet high, and passed underneath it through a low archway. Behind it, several towers rose even higher, turreted tops black against the stars. Lights glowed behind the windows, giving off a blue-green radiance that had looked more like the devilfish's glow than a proper fire.

In the center of the wall was an iron-barred gate. Standing beside it was an enormous woman, easily nine or ten feet tall, with skin the blue-white of old ice and frost-white hair. She wore a conical helmet and carried a long-handled ax whose blade glittered in the light as though it too were made of ice.

"I take it your memories don't include anything like that?" Alice said.

Flicker shook his head. "I told you someone would be using the gate."

"Who are they?"

"I don't know," Flicker said. "Pyros might. It's been a long time since we had contact with any other peoples. Does it matter? I don't imagine they pose any more threat to you than we do."

"I'm not going to force my way through," Alice said. She was slightly chagrined to find she'd automatically been thinking about how she would fight the ice woman. "I don't just attack people for no reason."

"What are we going to do, then?"

"Talk to them, for a start."

CHAPTER TWELVE
ERDRODR OF NO NAME

THE ICE WOMAN HEFTED her ax a little, testing the balance.

"Ho, there!" she said, voice deep but surprisingly melodious. "Travelers, are you?"

Alice nodded. "I'm Alice," she said. "And this is Flicker."

"I am Byrvorda the Keen-Eyes. It has been long since we have seen a human, and longer still since a fire-kin has visited our lands. What do you seek in the domain of Helga the Ice Flower?"

"There is a wild portal in your fortress, I think," Alice said politely. "We would like to go through it, and come back this way later."

Byrvorda frowned. "The curtain is within, aye. What business have you in the land beyond?"

"I'm going to visit the Palace of Glass," Alice said.

"The Palace?" The ice giant made a curious gesture with one hand, then spat in the ash at her feet. Her spittle made a tinkling sound as it shattered into frozen droplets. "You won't be coming back, then, more fool you. But it matters not. Helga the Ice Flower has decreed that the castle is closed to all outsiders until her return."

"When will she be back?" Alice said.

Byrvorda shrugged. "Who can say? Helga hunts in the land beyond the portal, and she will travel as far as her whim takes her. When she returns, we will feast."

"We're just passing through," Alice said. "We won't stay long in your castle, I promise."

"Helga's decrees are absolute, human," the ice giant said. "In truth, even when she returns, I do not fancy your chances. She is not fond of your kind, though I daresay she might keep the fire-kin for a pet. They have grown rare in these lands."

"Flicker is not a pet," Alice said.

"And she is not just a *human*," Flicker said, sliding his hand down his spear. "She is a *Reader*. Do you have any idea what that means?"

The giant shrugged again. "I have heard stories. Readers are said to be most formidable creatures, though I must say she does not look it." She cocked her head, hand returning to her ax. "Is it to be war, then, Reader? Will you match your strength against mine?"

"I'm trying to *help* you—" Flicker began.

Alice cut him off. "No, Flicker."

"Wise, for a human. You ought to be wise enough to give up your journey. The Palace is cursed."

"Can you tell us when Helga returns?" Alice said.

"You will know," the ice giant said. "The castle will come alive with feasting and song. If her hunt was a success, perhaps she will be in a generous mood."

"Perhaps," Alice said. "Thank you."

She turned away, following her footprints in the soft ash back toward the hill. After a moment's astonished silence, Flicker followed, hurrying to catch up.

"I got the impression from Pyros," the fire-sprite hissed, "that you were in a hurry."

"I am." Alice had checked the watch before coming down the hill. *A bit more than five and a half days. And I'm going to have to come* back *this way, even once I find the Palace.*

"Then what exactly are you doing?"

"Thinking," Alice said.

"You killed a *bluechill*," Flicker said. "Don't tell me that ice-thing scares you."

"Look," Alice said. "I know what you think of me, but I'm not going to hurt anyone if I don't have to, all right?"

Flicker stared for a moment, then shook his head. "Then we're just going to wait for Helga?"

"I'm going to eat something and try to get some sleep," Alice said. Even with time trickling away, she had to rest *sometime*. "I'm exhausted after all that climbing."

"What if Helga won't agree to let us through?"

"Then we'll find another way," Alice said. "Something better than smashing the front door down."

They made their camp in the shadow of a boulder on the hilltop, with a good view of the fortress and the plain beyond. Flicker made a fire in a small metal bowl, providing a measure of relief from the chill wind. Alice ate a joyless meal of cold dried meat, and watched in fascination as Flicker scooped up bits of flame with his bare fingers and popped them into his mouth like candies.

When she was full, she stretched out with her pack for a pillow. The ash made the ground surprisingly soft, and the rigor of the day's travel had left her so tired, she fell asleep almost immediately. For once, the memory of her father was content to leave her in peace.

She woke to Flicker shaking her by the shoulder. His hand was warm, even through her leathers, like a mug of freshly brewed tea.

"Reader," he whispered.

Alice blinked and sat up, ash cascading away where the wind had drifted it against her. "What's wrong?"

"Someone's come out of the fortress."

"Just one?"

Flicker nodded. Alice licked her lips, then unscrewed the top of her canteen and took a swallow of cold, clear water. The ash got everywhere—even the inside of her mouth seemed to be coated with the stuff, and everything she swallowed tasted burned. She put the canteen away and climbed carefully to the top of the boulder, where she could see down to the fortress and the plain.

The guard was still at the gate, but another ice woman had appeared. This one was smaller, and dressed in a long white robe instead of furs and armor. She carried no weapon, only a basket. After exchanging a few words with the guard on the gate, she started walking across the ash wastes toward their hill.

"If it comes to a fight, better up here than down there,"

Flicker said. "Who knows how many of them there are inside?"

"It won't come to a fight." Alice judged the ice woman's path for a moment. "Let's stay behind the boulder. We don't want to startle her."

"She doesn't *look* dangerous," Alice said.

"Aside from being twice our size," Flicker said.

That was hard to deny. This ice giant didn't have quite the intimidating size and bulk of Byrvorda, but she was still a good seven feet tall, taller than Mr. Black. She was thin, though, and something about her gangly frame made Alice think of a girl in her mid-teens. Her blue-white hair hung loose to just above her shoulders, and she wore a thin white robe that didn't seem adequate for the chill.

She climbed up to the hilltop, not far from the boulder where Alice and Flicker were hiding, set her basket down amid the ash, then looked over her shoulder at the fortress. Cupping her hands to her mouth, she said, in a ridiculously loud whisper, "Human! Human, are you there?"

Flicker caught Alice's eye. Alice shrugged, gestured for him to stay put, and got to her feet. The giant caught sight of her and took a half step back, eyes going very wide.

Alice raised her hands. "I'm not going to hurt you," she said.

"I . . ." The giant composed herself a little and coughed. "I am sorry. I have never seen one of you before. Byrvorda said you were no larger than an infant, but I did not expect . . . I mean . . ."

Her face colored from white to off-blue in what Alice guessed was a blush.

"It's all right," she said. "I'm Alice. What's your name?"

For some reason, this question made the giant wince. "Erdrodr," she said. "Erdrodr of no name."

"Why were you looking for me?" Alice said.

"Byrvorda was telling everyone at dinner that she'd seen a human and a fire-kin at the wall. A *Reader*, she said." Erdrodr peered at Alice a little closer. "Are you a Reader? You don't look like the ones in the stories."

"I am," Alice said, deciding not to mention that she was only an apprentice. "Byrvorda said we can't go through the gate until Helga comes back. Has she returned?"

"Oh, no." Erdrodr shook her head vehemently. "Even when she returns, my mother will never let you pass. She guards the curtain jealously."

"Your mother? You're Helga's daughter?"

Erdrodr nodded, a mournful look on her face.

"Could you speak to her for us?" Alice said. "If I can help somehow—"

"Mother is less likely to listen to *me* than she is to listen to you. But I *can* help you, if you can help me. I can get you inside the castle. But . . ." She hesitated, then blurted out, "You must make me a promise."

Alice blinked. "What kind of promise?"

"I must go with you. To the other side of the curtain. No matter what, you must allow me to come."

There was a long pause.

"You'd better explain a little," Alice said. "Do you mind if Flicker joins us? He has a spear, but I promise he's not a threat."

"Of course." Erdrodr scuffed a clear place in the ash with her foot. "We should sit. The guards may look this way, and I told them I was going to work on my sketches."

"All right." Alice waved, and Flicker got up from behind the boulder. Erdrodr had just settled herself on the ground, heedless of the smudges on her white robes. At the sight of him, the ice giant jumped back to her feet, so quickly that a startled Flicker pointed his spear.

"Oh!" Erdrodr said, staring.

"What?" Flicker said, raising his spear. "What's going on?"

Alice hastily stepped between the two of them. "Is something wrong?"

"No!" Erdrodr blinked and shook her head. "I have never seen a fire-kin before. I did not think . . . he is *beautiful*. The colors . . ."

Flicker's hair went briefly to a white-green, and Alice wondered if that signaled embarrassment.

"It's all right," Alice said to him. "I think she was just surprised."

Hesitantly, Flicker lowered his spear and came over. Erdrodr was rooting around in her basket, and after a few moments she produced a wooden slate and a stub-end of charcoal. Flicker flinched again as she straightened up.

"May I draw you? Please?" The ice giant stared at Flicker like an eager puppy. "It won't take long, I swear it."

"I . . ." Flicker's hair gave another spurt of green. "I mean, I don't *mind*, but . . ."

The ice giant was no longer listening. She sat down again, raising a puff of ash, and began furiously scraping at the board. Alice shifted around behind her, to watch the work in progress, and gaped in astonishment. The stack of paper held to the board with twine was rough and uneven, and the charcoal crumbled and split in Erdrodr's thick fingers, but somehow she compensated for all these difficulties. A picture of Flicker took shape, in delicate smudges of black and gray, capturing everything from the tilt of his nose to the way the light of his hair made the rocks at his feet cast shadows. In a few moments, Erdrodr lifted her hand, a frown fixed on her face.

"It's amazing," Alice breathed.

"It's not right," the ice giant muttered. "The colors *change*. I can't . . . bah." She tore the page from the stack and tossed it aside. "I am not good enough. Not yet." She let out a long breath and looked back at Flicker. "I am sorry. It is my passion, you see. The others think it foolish, but . . ." Her hands flexed, tightening into fists. "I cannot help it."

Flicker picked up the discarded page, stared at it curiously for a moment, then shook his head. Alice took a seat on a rock across from the giant, so the disparity in their heights wouldn't be so extreme. Flicker settled himself close by her side.

"That is the heart of it, really," Erdrodr said. "The drawing. Mother says it is no fit pursuit for a warrior, let alone a daughter of the first family. As long as I persist, she refuses to let me claim my name or my proper place."

"What does that have to do with us?" Flicker said.

Alice shot him a look, but Erdrodr didn't seem offended.

"She has forbidden me from joining the hunt in the land beyond the curtain," the giant said. "I must languish here, where there is nothing but rocks and ash to draw, while those of an age with me go forth to win their names. It is not . . . *just.* Mother is . . ." She paused. "Too cautious."

"So you want us to help you get through the gate?" Alice said.

"Why?" Flicker said.

"If I go to the other side and live to return, Mother will have no choice but to grant me my name and my place." Erdrodr bent forward, eyes shining. "Please."

Alice thought for a moment. "Why do you need *us*? You're already inside the fortress. Why can't you just go through?"

"The room with the gate is sealed while Mother is on the other side." The giant sat back, blushing again. "I have tried to steal the key, but Nordra the Warden keeps it out of my grasp. But I'm certain a mere locked door would present only a small obstacle to a Reader!"

Alice had to admit that was probably true. She looked at Flicker, who met her gaze and shrugged, as if to say, *You're the Reader. This is your show.*

"All right," Alice said. "If you can get us into the fortress, I'll get you through the door to the portal."

"You give your word you'll bring me through?" Erdrodr said. "You won't leave me behind?"

"I give my word," Alice said. "Now, how are you going to sneak us inside?"

The ice giant grinned, and rummaged once again in her basket.

CHAPTER THIRTEEN
A SUBTLE ENTRANCE

Y OU DON'T HAVE TO come, you know," Alice said.

Flicker stared miserably at the river. It was calm, to Alice's eyes. She wouldn't have worried about going for a swim, if it weren't so cold. But from the way the fire-sprite looked at it, it might have been Niagara Falls.

"Pyros told me to take you all the way to the Palace," Flicker said. "My memories of the other side may be useful."

"You've shown me to the gate. I'm sure that's enough."

He shook his head. "No. Get on with it."

They were at the bottom of the hill, out of sight of the ice giants' fortress. Erdrodr had told them to wait an hour, which Alice had timed precisely by the hands of the silver watch. Erdrodr had gone back to the fortress and made her own preparations.

Now Alice held the ice giant's gift. It was a sphere of ice about the size of her head, cool and slick like an enormous marble, heavy enough that she had to carry it in both hands. Alice had covered it with a ragged bit of bedsheet to keep it from freezing to her fingertips. When the hour was up, as Erdrodr had instructed, she tipped it into the water with a splash. The water was cold, but not frozen, so the ice ball ought to have begun to melt.

Instead, the exact opposite happened. Feathery tendrils of frost shot across the surface of the water, extending out from the sphere in a carpet that rapidly condensed into a solid surface. The expanding ice pushed the sphere a bit farther from the bank, still bobbing in the current. As the iceberg grew, it changed shape, ice creaking and snapping under the influence of an invisible force. The top hollowed out, and within a few moments Alice could see the shape of the thing that was growing.

It was a boat, made entirely of ice, with the sphere embedded in the deck at the very center. It looked like the small wooden rowboats that Alice and her father had taken out on the lake in Central Park, but much larger, as befit a craft designed for giants. Alice borrowed Flicker's spear and used it to pull the vessel up against the bank. The slope was shallow enough that they could step from shore to boat without even getting their feet wet, but the fire-sprite still looked deeply unhappy.

"Last chance to back out," Alice said.

Flicker shook his head. With a major effort of will, he stepped gingerly over the side of the boat. When it swayed under his weight, he hurriedly sat down, hugging his knees.

He and Ashes would get along. Neither of them likes to get wet. Alice put her pack in the bottom of the boat and climbed in herself, spear in hand. Erdrodr had assured her that the current would carry them downstream, into the fortress and up to a smaller gate, where the ice giant girl would be waiting.

The important thing was that they not be seen on the way in. Alice tossed the remains of her bedsheet-pack over Flicker like a shroud. Not being able to see the river seemed to comfort the fire-sprite, and he pulled the sheet tighter around himself. The fabric blocked the light from his hair, leaving Alice in almost total darkness. She waited a moment for her eyes to adjust, the bulk of the hill just barely visible in the starlight, and then she pushed them away from the bank. Using the spear like a pole, she shoved the little craft out into deep water, until she could no longer reach the bottom. Then there was nothing to do but hunker down beside Flicker and wait.

The current was so smooth that there was hardly any sense of motion, but soon they were rounding the side of the hill, the fortress looming larger by the moment. Alice could see Byrvorda still standing at the gate, but the river was some distance away from her, and the boat was nearly invisible in the darkness.

The current got faster, rocking the boat, and Alice pushed Flicker down and ducked her own head. The stones of the fortress swept above them as they passed under a low archway, the ice boat scraping alarmingly against the wall of the tunnel. Then, with a *clang*, they stopped. Alice raised her head slowly and found that she had enough space to stand, though the boat shifted under her feet. It was completely dark, without even the faint illumination of the stars.

Hinges creaked, and a blue-green glow appeared. Alice saw Erdrodr, standing in a narrow doorway, a lamp in one hand. The boat had come to rest in a square chamber, with a slimy stone walkway serving as a dock. The river roared on through the bowels of the fortress, but closely set iron bars kept the boat from being swept along with it. The air smelled of damp and mildew.

"No one's raised the alarm," Erdrodr said, "but we must hurry."

She extended her hand, and Alice took it, her own fingers impossibly slender against the giant's. The boat shifted, but she managed the quick step to the dock. Flicker, who'd thrown off the bedsheet and raised his head, squeezed his eyes shut with a queasy expression and sank back into the bottom of the boat.

"It's all right," Alice said. "It's just a little step."

"I can't," the fire-sprite said in a tiny voice. "It'll tip over, and I'll fall in."

"You cannot stay here," Erdrodr said, looking over her shoulder.

"Flicker . . ."

"Just leave me," he said. "I'll . . . I'll figure something out. Go on."

"Don't be an idiot." Alice pulled his spear out of the boat and held the butt end out to him. "Here. Grab on. You don't even have to open your eyes."

"I can't," Flicker repeated. "It's—"

Erdrodr made an exasperated noise and leaned over the boat, grabbing Flicker under his armpits. She might have been smaller than Byrvorda, but she was still strong enough to lift the fire-sprite like he was a child, his legs dangling until she set him down on the dock. Alice hurriedly grabbed his arm when he threatened to fall over.

"I must retrieve the boat," the ice giant said, bending down to work the ice sphere loose from the center of the craft. "We will need it, on the other side."

"What?" Flicker's eyes opened. "What did she say?"

"Never mind," Alice said. "Are you all right?"

"I'm . . ." He looked at the glittering surface of the water, swallowed hard, and averted his gaze. "I'm fine. Sorry. I didn't . . . I just kept thinking about falling in, and having that stuff all around me, and . . . urgh."

"You'll be fine." Alice patted his shoulder and handed back his spear. His skin was hot to the touch, and faint wisps of steam were rising from the damp stone under his feet.

"There." Erdrodr stood up, tucking the ice sphere into her oversized pocket. The rest of the boat sagged, rapidly melting back into the river. "Now, follow me, and be as quiet as you can."

The ice giant led them through a series of corridors and up a flight of stairs. They emerged on a covered walkway overlooking the central courtyard of the fortress.

Several buildings fronted onto a rocky square of ground, which Alice was startled to see was full of *trees*. Each tall, slender plant had its roots in a round basin full of rocks and water, and trunks and leaves alike were made of translucent ice, drinking in the faint starlight. Ice flowers bloomed here and there, petals carrying subtle hints of color.

Erdrodr must have noticed Alice's expression, because she made a face. "Those are my mother's pride. No other has bred blooms so large and colorful. It gave her her name, when she was younger than me. Helga the Ice Flower." She shook her head. "No one says *she* is less a warrior for it."

"They're beautiful," Alice said.

"I think she cares for them more than she does for me." The ice giant's lip twisted. "Come. This way."

At the end of the walkway, another door led them back inside. Another flight of stairs, down this time, opened onto a long hallway and then to a single massive door, ancient, hardened wood banded with metal bars and rivets. An iron plate just above the level of Alice's head bore a large keyhole.

"That is the door," Erdrodr said. "Nordra has the only key, and she is asleep in the guard tower."

"Is there anyone nearby?" Alice said.

"Most of the warriors are with Mother on the hunt. Only a few guards and *children* were left behind."

"Then I think we won't try to be subtle," Alice said. "Stand back."

She reached out with her mind and grabbed Spike's thread, pulling the dinosaur into the world with a *pop* of displaced air. Erdrodr jumped, slapping a hand over her mouth to stifle a yell. Even Flicker, who'd seen Spike before, looked startled. Alice grinned a little to herself as she gave the dinosaur mental instructions. He grunted, lining up on the door, and lumbered into motion.

As she'd found out when she'd entered his prison-book, Spike's strength and considerable bulk let him build up the momentum of a freight train. By the time he hit the door, the wood and metal didn't stand a chance. Timbers snapped and cracked, the hinges gave way with a squeal of tortured iron, and then the entire door came free, hanging from Spike's horns as he skidded to a halt in the room beyond.

"*What,*" boomed a huge voice, "is going on here?"

"Oh no," Erdrodr said. "No, no. Not *now.* She's not supposed to be back yet!"

As the dust cleared, Alice could see a group of huge ice

women, dressed in furs and leather and carrying enormous axes and bows, in the large, windowless stone chamber beyond the wrecked door. There were at least two dozen of them, and the one in the center, with a pair of ax handles sticking up over her shoulders, bore a distinct resemblance to Erdrodr. Her triple braid, which hung past her waist, was weighted with gold and silver rings. Her broad face was marred by a scar on her lip, which tugged at the corner of her mouth and gave her a perpetual scowl. She was a head taller than Erdrodr, towering several feet above Spike.

Behind the returned hunting party was something Alice had never seen before, a shivering, shifting curtain of light that hung in the air, rippling like a flag on a windy day. Rainbows scattered from its surface, as though it were a prism, but here and there it flattened out and she could glimpse something beyond it. She saw fragments of a blue sky, white clouds, and green foliage. *Another world. That's the wild portal.*

It was right there, not thirty feet away. *I could get there.* If she split into the Swarm, she could flow around the feet of the frost giants, leap through the portal before they could react. *They couldn't stop me.* Or she could have Spike clear her a path—she doubted he could fight all of

them, but it didn't have to be for long. *I could get there, and—*

And she'd leave Flicker and Erdrodr behind. Alice had no idea what the ice giants would do to a fire-sprite they caught sneaking into their fortress, but from Erdrodr's description of her mother, she couldn't imagine Flicker getting away with a stern talking-to. And while Erdrodr herself probably wouldn't be *hurt,* Alice had given her word to take her along. *She kept her part of the bargain. It's not her fault we happened to run into her mother . . .*

Flicker had lowered his spear in the direction of the ice giants. The weapon looked unimaginably puny compared to the massive axes the women were beginning to unsheathe.

Alice let out a long breath and released Spike's thread, the broken door crashing to the ground as the dinosaur disappeared with a *pop.* She met Helga's eye and raised her hands over her head in surrender.

At her side, she heard Flicker sigh.

CHAPTER FOURTEEN
HELGA THE ICE FLOWER

*F*IVE DAYS, ELEVEN HOURS *left.* Alice snapped the watch closed.

"Readers are supposed to be practically *gods*," Flicker complained. "What kind of a god lets herself get thrown in a cell?"

"The kind who doesn't want anybody to get hurt," Alice said. "Especially her friends."

"The one time I'm on a Reader's side, and I get *you*."

Alice had to admit she couldn't imagine Geryon submitting meekly to capture, or even speaking to the ice giant on any terms other than conqueror to conquered. *He'd probably have laid waste to the whole fortress. That's what makes me different from him,* she thought fiercely. *He* deserves *what I've got planned for him.*

The ice giants hadn't treated them too badly, all things considered. They'd taken their packs and Flicker's spear and walked them gently but firmly to this cell in the depths of the fortress. It probably would have been uncomfortably small for one of their own people, but it was larger than Alice's bedroom back in the Library. The last she'd seen of Erdrodr, the ice giant girl had been speaking frantically to her mother.

"We'll be all right," Alice said. "They can't keep us in here forever."

"Oh?" Flicker said. "Why not, exactly?"

He had a point. "I don't *think* they will," she amended. "And if they try, I'll—"

"Think of something," Flicker finished for her. "So far, that's worked out very well."

Alice was in the midst of trying to think of an appropriately cutting response when heavy footsteps came from outside. A key turned in the lock with a *clank,* and a heavyset woman opened the door. She had an ax strapped to her shoulder.

"Helga desires your presence," the ice woman said. "Follow me."

"What about Erdrodr?" Alice said, getting to her feet. "Is she all right?"

The ice woman did not answer.

Alice and Flicker had to jog behind the giant to keep up with her strides. For the hundredth time, Alice wondered if she ought to simply take hold of her threads and smash the giant aside. *There are too many, though. And I don't know the way to the portal.* Better to keep violence as a last resort, until time started to really run short.

They passed through more stone corridors, then cut out into the starlight and across the central courtyard, where several ice giants were tending the ice flowers.

The largest building facing the square had huge metal doors standing half-open. Inside, a broad timbered hall was occupied by a pair of long tables, where it looked like the feast Byrvorda spoke of had recently taken place. Joints from some large animal and smaller, bird-like carcasses were scattered across the tables, reduced to a mess of gristle and bones.

Only a half-dozen ice giants remained, clustered at one end of one of the tables. Just beyond them, in a large chair, sat Helga the Ice Flower. She still wore her furs and leather, and her axes rested against the arms of her throne. One of her massive hands was wrapped around a tankard. In front of her, Erdrodr was on her knees, head bowed. Alice was glad to see that she seemed unharmed.

Helga looked up as they entered, peering down at Alice and Flicker. Their guard led them through the big hall to stand beside Erdrodr. Alice tried to catch the giant girl's eye, but she didn't raise her head.

"The prisoners," the guard announced.

"A human," Helga rumbled, "and a fire-kin. Curious. And my daughter tells me that the human is a *Reader*, which is stranger still. It has been a very long time since we have crossed paths with one of that benighted breed." She shifted irritably on her throne. "Is it true, then?"

"It is," Alice said. She fought an urge to say "Your Majesty"—the place resembled nothing so much as a medieval throne room blown up to twice normal size.

"And are you here to enslave my people to your books?" Helga's scarred lip twitched upward.

"No," Alice said. "I just want to use the portal."

"That is what my daughter tells me," Helga said. "She is young, however, and more naive than she ought to be." Her eyes sought out Byrvorda, who was among the giants gathered at the table. "My Keen Eyes tells me you wish to visit the Palace of Glass. Have the mighty Readers grown so careless of their lives?"

Alice shook her head, not sure what to say. Helga yawned.

"No matter. Tell me, Reader, what did you promise my daughter, that she agreed to betray her family?"

"She came to us," Alice said. "She said she could get us to the wild portal, if we took her with us to the other side."

"I *told* you," Erdrodr said. "They—"

"*Silence*," Helga snapped. "When I wish you to speak, girl, I will say so. Reader, you did not think what you were doing was wrong?"

"I only want to pass through," Alice said. "Erdrodr told us—"

"No doubt she spun you a tale of woe. Cruel creature that I am, I keep her locked away for no reason other than malice." Helga's lip twitched again. "Did she tell you what happened the last time she was allowed to join the hunt? How she was nearly killed by a long-horn because she was busy *sketching* some pretty bug? Did you show the Reader your scars, Erdrodr?"

"That was two years ago," Erdrodr said. "I have grown, Mother."

"So you say. I see a silly girl still obsessed with her drawings. Until you demonstrate you're no longer a child, you will be treated like one."

Alice, standing beside Erdrodr, could feel her tension, but the giant girl lowered her head and went quiet.

"Well." Helga rolled her shoulders. "My daughter has pleaded quite eloquently on your behalf, Reader. She says that the idea of breaking you into the fortress was entirely hers, which is *exactly* the sort of foolish notion I expect from her. Since the only real harm done is a broken door, I believe I will be generous. You and your companion may pass through the curtain, and good riddance to you. If you wish to kill yourself at the Palace of Glass, it is hardly my concern." She waved a hand. "Bring their things and take them away."

"Thank you," Flicker said, bowing low. "We are very—"

"What about Erdrodr?" Alice said. "What will happen to her?"

Helga's face went cold. "I hardly think that is any of *your* concern."

"I gave my word that I would bring her through the portal," Alice said, not daring to look at either of her companions. "I don't know if that means anything among your people, but it does for me."

"Your *word*?" Helga's sneer broadened. "All the worlds know what the word of a Reader is worth. You had best go at once. I can feel my generosity waning by the moment."

"Go," Erdrodr said in a low voice. "It's all right, Alice. Just—"

"She comes with us," Alice said.

"*Now* she's willing to put up a fight," Flicker muttered.

Helga glared down at Alice, blue eyes gleaming with fury. "Are you challenging me, little Reader?"

"I don't want to challenge anyone," Alice said. Her heart was hammering, but she forced herself to meet Helga's gaze. "But I will, if that's what it takes to keep my word."

Muttering ran through the ice giants behind them. Helga's face twisted for a moment into a mask of rage that was quickly replaced with a superior smirk.

"Is that so?" she said softly. "How shall we compete, then? A race around the castle? Shall we see who can shift the heaviest weight? Who can make the climb to the top of the tower?"

Alice kept her expression neutral, but she was thinking frantically. She doubted even Spike's strength would let her out-lift, out-run, or out-climb Helga. The giant was twice her size, and her limbs were corded with thick muscle. *Maybe I could try to out-think her.* But intelligence glittered in those ice-blue eyes, and Alice had a nasty suspicion that if the ice giants had anything like chess or checkers, then Helga was a master of it.

Then it came to her, all at once, and she found a grin spreading across her face. *Of course.*

"Flowers," she said. "We'll compete with flowers."

A silence fell throughout the hall.

"Alice, no," Erdrodr hissed. "You don't know what you're asking—"

A deep, raspy sound cut her off, rising until it filled the great room and echoed off the walls. Helga was laughing.

"I will say this for Readers," she said, lips stretching in a wolfish smile that reminded Alice of the labyrinthine Torment. "You do not lack for courage. Or for arrogance. But unless you plan to be my guest until you can grow your own crop, how do you plan to hold this competition?"

"Give me a few minutes and one of your trees," Alice said. "If I can produce a more impressive flower than any of yours, then Erdrodr comes with us."

Helga was still smiling. "And if you cannot?"

"You let Flicker go," Alice said, "and I'll do whatever you like."

"Reader," Flicker whispered. "Are you sure about this?"

"Not at all," Alice whispered back. "But you told me to think of something . . ."

"I was hoping for something a bit less mad."

"Done," Helga said. "Having my own Reader would be a useful thing. Do you need a rest to prepare yourself?"

"No," Alice said.

"Then let's waste no further time."

They all gathered in the courtyard, and passersby stopped their work at the sight of their leader and the tiny visitors. Helga prowled among her trees, examining the pale flowers and running her hand across the petals. She muttered to herself as she went, finally halting in front of a particularly large specimen stippled with blue and red. The ice giant broke the flower off with a *crack* like an icicle snapping, and carried it in both hands back to Alice.

"This is the finest flower in my garden," she said, her voice softening. "Have you ever seen its like?"

It was beautiful, Alice had to admit. Layers of delicate ice petals, so thin that they looked as though they would melt under her breath, opened outward from a central bud. Some were tinted a very faint red, and others a deep, icy blue, giving the whole flower a dappled look. And, Alice was surprised to find, it had a sweet, cold scent, a bit like peppermint.

"If you wish to back down," Helga said, quiet enough that only Alice could hear, "I will permit it."

Alice looked around. The edges of the courtyard were full of ice women now, in robes, furs, and bits of armor. All their eyes were on her. Flicker looked as nervous as Ashes walking on the edge of a bath, and Erdrodr's face was ashen and pale.

"It's a beautiful flower," Alice said. "But I'll give it a try, if it's all the same to you."

Helga's scarred lip twisted into a sneer. "Then pick whatever tree you like, Reader, and let us see your magic."

Alice nodded and walked past Helga, to the edge of the grid of potted trees. She stopped at one that had no flowers at all, and put her hand against it while she took hold of the tree-sprite thread. She could feel the tree, ancient and tired, with only the feeble light of the stars to draw on.

She dug in her pocket and produced one of her acorns. With the tree-sprite's power in her, she could feel the energy packed into the acorn as it lay in her palm, a blazing star of the raw stuff of life. She tossed it into the ice tree's pot, where it fell into the water with a *plop*. There was no soil in there, only a tangle of roots and small rocks, and the acorn drifted down among them.

Touching the tree again, she willed its roots to find the acorn and break it open, absorbing the unexpected nourishment. Power thrilled through the tree. It wanted to grow, to shoot up like a weed, to drill its roots through the sides of its pot in a quest for more water. But Alice held it in check, directing all that energy into a single bud at the end of a long branch.

She closed her eyes and created the flower in her mind. It would be red, blue, and green, brilliantly colored instead of pale, and larger than anything she'd seen in the garden. The bud swelled, and she heard Helga's breath hiss. Alice grinned to herself, hand twitching minutely as she directed the tree. The yard was silent, except for the howl of the wind, as the flower bloomed.

Alice felt the flower opening, but it seemed *off*, the tree itself protesting against what she was pushing it to do. *No*, she thought. *Like this. Grow.* She bore down harder, forcing the bud to spread. Something was wrong.

Then Helga began to laugh again.

"Is that it, Reader? Is that what all your power can do?"

Alice opened her eyes.

The flower was blue and red and green, but it was a

far cry from the delicate, intricate mass of petals Helga had shown her. It was a mess, thick slabs of icy leaf interspersed with half-formed petals, most of them still rolled into tight tubes. As Alice watched, several petals cracked under their own weight and fell. Tentatively, she took a sniff, and nearly gagged at a scent like rotten meat.

"I . . ." Alice looked from the hideous flower to Helga's elegant bloom and back. "I'd like to try again."

"By all means." Helga smiled her wolfish smile. "I would hate for it to be said that you put forward less than your best effort."

Alice snapped the ruined flower off, letting it fall into

the pot to dissolve in the water. She closed her eyes again, reaching back out to the tree. There was still power left from the acorn, the tree fairly quivered with it, but she was suddenly unsure of what to do.

What happened? The flower had been so *clear* in her mind. *Why didn't it grow right?* She tried to picture it, concentrating—the colors, the petals—

It wasn't clear, she realized. Not really. She called Helga's flower to mind. The way the petals interlocked at the base, how they were attached to the plant, each row growing so as to leave room for the next. The way the color faded toward the tips of the petals as it was drawn out of the branch and into the flower. All the delicate manipulation of chemicals that went into the scent.

When Alice had bound her first creature, the Swarm, she'd found it difficult to control more than one of the little swarmers at once. Eventually she'd figured out that the trick was to *trust* them—she could control them, but trying to keep track of a hundred legs at once was a recipe for disaster. But the swarmers already *knew* how to run, and with practice she'd learned to leave them to it and only provide general instructions.

The tree *knew* how to make a flower. Helga had taught it, with years of breeding and care. *All I have to do is point it in the right direction, not tell it what to do.* To ask for help, rather than command obedience.

Please, she thought at the tree. *Grow. Like this.*

Another bud began to form. Alice felt it burgeon and swell, layer after layer of delicate petals growing inside it. Colors welled up, a subtle pattern that formed of its own accord, like frost sketching ferns on a windowpane. A surge of energy, and the bud was opening, spreading its petals wide, the branch thickening beneath it to bear its weight. A sweet, crisp scent filled the air.

Alice let her eyes open again. The flower was almost the size of her head. It was nothing like she'd pictured— in a thousand ways, the tree had crafted it on its own. And it was beautiful, an elegant pattern of subtly refracted color, like a rainbow captured in ice. Alice let out a breath she hadn't realized she'd been holding, then looked up at Helga, keeping her face carefully neutral.

"I think," she said, "that this is probably the best I can do."

Helga blinked, her eyes shining. She swallowed hard.

"Leave us," she said. Her voice was husky. "All of you." When no one moved, the note of command returned. "Leave us!"

The other giants backed away. Helga held up a hand.

"Erdrodr."

"Yes, Mother?" the giant girl said in a tiny voice.

"Bring our guests' things." Helga swallowed. "And whatever you're going to need for your . . . journey."

Erdrodr let out an excited squeak and hurried away. Alice found herself alone with Helga and Flicker in a suddenly empty courtyard.

"Do you know where these trees come from?" Helga said.

Alice shook her head.

"My grandmother brought the seed here, from our old home. Through the gate, across the world, and through *another* portal. The world beyond the world beyond. She gave the seed to my mother, who planted it here. She gave the trees to me when they were only sprouts. They suffered here, with only the stars for light, but I nurtured them and bred this strain." She shook her head. "Mother told me about the flowers she remembered, back when she was at Grandmother's knee. No matter what I did, my trees never matched the beauty she told me about, not here. Until now."

"The tree knows how to make the flower," Alice said. "It just needed a little push."

Helga nodded, staring at the huge flower as if hypnotized.

"What happened to your home?" Alice said.

"It froze," Helga said. "It was always a cold place, but it grew colder, until not even my people could stay. We fled through the portal into the world beyond, and then here when we found it suited us better."

Alice glanced at Flicker. *What was it he said? "The Heartfire began to weaken when they locked away the portals in their books and their libraries." Could these changes in the worlds be the fault of the Readers? When the portals are locked in books, does it weaken the worlds on the other side?* She pictured the Earth, her world, at the center of a vast web. Worlds linked to worlds by portals, spreading outward in an intricate tapestry, all nourished by power flowing from the true reality at the center. And then the doors slamming shut, the portals caught in a trap woven of words and magic, captured in libraries by the Readers and their labyrinthine servants. The lights of the web going out, bit by bit, the fires dimming.

It could be coincidence. Just because it happened to a few worlds doesn't mean the same thing happens everywhere. She shook her head. *Maybe Ending knows something. Or maybe we can get Geryon to tell us the truth, once we've caught him.*

"Listen," Helga said, shaking herself out of her reverie.

"I am Helga the Ice Flower, and let it never be said that I do not keep my word. But . . . Erdrodr . . ." She hesitated. "The world beyond is dangerous, and she is a foolish child. Is there no way you can leave her here, where she will be safe?"

"She wants a chance to prove herself to you," Alice said. "I can't tell her not to go where she thinks she has to."

"I suppose not." Helga sighed. "You truly mean to visit the Palace of Glass?"

"I won't let her come inside with me."

Helga shook her head. "Even Erdrodr knows better than to enter such a place. Is there no other way? Nowhere else you can find what you need? Our legends speak of monsters imprisoned there, horrors from beyond all the worlds. I do not know if I am worried that you will not return, or that you *will*."

"It has to be the Palace," Alice said. The Infinite Prison *is my chance to finally get revenge on Geryon. I'm not going to stop now.* "But I will keep your daughter safe and be as cautious as I can, you have my word."

"Thank you, Reader." Helga grinned, her scar making it lopsided. "I know well, now, what your word is worth."

CHAPTER FIFTEEN
THE LAND BEYOND

ALICE, FLICKER, AND ERDRODR stood in the basement room they'd so nearly reached the night before, with Helga and Byrvorda waiting in the empty doorway. Alice felt a touch of guilt at the sight of the demolished door.

"Sorry about that," she said.

Helga waved a hand. "It's nothing. You're sure you don't want more food?"

Alice's pack, depleted by the days in the realm of the fire-sprites, now fairly bulged with provisions. The ice giants' food—mostly smoked meat and hard bread—was a considerably better match for human physiology than the fire-oil. Flicker's own supplies had been augmented by a stash of kindling and dead leaves. Erdrodr had a much larger pack with supplies for herself, a collapsible tent made of hide and bone, and the sphere-boat.

"I don't think I could carry any more," Alice said.

"We'll be fine, Mother," Erdrodr said. She was bouncing in place, eager to be off. Her slate and a sack of charcoal hung from the side of her pack.

"Are you ready?" Alice said to Flicker. "And are you sure—"

"For the last time," Flicker snapped, "I'm not going back. Pyros told me to take you to the Palace of Glass, and I'm going to deliver you right to the front door."

"All right." Alice faced the gate. "Here we go, then."

The wild portal hung in the air. The ice giants called it a curtain, and Alice could see why; it looked like a cloth painted in shifting rainbow colors, flapping in an invisible wind. According to Helga, there was no special trick to passing through. You walked forward and . . . went.

Well. No percentage in hanging about. Alice gripped the straps of her pack and strode forward. A few steps took her to the threshold, and then one more took her—

—across.

It was a strange sensation, both like and unlike what she felt when she used a portal-book. There was the same moment of dislocation, as though she spent an infinitesimal time in a place *between* the worlds, neither on one side nor the other. But the portal-books had a sense of power, tightly controlled, waiting like a coiled spring, ready to serve the Reader who glanced at them. Here the power was diffuse, ragged, a wild surge of energy that rose as she stepped through and lapped around her like a wave. When it receded, she found herself blinking in bright light.

There was a proper sun here, she was glad to see, just edging away from the horizon. It was blessedly warm on her skin after so much time in the starlit world. She stood in a meadow, tall grass rising past her thighs, and ahead of her was a tree line that wouldn't have looked out of place back in Pennsylvania. She wondered, briefly, if the portal had somehow taken them back to Earth— somewhere in the southern hemisphere, perhaps, since it was mid-winter back at the Library.

But no. In the middle distance, a large animal raised its head. It looked a bit like a moose, but it had no *legs*, just a long body held in the air by hundreds and hundreds of tiny butterfly wings attached to its back. They fluttered in constant motion, each pair a different color.

"Oh!" said Erdrodr. "How wonderful!" She felt for

her slate with one hand, eyes fixed on the moose-thing, which stared back warily. "Just give me a moment—"

"I think we had better get moving," Alice said. "Or at least *I* should. You don't have to stay with us, Erdrodr. You've done everything you said you would do."

"And so have you," the ice giant said. She let her slate fall back. "But I think I will travel with you a while longer. I suspect my mother would want me to."

"We're happy to have you along," Alice said. "Flicker, do you have any idea which way to go?"

"I think so," Flicker said. He looked up at the sun, not bothering to shade his eyes, and stared at it long enough that Alice began to tear up in sympathy. "It's . . . going up. That's rising, yes?" When Alice nodded, the fire-sprite turned and pointed in the opposite direction. "Then we go that way for a while, until we find a wide river. And we follow it toward some mountains."

That sounded awfully vague for Alice's liking, but she didn't have anything else to go on. *If we find anyone here, we can ask them. Everyone seems to have heard of the Palace of Glass.* She let the fire-sprite lead the way, toward the trees.

"I want to draw that creature after all," Erdrodr said, her slate already out. Charcoal crumbled in her fingers as she sketched the form of the flying moose. "But go ahead. I will catch up."

It turned out that she could manage this without much difficulty, with a stride twice as long as Alice's. Erdrodr more than made up for her advantage in speed, though, with distractions. She wanted to draw *everything*, every animal and bug that was willing to hold still, and quite a few of the more interesting plants. Alice and Flicker started grinning at each other every time they saw something new, waiting for the startled "Oh!" and the scrape of charcoal on paper.

"She's certainly . . . enthusiastic," Flicker said as they strolled ahead of the ice giant girl. They'd passed through one belt of trees and emerged onto another grassy stretch, climbing up the side of a shallow hill. When they crested it, they saw the glitter of a stream winding its way into the middle distance, lined with scraggly bushes. "Though I hope she doesn't stumble into anything dangerous."

"Is there anything dangerous to stumble into?" Alice said. So far, all they'd seen in terms of animal life was the moose, several brilliantly colored birds, and a few beetles. They'd all been a rainbow of colors. Everything but the vegetation here seemed to have sprung from the saturated canvas of some mad painter.

"I . . . remember a few. The bluechills, but they live in the mountains. Some kind of big cat, I think? It's a bit fuzzy." He shrugged, glancing down at the stream with distaste. "I can see why my great-grandspark left this place behind."

As far as Alice was concerned, after freezing in the dark, the gentle sunlight and meadow of soft grass were the next best thing to paradise. *But if there's a stream, it must rain here.* That probably made it less than an ideal habitat for creatures like the fire-sprites.

After reaching the top of the hill and starting down the other side in silence, Flicker looked at Alice out of the corner of his eye.

"What?" Alice said.

"I have to ask," the fire-sprite said. "Could you really have fought your way through Helga and the ice giants, if you had to?"

"I don't know," Alice said. "That's part of the reason I didn't try."

"Part of the reason?"

"I told you. I don't hurt people if I don't have to." *Being a Reader isn't* always *about hurting people.* She thought of Geryon. *Just people who deserve it.*

"You *are* different," Flicker said after another moment

of silence. He stared ahead, not meeting her eyes. "You're trying to be, at least."

"I'm still figuring out what I'm trying to be."

"Are there others like you? Other Readers, I mean?"

Alice hesitated. *Dex,* she wanted to say, *and Isaac, and Soranna, and even Ellen.* After what they'd gone through in Esau's labyrinth, she thought of them all as friends. But while they'd been friendly to *her,* they were all Readers— they'd all used the prison-books, and showed as little concern as Alice had for cutting their way through the vicious creatures that had swarmed them on the fortress bridges. *Would they be willing to sit and talk with Flicker?* She didn't know.

Isaac would, she decided. *Even if I had to bash him over the head until he got the idea.*

"Maybe," she said. "I'm not sure."

"But not Geryon."

"No."

His name gave Alice a twinge of renewed anger. Her rage had been buried under the worries and trials it had taken to get this far, but it was still there, a red-hot coal hissing under a shovel-full of soil. Soon or later, it would surface.

"And you're going to . . . what, fight him?"

"If I can," she said.

"What happens if you win?" Flicker said. "To us, I mean."

"No more tribute," Alice said. "No more prison-books. I would never do that to you."

"But will you protect us?"

"Does Geryon?"

"Not against things like the bluechill," Flicker said. "I asked Pyros why we didn't hide from Geryon, or try to fight him, instead of giving him tribute. He said that if it wasn't Geryon, it would be some other Reader. Only the threat of Geryon's protection keeps the others from coming by and demanding their own tribute, or just taking what they want." He looked at Alice. "So if you win, will you be able to keep them away? All of the others?"

"I . . ." Alice shook her head. "I haven't thought about it."

Flicker shot her an unreadable look. "Maybe you should."

When the sun went down, they made camp amid a copse of trees, at the top of another hill. Erdrodr pitched the tent, which turned out to be a spacious thing, intended for several ice giants and more than big enough for her and two human-sized companions. Flicker built a fire in front of it, and Alice and the ice giant warmed their dinners over it while the fire-sprite picked up bits of the flame itself and licked them from his fingers. The stars here, Alice was pleased to see, stayed still like proper celestial bodies.

So far, they hadn't seen anything dangerous, which ought to have been reassuring. Alice couldn't put Pyros' and Helga's warnings out of her mind, though, and she kept a suspicious eye on the shadows around the camp. As she washed down some of the giants' hard bread with a swallow from her canteen, she felt suddenly, unutterably tired.

Five days left. She stared at the face of the watch, willing the second hand to run slower. *And it'll take at least a couple of days to get back to the portal-book from here. I'm running out of time.* She shook her head wearily.

"Someone should stand guard," she said. "If there are dangerous creatures around here, I don't want one of them sneaking up on us while we're all snoring."

"I'll keep an eye out," Flicker said. "Get some rest."

"Don't you need to sleep?"

"I don't think we sleep the same way you do," he said. "We rest, but we're not . . . you know." He frowned. "Unconscious."

Now that she thought about it, Alice couldn't recall seeing Flicker close his glowing red eyes. "You're sure?"

"Trust me." He shrugged. "You actually scared me the first time you went to sleep and woke up again. For us, it's a bit like dying and coming back to life."

Alice laughed. "Good enough for me. What about you, Erdrodr? Do your people sleep standing on their heads or something?"

"What?" The ice giant had been staring into the fire. "No. Why? It seems like that wouldn't be very comfortable."

"Never mind," Alice said. "I'm going to bed."

She crawled in through the tent flap, dragging her pack behind her. Erdrodr had brought three sleeping rolls along—it wasn't much more than a strip of shaggy hide, but Alice collapsed onto it as though it were the softest featherbed. She felt ready to drop off instantly, and was deciding whether to bother removing her boots, when the flap rustled.

"Reader?" said Erdrodr.

Alice opened her eyes reluctantly. It didn't help much.

Only a few scraps of illumination from the fire out-side snuck in through gaps in the fabric. Erdrodr was a shadow in the deeper darkness.

"What is it?" Alice said.

"I just realized I never thanked you, for what you did. I was so caught up in finally being here—"

"It's all right," Alice said. "We had a deal, didn't we?"

"I said I would get you to the curtain, and I didn't do it. You didn't have to go so far for my sake."

"Maybe not." Alice shook her head, invisible in the darkness. "It seemed like the right thing to do."

"It probably seems stupid to you, my wanting to come here so badly just to *draw* things. You've got something big and important to do, and I . . ."

"I understand," Alice said. "And I'm glad you decided to stay with us."

There was a pause. Alice let her eyes slide closed again.

"When you challenged Mother, I thought you were going to fight her," Erdrodr said, very quietly. "That's what the Readers do in all the stories, they fight. I thought the whole thing was going to end up teaching me some horrible lesson, where I got what I'd always wanted but only because you'd killed my mother, and I would learn to appreciate what I had only after I'd lost it, and . . . you know. The kind of thing that happens in stories." She sniffed. "Thank you for not hurting her. I know she and I don't get along all the time, but . . ."

"Yeah." Alice thought about warm afternoons lying in Central Park, and found tears stinging the corners of her eyes. "I know."

Chapter Sixteen
TURTLES ARE JERKS

THEY GOT AN EARLY start the next morning, and by noon they were in sight of the river. It was a big one, as wide as the Hudson in New York City, curving calm and flat through the grasslands. Alice, Flicker, and Erdrodr turned right, staying close to the bank, and made their way upstream. Soon, distant mountains darkened the horizon.

The river, Alice discovered before long, was inhabited. Big hummocky shapes broke the surface at regular intervals, moving upstream or down at a rapid clip. They were partially transparent, and swirls and whorls of color were embedded inside them, like Venetian blown glass.

Each one was a different color, from deep blue to soft green or even pale pink.

She might have thought they were small islands, moving under their own power, but one of them stopped and rose a bit higher out of the water, revealing a small, gnarled head that looked them over with black, unblinking eyes, and four huge flippers sculled gently through the water, holding it in place against the current.

"It's so pretty!" Erdrodr said, reaching for her sketch pad.

"Naturally," said the turtle in a deep, gravelly voice. "You, however, are ugly. And foolish, I don't wonder."

"What?" Erdrodr said, blinking in confusion.

"You can talk?" Alice said.

"That should be obvious to any right-thinking creature," the turtle said. "But as you are a little ape, I clearly should have expected less. Also, your nose is crooked."

"It is not crooked!" Alice said.

"Is so," the turtle said. "And your hair is stringy and frankly unappetizing. Really, each of you is a less impressive specimen than the last."

"Did you stop here just to insult us?" Flicker said.

"Yes," the turtle said, submerging again and swimming off.

"What was *that*?" Alice said, rubbing her nose.

Flicker shrugged.

"Your nose isn't *very* crooked," Erdrodr said.

The next turtle that passed by commented on their shabby state of dress and the shocking lack of proper accessories, while the one after that criticized their manners and breeding. After that, by common consent, they shifted their path some distance away from the river, sticking to the higher ground.

Alice's watch marked only four days and a few hours left when they stopped for dinner that night. She looked from the hills in her path to the mountains that were her destination and back again. *We're not going to make it.*

Their packs were getting lighter too. Alice had thought they'd had plenty of supplies, but Erdrodr's size came with a corresponding appetite. There was probably food to be had, in a land this lush, but searching would slow them down even further.

We could always try turtle soup, Alice thought sourly, watching the huge creatures, gleaming in the last rays of the sun, wend their way up and down the river below. At this distance, heads and flippers invisible below the surface, they looked like little boats.

Boats. She frowned at them, thinking of the ice raft still in Erdrodr's pack. *There's an idea. If only I can figure out how to bribe a turtle.*

It was kind of a plan, anyway. Alice sighed. *Flicker's not going to like it.*

The next morning, Alice interrupted the first turtle that stopped to insult them.

"I was wondering," she said, "if we could make a deal. We need to get up the river, you see."

"Your intellect," the turtle continued, "is clearly inferior, even for an unfortunate of a minor race such as yourself. I think—"

"Yes, yes," Alice broke in. "We're all terrible. You and all your friends have been telling us."

"We *are* extremely perceptive," the turtle said.

"But in return for your help pulling our boat upstream," Alice continued, "we could do a favor for you."

"Oh?" The turtle's head turned toward her, black eyes gleaming. "As it happens, there *is* a favor I need, one even such an inferior creature as yourself should be able to help me with. There's a spot on my back I can't scratch. Flippers, you see. If you would climb aboard and give it a tickle, I would be *most* obliged, and I'd be happy to take you anywhere you want to go."

This is going to be easier than I thought. Alice shrugged out of her pack and went down to the bank. The turtle shuffled closer, so Alice could scamper through the shallows and up the steep curve of its shell. The glassy, colorful substance was slick underfoot, so she moved on all fours, keeping her hands flat on the huge pebbly surface.

"A little farther to the left," the turtle said. "Up a bit. A bit more. Ah, yes. There you are."

It was hard to imagine a shell *itching*, but Alice had no idea what it felt like to be a turtle. She scratched at the glassy stuff tentatively.

"Oh, yes," the turtle said. "That's absolutely the spot. Keep that up."

"Alice?" Erdrodr called. "Are you all right?"

Alice looked up from her task and found that the turtle had pushed off from the bank, swimming out into the middle of the river. She waved at the ice giant and said, "Do you think you could take me back to the bank? I don't want to get wet."

"That would be a tragedy," agreed the turtle. It immediately began to submerge, great shell sinking beneath the water, leaving Alice treading water in the middle of the river.

"Stupid ape," the turtle scoffed. "An *intelligent* creature would never have believed such a thing. As a superior race, we would never get an itch in a place we were unable to scratch." Then, without waiting for an answer, it ducked its head back under and went on its way.

Alice struggled back to the bank in her clothes and boots, hauling herself out of the river a few hundred yards downstream from the other two, where the current had carried her. She lay on the dirt for a while, breathing hard, then got to her feet and trudged back up to meet them.

"Turtles," she said, "are jerks."

"Looks like it," Flicker said. Alice thought he might be fighting back a grin.

"They certainly don't seem very friendly," Erdrodr said. "Should we try talking to the next one?"

"Yes," Alice said. "But first I think we should make sure we've got its full attention."

It was warm enough that Alice had stripped off her soaked outer garments and laid them out to dry in the sun. She wrapped herself in her sleeping roll and glared down at the three sheets of parchment she'd dug out of her pack.

"Those are the things you tried to use on the bluechill, aren't they?" Flicker said. "I thought they didn't work."

"There's something wrong with them," Alice said. "I'm going to see if I can fix it."

She closed her eyes and reached out with her mind, feeling the magic embedded in the pages. Part of the web she'd so carefully laid down was torn and flapping loose. Alice let herself flow through the links and joins of the spell, feeling for the path the power would have to take.

Oh. She felt like slapping herself on the forehead. There was a *loop* in the spell, a place where the energy fed back against itself. *No wonder it didn't work before. It was drawing more and more power from me, trying to be stronger than itself, until the spell couldn't take it anymore.* A bit like a short circuit, if Alice was the battery. *Ending was right when she said I ought to test it.*

Now that she could see where the web had broken, redirecting the flow to eliminate the loop was easy. A few tweaks, and the spell was whole again. *And hopefully* fixed *too.* She felt for the three pages, gathered them up, folded them over, then opened her eyes. Flicker sat on a nearby rock, idly pulling dry leaves from a bush and incinerating them on his palm in little puffs of smoke.

"Where's Erdrodr?" Alice said.

"Up the hill a ways, drawing a bug. Did you figure it out?"

"I think so. I'll leave two of these here for you to set up. Make sure they're spread out, and *don't* stand between them." As a magical creature, Flicker would be caught in the ward as well. "In fact, you two ought to hide once it's set up. I've got an idea on how to play this."

Chapter Seventeen
HITCHING A RIDE

AFTER EXPLAINING HER PLAN to Flicker and sending him off to corral Erdrodr, Alice took off her shoes to leave with her other things drying on the bank, tucked one of the three parchments into her undershirt, and walked back down to the river's edge. Another turtle cruised past and gave her a superior look as she waded into the shallows.

With a deep breath, she wrapped the devilfish thread tight around herself. Transitioning from air- to water-breathing was always hard. As her body shifted and changed, there was a moment of confusion and panic; she flopped ungracefully into the water as a huge, toothy, Alice-sized fish. She wriggled out of the shallows and into deep, cool water, savoring the feel of the river as it sluiced through her gills.

Green light from luminescent patches on her sides illuminated the sandy bottom of the river, and smaller fish darted out of her way in terror. She suppressed the instinctive urge to snap at them as she crossed the river, fighting against the current. When she felt her back break the surface, she released her grip on the devilfish thread and changed back into a girl, standing hurriedly and gulping fresh air.

The parchment had gotten a bit damp, but not soaked— it had gone to the same who-knows-where place that her clothes went when she transformed—and Alice flapped it in the air to dry it as she hiked up the bank. She pulled on the Swarm thread to give her skin a bit of toughness, mostly for the sake of her bare feet, and pressed on until she reached a stand of bushes that would hide her from the river. There she paused, searching the opposite bank, until she found the tiny figure of Flicker. The fire-sprite jumped up and down, waving his arms, and Alice waved back.

She settled in behind the brush, peeking through a break in the foliage. If Flicker had done his job, the other two parchments were widely separated on the opposite side of the river, making a triangle that stretched all the way across. When Alice Read the spell, anything magical inside that triangle would be trapped. *Assuming it works properly this time.*

She let a couple of turtles pass by, headed downstream, and waited for one that was going in their desired direction fairly close to the bank where Flicker and Erdrodr were hiding. It was an especially large specimen, with dark green swirls in its shell. Alice opened the parchment and Read.

She felt the magic spring into being, pulling energy from her, but it was nothing like the terrifyingly rapid drain when they'd fought the bluechill. A white-walled triangle enclosed a sizable section of river, steadily becoming more solid and opaque. The turtle, oblivious at first, swam on until it ran into the upstream side of the ward. It hit the wall with a crackle of magic and raised its head from the water.

"I say!" the turtle exclaimed. "What's going on here?"

The wards contracted. The turtle swam back and forth, brushing the walls with its flippers, but it didn't thrash against them as the bluechill had. It wouldn't have mattered in any case: This time, the spell was working. Alice allowed herself a triumphant smile.

Leaving the parchment where it was, she jogged down to the river, turned back into the devilfish, and, careful to enter the river downstream of the turtle, swam across. She pulled herself out behind a rock, hidden from the turtle, and wandered up the bank with a casual air, as though she'd only been stretching her legs.

"This is intolerable!" the turtle said. "Help. I say, help!"

The ward had reached its smallest size, a triangle barely larger than the turtle itself. The big creature was thrashing its fins, churning the surface of the water to a froth to no avail.

Another turtle, gliding downstream, raised its head from the water and looked at the prisoner.

"What's going on?" it said.

"I'm stuck!" said the first turtle. "Help me out of here, would you?"

"Tough luck," the second turtle said. "You should have been smart enough not to get trapped in the first place."

It swam off as Alice walked up. The ward was still translucent enough to see through, but the turtle was so agitated, it took a few moments to notice her.

"I say, human!" it said, thrashing to turn around and face her in its tight confinement. "Something's got me trapped!"

"It looks that way," Alice said sympathetically.

"Get me out of here at once!" the turtle said.

"Not to be too blunt," Alice said, "but why should I? I'm not feeling especially well-disposed toward you turtles at the moment. You've been insulting us all day."

"My compatriots are most ill-mannered," the turtle said. "But if you let me out, I promise I will do nothing but sing your praises. All the right turtles will hear how generous you are."

"The opinion of turtle society is not terribly important to me," Alice said, and yawned theatrically. "As it happens, I'm in a bit of a hurry. Good luck with your predicament."

"Wait!" the turtle said. "Please. There must be something a superior creature such as myself can offer you."

"Well." Alice made a show of considering the turtle. "Could you pull a boat?"

"Of *course* I can pull a boat." The turtle slapped a flipper against the ward, eliciting a crackle of magic. "Get me out of here and I'll pull you wherever you like."

"How do I know you won't just swim off?"

"I am a turtle of my word," it said. "If I break a promise, even to a human, the whole river will know that Estevius Forthright Nichol-Flatley is no trustworthy turtle."

"Did you hear that?" Alice shouted at another turtle cruising upstream.

"I did!" it called back. "And he's almost as stupid as you are, but you're a sight uglier!"

"All right," Alice said to Estevius. "As it happens, I'm a bit of a magician. One moment."

She made a few meaningless gestures and muttered some arcane-sounding gibberish under her breath, then released the ward. Without her energy feeding it, the spell decayed, and the walls of the ward thinned and vanished.

"Oh, thank you!" Estevius said, swimming around in circles. "For a human, you are a surprisingly considerate creature. Practically demi-chelonian."

"Don't forget your promise," Alice said.

The turtle bobbed its head. "Fetch your boat, and I will tow it for you. But quickly, now! I have a salon to attend, and if I'm late, the others will be most sarcastic at me."

Even a trustworthy turtle, Alice decided, was not exactly pleasant company.

"And he doesn't wonder about where the trap came from?" Flicker said.

"Turtles are jerks," Alice said, "but I don't think they're very smart."

She and Flicker watched the ice boat grow outward from the sphere Erdrodr had dropped in the water. Alice had crossed the river to retrieve her ward, folding it carefully back into her pack along with the others. She'd dressed in her now-dry garments and made sure the silver watch still worked after its dunking.

"Are you going to be all right?" Alice said.

"Fine," Flicker said, staring at the boat. "I'll be fine."

"If you . . . get wet," Alice said carefully, "what would happen? Would it hurt you?"

"Not . . . hurt." Flicker looked pained. "It's hard to explain. Can you imagine the most disgusting liquid you can think of?"

Alice nodded, picturing something suitably vile.

"Now think about falling into a whole river of it."

"Urgh."

"Yeah." Flicker looked down at the boat again. "I'll be fine."

"The harness is ready!" Erdrodr said. She held up a mass of thin brown rope. "I had to tie together all the lines from the tent, but I think it will hold."

"Perfect." Alice took the rope and went over to the turtle. "Will it be all right if we tie this to your tail?"

"My mighty tail has borne heavier burdens," Estevius

said, sniffing. He raised the appendage in question, a thick, stubby green thing, out of the water. "Tie away."

Alice wrapped the rope tight, tied it off, and tested it with a tug. Once she was certain it was secure, she walked the line back and tied the other end to the ice boat. Flicker was already aboard, crouching in the back under a pile of canvas from the tent. Erdrodr carried his spear, which was more of a stick in her huge hands.

"All ready!" the ice giant said.

"Flicker?" Alice said. "How do we know when we've reached our destination?"

"There's a mountain," Flicker said, voice muffled. "A tall single spire, with three separate peaks, like a crown. We want to get off right at the base."

"All right." Alice climbed into the craft, producing a moan from Flicker as it rocked. Erdrodr pushed them away from the bank with the spear, and Alice waved at the turtle. "Let's go!"

She had to admit that in spite of the caustic tongue he apparently shared with all the other turtles, Estevius was quite a swimmer. The weight of the boat didn't slow him at all, and his powerful flippers pulled them upstream at a steady pace, even against the current. The hills on

either side of the river slid past with a satisfying rapidity, and the mountains drew closer. Alice checked the watch again as the sun sank toward the hills. *Three days, twenty-two hours. Still cutting it close, considering I have no idea how long I'm going to take at the Palace itself.*

Flicker, curled up under the tent, showed no interest in conversation, so Alice sat beside Erdrodr. The giant perched in the stern of the boat, sketch board in hand, using a piece of crumbling charcoal to do an amazingly lifelike rendering of Estevius' shell, complete with the tiny ripples he made as he glided through the water.

"Do you always use charcoal?" Alice said.

Erdrodr sighed. "I tried with ink, once, but it always spatters from the quill. I was going to make myself a brush, but Mother told me to stop wasting the ink, so I never got around to it. There's always plenty of charcoal."

It was odd, the things you took for granted, Alice thought. She had a hard time imagining what it would be like to grow up without *pencils,* for example. Or spending her whole life underground, never seeing the sky. *And knowing that every few years one of your friends or family was going to be taken away to be trapped in a book, and never, ever set free . . .*

She shook her head. What Flicker had said, about protecting his tribe from the other Readers, had needled her. She was loath to admit it, but if it came to an actual *fight,* she wouldn't have a ghost of a chance against Geryon or any one of his peers. She'd watched the battle between him and Esau in the magic mirror, and it had been like a war between ancient gods. Even if she *could* trick Geryon, capture him, then what would she do when someone like Esau came for the fire-sprites? *For that matter, how many other groups is he "protecting"? How would I even find them all?*

"Can I ask you something?" Alice said, leaning against the side of the boat and trailing one hand in the water. The fish she'd seen earlier darted about, agitated in the turtle's wake.

"Of course," Erdrodr said, not looking up from her sketch.

"You said you'd heard stories about Readers. What kind of stories?"

"It's . . ." Erdrodr looked up at Alice, then back down at her drawing. "They are just stories. I know most of them are not true."

"It's all right. Tell me."

"Readers are . . ." The giant sighed. "Not evil, I think, but not good, either. *Capricious,* above all else. Powerful.

Figures to be appeased, or bargained with at great peril. To make a deal with a Reader is to risk your very essence out of desperation."

Like we would say "a deal with the devil." It wasn't every day you found out you played the role of the ultimate villain in someone else's fairy tales. "Had any of you ever met a Reader?"

Erdrodr shook her head. "We negotiated, a few times, with creatures who claimed to represent some Reader or other. They barter with us. And when the nations meet, there's always someone whose cousin's cousin has seen something incredible." She shrugged. "I never placed much credence in any of it."

"You don't seem afraid of me," Alice said.

"Why should I be?" Erdrodr held her drawing at arm's length, looking from it to the turtle and back. "You risked yourself for me, when you didn't have to."

"Thanks," Alice said.

"For what?"

"Never mind." The sun was setting, and Alice had to shade her eyes, but a tall shape up ahead was casting a three-pronged shadow across the water. "I think we're nearly there."

CHAPTER EIGHTEEN

THE PALACE OF GLASS

"THANK YOU, ESTEVIUS," ALICE said as they unhitched the turtle from the boat.

"It was the least I could do after your timely rescue," Estevius said, a bit puffed up with his own heroism. "I must say, you are the least unintelligent human I have ever met."

A compliment from a turtle? Alice frowned, then sighed. "You haven't ever met any other humans, have you?"

"A state of affairs that I devoutly hope continues!" Estevius said cheerfully. "Best of luck with whatever adventure your dull mind has dreamed up for you."

He slid off, head slipping beneath the surface of the river.

Finding the right place hadn't been difficult. The ice boat was tied up to an actual dock, albeit a very old and weathered one. It was a slab of marble, pitted and worn by the elements, with small, nearly faceless protrusions that might have once been statues. Alice had tied the rope around one of them, and she and Erdrodr had helped Flicker ashore.

Now they stood by the river's edge, looking up the mist-covered slope of the mountain. It was littered with marble columns and low, fragmented walls. Trees grew up between them, small pines thick with needles, and here and there was a boulder or a patch of fallen rock. Running directly up from the dock was a staircase, made of broad marble flagstones, that switchbacked uphill until it was swallowed in the mist.

Alice had been expecting something more intimidating. Ending had warned her that the Palace could drive her mad. Pyros had told her that the place was a prison, and prisons normally had walls and guards. And Helga had said something about monsters from beyond time and space, but all Alice could see was some old statuary and a bit of fog.

Of course, where magic is involved, appearances don't mean much. I'm only here to find The Infinite Prison. The last thing she wanted to do was let anything *out*, especially if it might find its way back through the portal to the ice giants and the fire-sprites.

"Well," Alice said. "I think it's pretty clear where I need to go. You two stay with the boat until I get back."

There was a long pause. Flicker and Erdrodr looked at each other.

"Are you sure—" Flicker said.

"Do you think—" Erdrodr said.

"No," Alice said. "I told Pyros I would go up there alone, and I said the same thing to Helga."

"But . . ." Flicker stopped, hair flaring a sickly yellow green. "I mean, what if—"

"We'll wait here," Erdrodr said firmly, "until you come back."

"Thank you." Alice shrugged out of her pack and made sure the last of her emergency acorns was still in her pocket. "I'll be as quick as I can."

The steps were broad and shallow, sharp corners rounded off by the passing centuries. It wasn't long before Alice lost sight of the river, though Flicker's hair glowed through the gathering mist for a few minutes longer. Then that too was gone, and she was climbing alone in a world of ancient marble and cold, dripping pines. Columns had once lined the steps, but most of them were broken, and some had toppled altogether and lay among the moss and bushes on the rocky slope. Periodically there was a statue on a pedestal, missing arms or legs, face weathered into a featureless oval.

There was still nothing that looked dangerous, but the silence was eerie. The mist muffled the noise of the river, and before long the only sound on the mountainside was the scrape of Alice's boots against the stone. There was no birdsong, no rustle of small animals in the grass, not even a breeze to stir the trees. Alice found her breath coming faster. When she caught a flash of movement, she froze in place, reaching for her threads.

"Hello?" she said. The mist swallowed the words as though she were swathed in rolls of cotton.

When she took a cautious step forward, something moved again. Alice raised her hand, and finally caught sight of a small figure farther up the mountain, repeating the gesture. She squinted, taking another step closer.

It's a mirror. She shook her head. *I'm jumping at my own reflection.*

To be fair, she thought as she got closer, it *was* hard to

see. The mirror was the size of a shop window, standing at an angle off to one side of the marble staircase. The mist blurred the edges. If not for her own image, Alice would have had a difficult time picking the thing out from the ruin-filled forest it reflected.

There was another mirror across from the next switchback, and then two more side by side, so that for a moment a pair of mirror-Alices climbed beside her. Other mirrors were set deeper in the forest. None of them were within arm's reach of the path. She kept climbing, and the mirrors multiplied with every turn, showing reflections of reflections of reflections. Dozens of Alices, then hundreds, followed by her side.

At last, the staircase reached a flat space, a broad circular courtyard floored with weathered marble. It was surrounded on every side by towering mirrors, smooth and perfect. As soon as Alice stepped in among them, she was multiplied into infinity, versions of herself receding into the distance in every direction. She turned in a slow circle, and they all turned with her, like an army on maneuver. The staircase ended there.

"Hello?" Alice said again. Here, among the mirrors, the word echoed on and on, down to the very cusp of hearing. "Is anyone there?"

One of the mirror-Alices turned around. Alice's voice caught in her throat. It looked exactly like her, of course, down to the last detail; but where her face ought to be, there was a blank white mask, as smooth as porcelain.

"Hello." It was Alice's own voice, echoed back at her.

Alice raised a hand tentatively. All the mirror images moved with her, except for the masked figure, which stood absolutely still.

"It has been a long time since we had a guest." The voice was still Alice's, still had the *quality* of an echo, but it spoke words she never had. The mirror image bowed elaborately, hair falling around her masked face. "It can be quite lonely up here. Be welcome."

"Thank you," Alice said. "I've come a long way to find you."

"I can imagine," the mirror image said—Alice thought she was speaking, anyway, though the voice seemed to come from everywhere at once now. "But where are my manners? We must show a guest proper hospitality."

The image in the mirror shifted and swam. The masked Alice was suddenly standing in a grand ballroom, ablaze with the light of crystal chandeliers and sumptuously decorated with exotic hardwood and gilt. A table beside her was heavily laden with food and drink, platters of carved meat steaming gently beside potatoes swimming in butter, pies and sugary confections, fruit and nuts and cheeses. The mirror-Alice's clothes had been replaced with a gown the likes of which Alice had never seen, all green silk and blue lace and long, elegant folds. Her hair was perfectly coiffed into a neat wave, and diamonds sparkled at her ears and on her wrists. Only the mask was the same, as blank as an empty sheet of paper.

Alice looked over her shoulder. The ballroom was repeated, over and over, mirrors multiplying on forever. Every Alice but her was splendidly dressed; when she moved her arm, a thousand images moved with her in delicate folds of lace. But, she realized with a start, each of the others was *different*, each a new variation of cut or color more spectacular and beautiful than the last. She looked down at herself, still wearing her scuffed, practical leathers, and felt a little out of place.

Curiously, she reached out a hand toward the banquet table. It looked close enough to touch, and all the other Alices reached with her. But her fingers found a pane of cold glass, inches from the food. When she looked around, every other Alice had picked up something from the table and begun to eat.

"I apologize," the masked figure said. "All we have to

offer, truly, is tricks of the light. But we do the best we can."

"Thank you," Alice said, thinking it was best to be polite. "It's beautiful."

The mirror image inclined her head. "We are so *very* glad of your company. What brings you here, from far away?"

"I'm looking for something," Alice said. "A book. It's called *The Infinite Prison*."

"That old thing?" The masked figure laughed. Alice felt strange, hearing her own laugh echoing around her. "Of course you can have it. Here."

The mirror-Alice turned to the table and picked up a small, leather-bound book that Alice hadn't noticed there a moment before. She flicked through the pages, shrugged, and snapped it closed again.

"Catch," she said, and tossed the book at Alice. Alice brought her hands up automatically, at the same time not expecting anything to reach her—*it's only a mirror, after all*—

The book fluttered open, bouncing off her hands, and she grabbed it before it could fall. Long practice made her avert her eyes until she got the book properly closed. It was light, and the cover was worn, but she could just make out an image tooled into the leather, two identical men staring at each other.

"Thank you," Alice said.

"It's been lying around in a corner all these years. We're glad to be rid of it." The mirror-Alice's voice had a pleading note. "But there must be more we can do for you. We're so alone here, and you've come so far."

"Do for me?" Alice looked over the food. "I don't suppose you could throw me one of those apples?"

"I'm afraid not. The book was given to us, long ago, and aside from that, all we have are—"

"Tricks of the light," Alice said. "None of it is real."

"But," the mirror image said eagerly, "tricks of the light can be useful things. We can *show* you anything you desire. Any time, any place, any person. Whatever you like."

Alice hesitated. She felt like she should leave—she'd gotten what she came for, with no difficulty at all, and asking for anything more seemed like pushing her luck. But the mirror-Alice sounded so eager, so *lonely*, blank mask leaning forward until it was practically pressed against the glass.

Could they show me my father? Even Readers couldn't just call up a view of the past from nothing. Pyros' warning, and Helga's, floated across her mind. *It could be a trick.* She decided to test them first.

"Well," Alice said. "I wouldn't mind seeing my old house again. The way it was a few years ago, before—"

And suddenly she was standing in it.

Chapter Nineteen
VISIONS

S HE WAS IN THE front hall, with its grand staircase
and walls hung with her father's favorite paintings. In
later years, the sitting room had been closed up, its furniture covered in dust cloths, and some of the paintings
had been sold; but this was the old house at its height in
1929, when the good times looked as though they might
go on forever.

Servants bustled everywhere, footmen in black jack-
ets and maids in long skirts, cleaning and polishing. It
was the night of the first big party at which she'd been
allowed to sit with the adults when company came over.
She'd been ten years old.

She looked down. The ground under her feet was still

marble flagstones, and the sky over her head was still a misty gray. But the mirrors all around her reflected the house in such detail that she could almost believe she'd stepped back in time. *Back to another life.* Normally it felt like those memories belonged to another girl, another Alice. *Or just a dream I was having before waking up.*

"Is it to your liking?" The mirror image stood unobtrusively in a corner of the hall, still in her party dress. Behind her, peeking out from a doorway, Alice saw two more copies of herself, both wearing blank-faced masks.

"It's amazing!" Alice said. "There's my old tutor Miss Juniper, and father's man Cooper. And Elpseth, who left when she had a baby. And old Mr. Spiven." She'd forgotten how many servants they'd had in the old days. They'd always been kind to her. She found herself blinking back tears. "How did you know about all of this?"

"Time and distance are illusions when you look from this side of the glass." The mirror image leaned forward again, eager. "What else? What else can we show you?"

Alice wavered, a wave of fatigue running through her. It had been a *long* climb up the marble steps, and a trying day even before that.

"Can you show me what's happening *now*?" she said. "Somewhere else?"

"Of course, of course. It's all the same, from where we stand."

Alice frowned, still not convinced. "Then show me Mr. Black."

The scene in the mirrors shifted in a flash, and Alice was looking in on the Library storeroom, where she'd once played a deadly game of hide-and-seek with the big servant. Now he was shifting sacks and boxes, muttering to himself as he rearranged the supplies and restacked the crates.

It certainly looks like Mr. Black. "What about Ashes?" she said.

The mirrors changed again. She was standing in the library, among the dusty shelves, watching a small gray cat stalk silently forward with tail outstretched. A white mouse came into view, sniffing the air, and Ashes leaped. The mouse, too quick for him, darted under a shelf, and he landed in a puff of dust and sneezed.

Alice grinned as she watched him look around, to see if anyone had noticed his failure. Satisfied that he was alone, he gave his dusty paws a couple of licks and sauntered off.

"All right," she said, warming to the idea. "Can you show me Isaac?"

There were four of the masked creatures now, standing two to each side of the mirror, watching her with their blank faces. She was aware of movement around her, more of them filtering in. They were shy, but so awkwardly eager to please, it was cute.

This time, the mirror cleared to show the inside of a cave with a huge pool of water, hot enough that steam rose into the air and condensation dripped from the walls. Isaac, dressed in his tattered coat, entered with a box in one hand and a lantern in the other. He set them down by the side of the pool and heaved a sigh.

"Would it kill him to get a proper shower?" Isaac said. He unlaced his shoes and pulled them off, then shrugged out of his coat. "I mean, we've got the hot water, it should just be a matter of plumbing. There must be a book somewhere with a plumber in it."

He pulled a bar of soap and towel from the box, then went to pull up his shirt. Alice put a hand over her eyes.

"That's enough," she said.

When she peeked through her fingers, the mirrors had gone back to showing the marble courtyard. Reflected Alices were everywhere, dozens of them, standing all around the circle of mirrors in their colorful dresses. Every one wore a blank-faced mask. Alice waved at them, feeling a little light-headed.

"What next?" the mirror image said. It could have been any of them, or all of them. "Who next?"

"Show me . . ." Alice wrinkled her forehead. It felt as though she was *missing* something, something important. Her hand reached toward her pocket, then stopped. Her thoughts had gone hazy. "Show me Geryon."

The old Reader sat on one side of a table, looking across at another old man. A chessboard sat between them, yellowed ivory pieces arrayed against glittering obsidian. His opponent was a black man with a frizz of gray hair and a nose like a hawk. Geryon glanced down at the board and scratched his enormous sideburns, and a knight slid forward and to the left of its own accord.

"Then you agree that it may be a problem," he said.

"It may *develop* into a problem," the other man said. He reached out, put a finger on a pawn, hesitated. "The labyrinthine have never been so restless, but we still hold the whip hand."

"Do we?" Geryon watched as the other man's finger tapped the pawn. "Sometimes I wonder."

"They need our power to keep the Great Binding intact.

If we wanted to, we could simply let the prisoner escape."

"And what then?" Geryon said. "How well would we fare without the power of the labyrinthine?"

"Well enough. Some of us were old even before the Binding, you know."

Geryon frowned. "Are you going to move that pawn, or just polish it?"

His opponent looked down at the board, sighed, and pushed his pawn forward. "I could never get the hang of these new-fangled games . . ."

Alice shook her head, and the image faded away. Her weariness had increased. She felt as though she were wearing her pack, and it had been loaded with lead weights. She took a step forward, putting one hand on the mirror for support, and found the glass cool and slick against her palm.

"What else?" the mirror image said. "We can show you anything."

"Anything," the echoes repeated, over and over. "Anything."

Alice's mind was as slow as molasses. Her mouth seemed too thick to shape words.

"I want to see," she said, "my twelfth birthday. My father . . . gave me a present."

"Of course," the mirror image said, echoes chattering beside it. "Of course . . . of course . . ."

The mirror showed her father's study, with its big desk and electric lamp. He sat in his familiar chair, fiddling with the bow on a brown paper package. The door opened, and Alice watched herself enter, wearing a pretty striped dress, a ribbon in her hair, and a blank, porcelain mask.

"Alice," her father said, smiling the smile she loved so much. "Have you been having a good birthday?"

"Yes!" Alice ran to the desk. "Cooper took me for ice cream and soda, and we watched them fixing the big clock down in the square. I want to learn how to fix clocks!"

Did I really sound like that? Alice had always thought of herself as grown-up for her age, but the image in the mirror looked like . . . well . . . a child. A normal, happy girl of twelve. *As opposed to . . . whatever I am now.*

Her father looked taken aback, but his smile broadened. "I'm sure you'd make a fine clocksmith. Is that what they're called? Clocksmiths?" Alice shook her head, giggling, and he cleared his throat noisily. "In any event, I found this in a shop the other day and thought you might enjoy having it."

He pushed the package toward her, and she grabbed it eagerly. "Can I open it?"

"Go ahead."

The mirror-Alice worried at the bow, then slid the ribbon off entirely and tore the paper. There was a book inside, of course. It was an old, battered book, the gilt lettering on its spine nearly illegible. Alice remembered it perfectly. A collection of Greek tragedies, printed in the eighteenth century, a fine piece for any library.

"I thought," her father said, a little gruffly, "that as much as you love books, it's time you started your own collection."

"Oh, thank you!" The blank-faced Alice rushed past the desk and wrapped her arms around her father as far as they would go. He hugged her back, then lifted her off her feet, eliciting a delighted laugh.

Alice, the real Alice, found her eyes full of tears. She leaned on the mirror, glass pressed against her forehead.

Her skin felt clammy and slick with sweat. The mist was getting thicker—even the other side of the courtyard was hard to see, and mirror-Alices continued to gather all around. They had changed, they'd all changed. The masks were no longer blank, but split by a black slash of a mouth, crosshatched into huge, white teeth.

"Ask," the mirror image said. "Ask, ask, ask."

"I . . ." Alice was breathing hard. It was difficult to get enough air in her lungs. "Can you show me . . ."

"Yes?" the mirror image said.

Deep in her befuddled mind, a bit of curiosity remained.

"My mother," Alice said. "I want to see my mother."

She had no memories of her mother, and her father had never even showed Alice a picture. On the one occasion she'd asked him directly, he'd told Alice she was dead, and the thunderous look on his face was such that she'd never dared mention it again. She'd always said that she didn't *need* a mother, that her father was enough. And that was true, but it would have been nice to at least see her face.

"Mother," the mirror image whispered. "Mother . . ."

The creature sounded a little vexed, as if something wasn't working right. The mirror flickered, like a movie at the end of the reel, and then went totally, utterly black, leaving the mirror-Alices standing in an impenetrable void.

"Mother?" the echoes whispered. "Mother . . ."

Alice slumped against the mirror, sinking to her knees. She was tired, so tired, and while some part of her mind knew that something was badly wrong, she didn't have the energy to care. Much better to lie here, pressed against the chilly glass, and wait. Wait for . . .

"Mother?" Her own voice, twisted and echoing.

"Strange."

"Dark."

"Meaningless. Had our fill. Take her."

"Take her. Take her . . ."

Alice felt fingers on her arms, her shoulders. Hands as cold as the mirror, reaching out to take hold of her. The glass under her cheek *rippled* like water.

"Take her. Take her . . ."

Something moved in the depths of the void behind the mirror. The faintest twitch, darkness against deeper darkness. Then an eye appeared. Not a human eye—this was a vast thing, as big as Alice, with a silver iris that seemed to glow against the utter blackness. The pupil was a vertical slit, like a cat's, but this was no cat. It was profoundly *alien*—not a mammal, not a lizard or a snake, not anything that had ever walked the earth. Something *other*.

And yet, Alice thought, there was the faintest sense of familiarity, of recognition.

Alice.

The voice sounded in her mind. It reminded her of the Dragon, the way it had spoken to her when she'd entered Esau's fortress. But this voice was older, smoother. In some way Alice couldn't quite understand, it seemed *kinder*. She ought to have been terrified, but she felt nothing but a wave of gentle concern.

Alice. Wake up.

I'm ... tired. So tired ...

You are in danger. Wake up now, or sleep forever.

I can't.

You can.

The great eye shifted its gaze, pupil narrowing. Alice turned her head, an effort that was almost too much for her, and heard the tiniest sound. A *snap,* like a twig breaking underfoot.

There was a crack at the bottom of the mirror. It was only a few inches long, crooked like a bolt of lightning.

Wake up. The voice grew fainter. *I will see you again.*

The eye closed, leaving only darkness.

Alice stared at the tiny crack. She took a deep breath, what felt like the first real breath she'd taken in ages. Something was falling away from her mind, like she was pushing herself up from under a heavy sheet. She was still unutterably tired, but her lassitude was replaced by sudden fear, and her heart broke out of its lazy rhythm and slammed in her chest.

They were *pulling her into the mirror*. Very slowly, inch by inch. The mirror-Alices had gathered around, taking hold of her arms, her legs, her hair, and bit by bit they were lifting her up and taking her into their domain. It felt like slipping into a very cold bath—her left hand was already inside, and her fingers tingled and then went numb.

She jerked her right hand, but there were too many of the mirror creatures, and she was too weak. Desperately, she scrabbled for her threads, but she didn't have the mental energy to hold on to them, and they slipped through her grasp as though they were made of the same slick glass as the mirror.

"Ours," the mirror images whispered in her ear. The mouths on their porcelain masks had twisted into broad, toothy grins. "Ours, ours, ours forever."

Alice jammed her right hand into her pocket, pulling

hard against the grip of the mirror images. Her fingers found the silver watch, fumbled past it, and took hold of the last of her acorns. She put all the energy she had left into a grab for the tree-sprite thread, and for a bare moment she had it. She let its power stroke the acorn.

Grow, she told it. *Just grow.*

Then she flicked it, between finger and thumb, at the base of the little crack in the mirror.

The back of her head tingled as it passed through the glass. Cold hands were on her face, playing over her cheeks, poking at her eyes and the corners of her mouth. Curious fingers traced the pale scar, barely visible now, that the Swarm had left on her cheek during their first encounter.

"Sleep." The whisper was right in her ear now, cold breath tickling her neck. "Sleep, and dream, behind the glass . . ."

The acorn split. A green shoot wound up from the broken seed, following the path of the crack in the mirror. When it reached the end, it hesitated for a moment, pulsing with the unstoppable energy of life. There was a moment of strain, and then, with a sound like a gunshot, a spiderweb of fractures raced through the mirror. A section of glass fell, shattering on the marble with a merry tinkle.

"What?"

"What?"

"How?"

The hands pulled away from Alice, and she pushed herself forward. She came free of the mirror with an effort and a soft sucking sound, as though she'd been stuck to a bed of taffy. Mirror-Alices raced around the courtyard, painted mouths gaping wide with triangular teeth. The growing tree's roots burrowed down between two marble slabs, thickening as they reached the soil underneath. The tree shot upward, twisting as it grew, slamming a branch into the neighboring mirror and smashing it into fragments. Glittering shards of glass filled the air.

"No!" The mirror image's voice rose to a shriek, no longer resembling Alice's. "No, no, no!"

"Kill her!"

"Kill her!"

Alice stumbled to her feet. The tree smashed another mirror, but the slivers of glass didn't shatter against the flagstones. They curved through the air instead, homing in on her like a cloud of bees. She snatched up the book and pressed it against her chest, pulling as hard as she could on the Swarm thread to harden her skin. Then she ran, eyes squeezed shut against the slashing fragments, pounding down the marble staircase at a breakneck pace. Behind her, the mirrors shattered, one after another.

"It's been too long." Flicker's voice.

"It has not been that long," said Erdrodr.

"It's nearly night."

"What are you saying? That we should leave her?"

"I'm saying that we should go up there," Flicker said. "I—"

"The boat!" Alice shouted, as soon as she could manage a breath. She sprinted down the stairway, book clutched tight in one hand. Her clothes hung off her in tatters, sliced to ribbons by flying glass. "Get in the boat!"

"Alice!" Flicker said, getting to his feet. "What—"

"Get in the boat!" she shouted, jumping down the last few steps. Erdrodr had already stepped aboard, and Alice took Flicker's hand and dragged him over the side. The little craft rocked dangerously, and Flicker went still, his hair flaring red. But Erdrodr already had the spear in her hand, steadying them against the dock and then shoving them out onto the river. A quick slash cut the rope, and the current took them.

The mountain seemed to *writhe,* mist swirling with a thousand flying splinters of glass that shattered against the marble columns and sliced the branches from the trees. Alice watched them curve and dance in the air above the dock, shredding the surface of the water to a froth.

"Alice?" Flicker said. "Are you all right?"

He only uses my name after I nearly get killed. "Can the shards reach us?"

Erdrodr peered over the back of the boat. "I do not think so. We are leaving them behind."

"Good." Alice let her eyes close, squeezing the book tight.

The cover tingled against her fingers, and there was a faint sound, like a tiny crackle of static.

CHAPTER TWENTY
FAREWELLS

ALICE WASN'T SURE EXACTLY when she'd fallen asleep. She'd fought it as long as she could, but somewhere on the long, dark trip downstream, fatigue had caught up with her. The mirror-things had been draining her life, sucking her down to a husk before pulling her into the mirror to do . . . who knew what. Her dreams were dark, full of toothy grins and huge, slitted eyes, and a static buzz that seemed to fill the world.

She woke up in a bed, which was a definite improvement. It was in a stone room, with blue-green lanterns hanging on the walls. Even without these clues Alice would have guessed she was back in the giants' fortress; the bed was big enough to sleep half a dozen human adults.

When she sat up, she found that she wore only her underthings, which had been mended with surprisingly delicate stitches. Underneath, the slashes she'd gotten from the flying glass were sealed up under what felt like scabs made of ice, the cold pleasantly numbing the wounds underneath. The rest of her clothes were neatly folded by her feet, with *The Infinite Prison* and the silver watch sitting on top of them.

Erdrodr was sitting in a chair beside the bed, charcoal in hand, focused on her sketch pad. Alice cleared her throat, and the giant girl looked up.

"You're awake!" She set her slate aside. "How do you feel?"

"Remarkably well," Alice said. Her mind felt wonderfully clear. She leaned forward and clicked open the watch. *Thirty-six hours left!* "I've been asleep for *two days*?"

"You weren't injured that badly," Erdrodr said. "But you wouldn't wake up."

The mirror-things took too much of my energy. Alice let out a long breath. She had thirty-six hours to make the trek back to the portal-book near the fire-sprite village. *I can make it.*

"You haven't opened the book, have you?" Alice said. "It might be dangerous."

"We know better than to investigate any book carried by a Reader," Helga said from the doorway. "And do you feel entirely yourself?"

"Mother!" Erdrodr said. She turned to Alice and shook her head. "She insisted on keeping you under guard while you slept, 'just in case.'"

"The Palace was dangerous, but I believe I escaped mostly intact." Alice inclined her head, the best bow she could manage from her sitting position. She felt an almost irresistible urge to be up and moving. *The Infinite Prison* was right there, her revenge against Geryon almost within her reach. *Just a little further.* "Thank you for taking care of me."

Helga waved a hand. "You have been to a place of legend and survived. It honors us to have you." Her eyes went to Erdrodr. "And you kept your word about keeping my daughter safe."

"The nation has given me a name!" Erdrodr said in the excited tones of someone who couldn't keep quiet any longer. "Erdrodr the Artist."

"That's wonderful." Alice was no expert on ice giant

society, but it clearly meant a great deal to Erdrodr. "I'm glad I could help."

"I'll never forget this," Erdrodr said.

"Nor will I," Alice said. "Where's Flicker?"

"Downstairs." Helga took Erdrodr by the shoulder. "Come, daughter. Give the Reader a chance to dress. And there are still many who wish to congratulate you."

Erdrodr waved to Alice, then followed her mother. Alice climbed out of bed, wincing a little as the skin stretched around her ice-covered cuts, and put on the rest of her clothes. *The Infinite Prison* gave a tiny crackle when she picked it up, like a momentary growl of static. She opened her pack and shoved the book way down at the bottom.

Thinking back to the mountain made her shiver. It felt like she'd been in a dream, saying things that made no sense in the cold light of day. *I should have run for it as soon as I got the book.* The mirror-things had been inside her head from the moment she arrived, clearly.

The huge, lidless eye, silver and alien, *ought* to have been scary, but it wasn't. *It felt . . . warm. Like it cared for me.*

She shook her head. Whatever the mirror-things had shown her, they'd obviously done it for their own reasons, to keep her busy while they drank her life. *I'd be a fool to believe any of it. I've got the book, and that's what matters.* Revenge on Geryon. *I'm almost there.*

She and Flicker said good-bye to Erdrodr, and Alice promised that she'd try to come and visit. Erdrodr fought back tears, and Helga told them they would always be welcome.

"I talked a bit with Helga," Flicker said as they hiked through the ash wastes. "She's going to bring some of her people to visit the village. I think we could help each other—with the Heartfire getting smaller, we could trade with them for food. They don't have much metal or glass."

Alice nodded. "That's good."

"Some of the elders won't like it," Flicker said. "We've always kept to ourselves. But I think Pyros will agree with me."

"I think you're right," Alice said.

For a while, they walked in silence.

"I thought about what you said," Alice ventured. "About who would protect you, if Geryon fell."

"And?"

"I don't know," Alice said. "I need to think harder." She offered him a wan smile. "But before now I didn't know I had to think about it. So that's something, I suppose."

Flicker patted Alice on the shoulder. "Keep thinking."

Flicker offered to take Alice back to the village to rest, but Alice insisted on going directly to the portal-book. *I can't afford any more detours.* She couldn't bear to think that she'd come so far and found what she was looking for, only to come up short by a few hours. They followed the winding lava tunnels accompanied only by Ishi, who met up with them with a good deal of barking and smoky breath.

"Actinia will be disappointed he didn't get to see you again," Flicker said when they'd reached the portal chamber. The book, an exact twin of the one Alice had used to get here, sat just where she'd left it.

"I'll be back, I expect," Alice said. "I hope, anyway." According to her watch, she had twenty-three hours to go.

"We'll look forward to it." Flicker frowned, glancing at his feet. "I'm sorry if some of the things I said were harsh. It wasn't fair."

"It's all right," Alice said. "I understand. The Readers have hurt you."

"But *you* haven't. You're just as stuck as we are. I hadn't . . . realized that."

Alice grinned at him, and he smiled back. It wasn't much, but it was a start.

As she went over to the portal-book, Flicker cleared his throat, a sound like a fire spitting sparks.

"Alice," he said. "Be careful, all right?"

"I will." She reached into her bag to touch *The Infinite Prison* one more time. The faint buzz of static set her teeth on edge, but its presence was reassuring. *Almost there.*

Alice flipped open the front cover of the portal-book, and read:

Alice had forgotten how awful it was on the other side of the portal . . .

Alice had forgotten how awful it was on the other side of the portal, hot as an oven with the air full of noxious smoke. She ran for the shelves as fast as she could, her boots leaving little patches of burned rubber on the rocks behind her. When she reached cleaner air, she took a deep breath, then slid between the great stone monoliths that guarded the edge. As she wriggled through, space twisted around her, and stone became wood. She popped out from a crack between two bookshelves, back in the library, and breathed the familiar scent of ancient paper and dust.

Ashes was waiting for her, sitting with his paws together and his ears flat. Behind him, Ending's yellow eyes glowed.

"Alice," Ashes said. "You're okay?"

"Did you retrieve the book?" Ending rumbled.

"I got it." Alice patted her pack triumphantly, but neither of them seemed to share in her cheer. "What's wrong?"

"Geryon returned this morning," Ending said. "One day early."

Alice's hand went into her pocket, gripping the silver watch tight.

"He asked to see you," Ashes said miserably. "As soon as you returned."

Chapter Twenty-one
CARDS ON THE TABLE

ALICE'S MIND FELT LIKE a car tire in deep mud, spinning madly with no traction.

"He got back . . . early?" she said. All she could think was, *That's not fair.*

"I assume it was his intention from the start," Ending said. "He must already have been suspicious of us."

"He sounded angry when Mr. Wurms told him you were off in the library," Ashes said. "He's had me waiting here for you ever since."

"But . . . what are we going to do now?" Alice looked from Ashes to Ending and back again, then shook her head, trying to collect her scattered thoughts. "We can't just give up. There has to be something we can do."

"I see two options," Ending said. "The first option, most likely to succeed, is that you blame me for everything. Say this endeavor was my idea from the first. I think he will believe you, and while you may be punished, it will not be severe."

"But if we do that," Alice said, "he'll think you're rebelling like Torment, trying to get me to murder him. He'll—" Alice stopped. She didn't know *what* the Readers would do to a rogue labyrinthine, but it couldn't be good.

"He'll bind me away," Ending said. "Like the Dragon. An ironic fate, given our history."

"Mother," Ashes hissed, "you can't be serious."

"I am only facing the truth as I see it," Ending said. "If Alice wishes to do this, I cannot stop her."

"What's the second option?" Alice said.

"Ashes," Ending said. "Perhaps you could keep watch on Mr. Wurms for us?"

Ashes bristled, his hair standing on end, but a low growl from Ending silenced his protest before it began. He stalked away haughtily, tail lashing in his wake.

"It is best that he not be involved. For his sake, if something goes wrong." Her golden eyes followed Ashes for a moment, then returned to Alice. "The second option is to attempt to complete the plan. To trap Geryon with *The*

Infinite Prison. But if his suspicions are already raised, I can see only one way to do it, and if you fail, then you will bear the full force of his wrath."

"I'll do it," Alice said immediately. "I'm not going to hang you out to dry, not now."

"Somehow I thought as much," Ending said. Her huge eyes were hard to read. "Come with me, then."

"Geryon doesn't know yet that you've returned," Ending said as they walked. "We'll have a little time to prepare, at least."

They reached the nook where Alice had practiced her Writing.

"Sit down here." Ending indicated the familiar wing-back chair. "You're going to transfer the trap spell from *The Infinite Prison* into this volume." Ending nodded at a slim book bound in tatty red fabric on the small table.

"Geryon keeps a book in his study that contains his innermost wards and protections," Ending continued. "He uses it when he requires the utmost security. If he suspects that you and I have betrayed him, he will certainly activate them when he speaks to you. It happens to be almost identical to the one I have here.

"You will have only one chance. You must swap the

books, so Geryon opens the trap and Reads it before he realizes what has happened."

Alice dug the *The Infinite Prison* out of her pack and looked at it with her inner eye. The spell inside was far more complicated than the simple wards she had created on parchment. She could see certain basic similarities, but the full depth of it was well beyond her understanding. Her heart sank for a moment as she traced the web of power that ran through the book.

"How can I transfer something this complicated?"

"Examine it closely. The trap, which binds the Reader, is only a small part. The majority is the prison that *keeps* him bound, and that can remain here."

Alice looked more closely. Ending was right—most of the spell was an endless loop, turning back on itself over and over like a tangled ball of yarn. The trap hung from it, a vicious, jagged thing, connected by a few thin strands.

She found her attention drawn to the prison, though. It was hard to see what lay at the very center, but she felt like there was something *moving* there, and she felt a tingle in her mind. An odd buzz, like radio static, that almost seemed to shape itself into words. Into her name.

"Alice . . ."

"Are you sure this is a good idea?" Alice said, blinking

her eyes and coming back into the real world. "What if I get it wrong?"

"There is a risk," Ending said. "But this is the only path we have left. The only way for you to get your revenge."

Anger flared, and Alice gritted her teeth. She opened her inner eye again and got started.

It wasn't easy. Even the trap spell, the smaller part of *The Infinite Prison*, was too massive for her to get ahold of at once. She had to grab the biggest chunk of the spell that she could manage to keep in her grip at once, gently detach it from the rest, and move it from one place to another. Once it was settled, she went back for the next piece, re-creating the connections between them as best she could where they seemed to fit. It was like moving a jigsaw puzzle, lifting up chunks of pieces and fitting them back into place. Only they were more fragile than that—*a jigsaw puzzle made of cobwebs, maybe.*

It took a good deal longer than she'd expected, and she had to rest between one chunk and the next, when her mental grip started to weaken. During one of these pauses, she told Ending what had happened when she'd tried to use the wards, and how she'd had to repair them afterward.

"A feedback loop," Ending said, sounding a bit smug.

"Yes, that makes sense. It's one reason I wanted to test the spell. But it was fortunate for you that it burned out when it did."

"Why?" Alice said. "The bluechill got loose and nearly killed us."

"If the spell had held, it would have continued to drain your energy at an accelerating rate. That would have killed you just as quickly."

"Oh." Alice remembered the sensation, like the blood was being piped out of her body and replaced with something thick and cold. She shivered. "Will we get a chance to test this one, do you think?"

"Unfortunately not," Ending said. "There is no way to test it without becoming trapped in it yourself. But on the other hand, a spell draws its power from the one who Reads it, which in this case will be Geryon. If something goes wrong, he will bear the consequences."

"I don't want to kill him," Alice said. "I told you that."

"We won't," the labyrinthine said. "I would worry more about yourself. If the spell doesn't hold, or Geryon catches you trying to make the switch, he will not hesitate to kill *you*."

Alice paused.

"You've done a great deal for me," she said. "And I don't

want to seem ungrateful. But I have to know. Why?"

"Why?" Ending said.

"Why *me*? I know why *I* am taking this risk. I know what I have to gain. But why are you helping me? Do you want revenge on Geryon? Or is it something else?"

There was a long silence. Alice tried to match Ending's luminous gaze.

"What you have to understand," Ending said eventually, "is the relationship between the Readers and the labyrinthine."

"The labyrinthine serve the Readers, don't they?" Alice said. "Not as bound creatures from a prison-book, but like Mr. Black or Mr. Wurms."

"Not like them," Ending said. "Such creatures serve because they are promised rewards, or in exchange for favors. Someday they may leave their master's service and seek another. But we labyrinthine have served the Readers since the very beginning, and will serve them forever, if they have their way. Without us, without the labyrinths, they could not maintain their libraries. The books *leak*. So much magic, in such a small space, is only stable with our efforts."

"But you said the Readers haven't bound you," Alice said.

"We are too strong for that," Ending said with a hint of pride. "They must blackmail us instead. There was a creature, long ago, that threatened to destroy all labyrinthine. We could not defeat it, so in desperation we bargained with the Readers, exchanging our servitude for their help. They combined their efforts—the first and last time they have worked for a common purpose—and created the Great Binding, locking the thing away. But they still hold the key. We serve them to ensure that the creature will not be released."

Ending's voice had lost its usual sly, knowing tone. Alice was quiet, thinking hard.

"We all suffer, but some of us bear it better than others," Ending said. "Torment, for example, has always been half-mad. But he is not the only one to dream of turning on his master."

"So why haven't you betrayed Geryon before this?" Alice said. "Like I said, why *me*? I'm a Reader, just like he is."

"Because I am *not* mad. Torment's fate was sealed when he slew Esau. The Readers will bind him into a prison-book, and there he will stay until the end of time."

"Am I just a tool, then? Someone to take the blame?"

"You don't trust me," Ending purred.

"I don't know." The Dragon had warned her, before it had gone to sleep, that Ending exploited everyone around her as naturally as she walked and breathed. "But I'd like you to answer: If this works, where does it leave you? What do you *want*?"

There was a long pause.

"Have you thought about why we need to use the trap to capture Geryon?" Ending said.

"Because he's too powerful for us to fight?"

"It's not only that. Suppose we *could* fight him. Suppose we won, and you killed him."

"I never said I would *kill* him," Alice said. There were things you didn't do unless you absolutely had no choice, and killing a *person* was at the top of that list, no matter what terrible things he'd done to you. She remembered trying to explain herself to Flicker. *I am better than Geryon. I have to be.*

"This is only hypothetical," Ending said. "Suppose you did. What then? What would happen to all the creatures in his domain?"

"Flicker told me," Alice said, "that Geryon protects the fire-sprites from the other Readers. He asked me what I would do if I got rid of Geryon."

"Precisely," Ending said. "They are not so different

from we labyrinthine in the end. If Geryon *died,* the other Readers would descend on this place, to claim me as a servant or bind me away. And, in the long term, we will always need the Readers. Someone has to maintain the Great Binding."

"But if Geryon is only trapped . . ."

"It will be a long time before word gets out," Ending said. "Fear of him will keep the others at bay. We will have a long time to work."

"To work on *what?* What does this have to do with me?"

"As I said, we will always need Readers. *I* will always need a Reader to serve." Ending's tail lashed. "For a long time, I have been waiting for the *right* Reader. First of all, she would need to be powerful, powerful enough that, in time, she could become the equal of Geryon or any of the others."

Alice blinked. Geryon had told her she was strong for an apprentice, but he hadn't said anything like *that.*

"And second," Ending said, "she would need to be . . . *kind,* for lack of a better word. Willing to treat magical creatures as equals. Someone with whom I could be *partners* rather than master and servant. Only such a person would be able to help me.

"For a time, I thought it was impossible. The Readers bring in their apprentices young. You've met some of them. The Readers teach them the old ways, molding them in their own image. When, by chance, I happened to find you before anyone else, and understood the depth of your talent, I knew what I had to do. I protected you from discovery as long as I could, so you would grow up outside the system. I hoped it would be enough."

"Then Mr. Black found out about me," Alice said, thinking back.

"Yes, my protection was fraying. And instead of reporting back to Geryon, Mr. Black sold the information to Esau. My power kept Esau's fairy, Vespidian, from simply taking you for himself, but when your father left on the ship, I could no longer shield him."

"Esau found my father, on the *Gideon*," Alice said, chest clenching. "And he assumed I was with him."

"Yes," Ending said. "After that, I knew I had to bring you here, ready or not. So I told Geryon I'd found you, and he arranged the rest."

"You never told me any of this," Alice said.

"I wasn't sure what you would do if I did," Ending said. "Have you considered that *I* was never sure I could trust *you*? The wrong word in Geryon's ear, and things might have gone very badly."

Alice was silent. Ending yawned, fangs gleaming.

"You want me to be your Reader?" Alice said.

Ending nodded. "Now do you believe me when I say our interests are aligned?"

"I think," Alice said, "I do."

"Then finish the spell."

Alice put her hand back on *The Infinite Prison*, feeling the tiny growl of static. She closed her eyes and went back to work.

Chapter Twenty-two
THE INFINITE PRISON

ALICE EDGED UP TO the study door, red book under one arm, Ashes sticking close by her heel. Her stomach felt queasy, and her heart was already hammering.

One chance. She tried to keep her breathing regular. *One chance to turn the tables on him once and for all.* She closed her eyes and replayed the image of the *Gideon's* destruction for the thousandth time, fanning the anger in her chest to white heat. She pictured all of the terrible things she'd wanted to do to Geryon, recalled every minute she'd spent listening to him and pretending she didn't know he was a murderer.

One way or another, this is going to be the end of it.

She raised her hand to knock on the door.

"Alice," Ashes blurted. "I don't know what you and Mother have cooked up, but it's not too late to back out."

"Yes," Alice said quietly, "it is."

Ashes rubbed his head against her ankle. Alice blew out her breath and knocked on the door.

"I've brought Alice," Ashes said.

"Very well," Geryon's voice came through the wood. "Alice, come in. Ashes, you are dismissed."

"You don't want me to stay?" Ashes said, very quietly.

Alice bit back a quip about Ashes' usual habit of abandoning her in a crisis. Instead she scratched him behind the ears and shook her head.

"I'll be all right," she said.

"You'd better be." The cat slunk off, looking miserable.

Alice opened the door and walked down the short hallway. It led past the vault room, which housed Geryon's most dangerous books, past the padded chamber where she'd first practiced finding her threads, to the study, where Geryon waited behind a cracked door.

Alice paused. She had to get the book into place without Geryon noticing the switch. Taking hold of her threads, she pulled a couple of dozen swarmers into being around her. Four of them got into a square, and she laid the red book on their backs.

Here goes nothing.

Leaving the swarmers behind for the moment, she pushed the study door open and went inside. Geryon sat at his desk, examining a book by the light of an oil lamp. He looked up as she came in, and gave her a brief smile absolutely devoid of humor.

"Hello, Alice," he said. "You look like you've been in the wars."

The ice giants had stitched up the holes in her coat, but there was no disguising the fact that it had been six days since Alice had washed, or changed her clothes, or slept in her own bed. Her hair was a tangled rat's nest, thick with dirt and ash, and her skin was smudged with grime and sweat. The ice-bandages had melted, leaving her mottled with half-healed cuts and bruises.

"Mr. Wurms tells me you went off into the library," the old Reader went on, glancing back at the book on his table. "Would you care to explain yourself?"

"It's a long story, sir," Alice said stiffly, letting a little bit of her nervousness into her voice. *He expects me to be afraid, after all.*

At the same time, she looked around for the red book that matched the one Ending had given her, but she couldn't see anything that seemed close. There were *hun-*

dreds of books in the room, piled against the walls and tossed carelessly into corners. *If it's buried under something, I'll never get to it!*

"I daresay," Geryon said. "I'm listening."

Calm down. It has to be easy to get to, if it's such an important defense. He wouldn't leave it under a pile. Geryon was now looking down at his desk, and Alice risked turning her head. *There* it was, behind her, on a side table just beside the door. She took a step sideways, putting her body between it and Geryon.

"I heard a rumor," she said. "That there was a lost book on the other side of one of the portals."

Geryon looked up. "Heard a rumor from whom?" he snapped.

"Isaac." The lie came easily. *I just have to keep him talking...*

Behind her, under her careful mental direction, the four swarmers crept into the room with the trapped book on their backs. The rest of the swarmers followed, a flowing black mass, moving slowly so their claws wouldn't catch on the carpet.

"Isaac told me about it," Alice invented. "He said that he'd eavesdropped on his master trying to figure out how to get to it through one of our portals."

"And you offered to get it for him?"

"No, sir!" Alice said. "Please believe me. I was going to get it for *you*."

The swarmers had maneuvered the book to the base of the side table. Two of them climbed up one side of it, claws scratching as they dug into the wood. Alice pretended to cough to cover the sound.

"Why would you do that?" Geryon said. "Instead of just telling me what you heard?"

"I . . ." Alice hesitated, as though she were about to cry. Her head throbbed. The pressure of trying to direct the swarmers while keeping a straight face was like trying to think in three different directions at once. "I knew you were angry with me. After the century fruit. I thought . . ."

The two swarmers made it to the marble tabletop, scurried around the real red book, and started pushing. It slid easily over the polished surface, and just as it was about to fall, Alice brought her hands up to cover her face, the motion drawing Geryon's eye. Behind her, the book fell among the swarmers, whose rubbery bodies silently absorbed the impact. She had to bear down hard to prevent them from making *quirks* of triumph. *Now for the difficult part.*

"Spit it out," Geryon said, disgusted.

"I thought I could make it up to you by getting the book," Alice said, sniffing. "I just wanted you to be happy with me again. And when you said you were going away, I thought . . . maybe this was my chance."

The swarmers couldn't climb and carry the book at the same time. Alice had six of them stand side by side, and four more clamber on top of those, and so on, forming a ramp. But the little things weren't tall enough. *I need more.* Carefully, very carefully, she pulled on their thread, letting more of them appear around her feet. She locked eyes with Geryon, silently willing him to hold her gaze.

It worked, and he continued to glare at her, tugging absently on one of his long sideburns. Then, suddenly, he got to his feet. Alice's heart double-thumped. *Did he see them?*

"Alice Creighton," he said. "You are a terrible liar."

"S . . . sir?" Alice didn't have to fake the quaver in her voice.

"I met with my fellow Readers," Geryon said, looking down at her from his full height, "to determine what happened in the matter of Esau's death. We . . . inquired. Do you know what we found?"

"No, sir." Alice took a step back, as though terrified, the better to obscure the swarmers from Geryon's view.

There were enough of them now to form a ramp all the way to the top of the table, and four of them started shoving the book up across the backs of their fellows.

"I always thought your story was fishy," Geryon said. "You were never clear on exactly how you'd defeated Torment. A gang of apprentices, defeating a labyrinthine? Unlikely." He leaned closer. "I know you had help."

"I . . . I'm not sure what you mean, sir."

"Don't play stupid. *Someone* helped you through that labyrinth. We couldn't trace who it was, but I have my suspicions." He grinned again, showing his teeth. "You've always been friendly with this *Isaac*, but I see it goes further than that. Tell me, what has Anaxomander promised you and Ending for turning on me?"

"I don't know what you're talking about!" Alice said desperately. "Ending helped me in the labyrinth, I should have told you that, but she asked me to keep it secret, and I didn't see the harm—"

"Didn't see the *harm* in keeping secrets from me? Don't expect me to believe that."

The swarmers pushed the book onto the table, edging it back into position where the real book had been. As they were setting it down, one edge slipped on the slick marble, and it dropped into position with a slight *thump*.

Geryon's eyes flicked over. Alice dropped to her knees and began to sob loudly. She released the thread, summoning a particularly loud moan as the swarmers vanished with faint *pops*.

"I'm sorry," she bawled as she hadn't done for real since she was four years old. "Please. Don't hurt me."

Geryon's eyes narrowed. "Is this supposed to arouse my sympathy?"

"I just . . . Ending said . . ."

"I don't know what game the two of you are playing," Geryon said, walking past her, "but I'll soon find out. That treacherous cat will not be able to help you *here*. And then we'll have the truth of where you went while I was away."

He went to the side table and frowned for a moment at the red book. Time seemed to slow to a crawl. Then he snatched it up and flipped the cover open.

"I can see," he muttered, "that I made a mistake with you—"

Then his expression changed to a wild anger, and he dropped the book as though it were a poisonous snake. He rounded on Alice, who had gotten back to her feet.

"*You*—" he shouted.

Alice took a step back. Something formed in the air

around Geryon, a sphere just a bit bigger than he was, translucent at first but rapidly solidifying. It was a mirror, a curved one, like an enormous drop of mercury, and Alice could see herself reflected huge and distorted in the outer surface.

"Alice!" Geryon's shout was twisted, like he was speaking into a malfunctioning loudspeaker. *"You* stupid *girl! You don't knooooooo—"*

The voice rose into a scream, not a human shriek but the sound of metal twisting against metal. It climbed higher, through fingernails-on-a-chalkboard and into an impossible, inaudible vibration that bypassed the ears and clawed at the inside of Alice's head.

Something flickered across the surface of the sphere. A crude face, two black holes for eyes and a slash for a mouth, bent into a slight smile.

"Alisssss..." It wasn't Geryon's voice. Static buzzed and popped, drawing the word out into a hiss. "At lassssst..."

The metallic sphere bent, twisted, as though something were pushing on it from the inside, and the face vanished. The air was hot and tasted of ozone, and bolts of lightning flickered between the sphere, the desk, and the walls.

Then, when the phantom sound had convinced Alice

that her head would pop like an over-inflated balloon, it all stopped at once. The sphere shrank to a point above the book, then disappeared, and the trap-book snapped itself shut and landed neatly in the chair where Geryon had been sitting. The lightning vanished, leaving only scorch marks on the furniture. Alice slid down the wall until she was sitting on the floor, her legs suddenly too weak to support her.

It . . . worked? She blinked. *Did it work? What was that other voice?*

But it must have worked. If Geryon had *escaped*, he'd already have torn her limb from limb. *It worked. It worked!* He was stuck, trapped where he couldn't hurt anyone until *she* chose to let him out. *I got him!*

"That," she said in a weak voice, "is what you get for hurting my father."

She'd imagined saying that would be more satisfying.

The outer door of the study opened. Mr. Black rushed in, with Ashes hot on his heels.

"What in all the hells was *that*?" the big servant yelled. "Master? Girl?"

"Alice?" Ashes said.

"I'm here," Alice said from her position by the side of the door. She struggled to her feet.

"What *happened*?" Mr. Black said. "Where's the master?"

"You felt it?"

"Of course I felt it," Mr. Black said. "I should think everyone within a thousand miles who has an ounce of magic in them felt *that*."

"It *was* rather hard to ignore," Ashes said. "Was Geryon here?"

"He . . . was." Alice thought very quickly. "He was investigating that book. I think . . . there must have been some kind of accident."

"Oh, no." Mr. Black's face, as much of it as was visible behind his wild hair, went pale. "Oh, that's not good."

"I'm going to take it to Ending," Alice said, snatching up the trap-book. She could feel the spell inside it now, humming away, power crackling across her fingers. "She'll know what to do."

"Wait," Mr. Black said as Alice ran past him, book clutched to her chest. "You can't trust that bloody cat, not if the master's gone! Alice!"

Alice shook her head, running out into the yard without bothering to fetch her coat. Ashes kept pace beside her, for once not complaining about the snow. They ran together to the bronze door of the library, and Alice wrenched it open, hinges squealing in protest.

For the first time Alice could remember, Ending was there in the anteroom, yellow eyes ablaze.

"You felt it too?" Alice said.

Ending nodded. "Something," she said, "has gone very badly wrong."

Chapter Twenty-three
LIGHTING A BEACON

"Bᴜᴛ ᴛʜᴇ sᴘᴇʟʟ *worked*," Alice said, putting a hand on *The Infinite Prison*. The disconcerting buzz had vanished. "It's holding. I can feel it."

"It worked," Ending said. She padded back and forth, more agitated than Alice had ever seen her. "The problem is that *everyone* felt it. Geryon must have had a personal ward I didn't know about. When it collided with the spell, it radiated energy on an incredible scale. The very fabric of the labyrinth itself seems to have been affected. An old Reader could sense power like that on the other side of the planet. My brothers and sisters are contacting me to ask what happened. When I don't have a good answer for them, they're going to come and investigate. And half the library is going mad."

Ending looked over Alice's shoulder, eyes distant as she felt the weave. "Every creature on the other side of a portal is trying to get through, and some of them are succeeding."

"What do we do?"

"You'll have to speak to them."

"*Speak* to them?" Alice said. "What am I supposed to say?"

"Reassure them," Ending muttered. "They are gathering right now, and Ashes should be back in a few moments with Mr. Black." Ending had summarily dispatched the cat back to the house the moment Alice and Ashes had appeared in the library.

"How am I supposed to reassure anyone?"

"I don't care," the big cat snarled. "Think of something. A few jittery sprites are hardly our biggest problem right now! It won't be long until the other Readers respond. I'm trying to stall . . ."

She vanished into the shadows with a swish of her ebony tail. Alice turned and saw that the aisle she'd come down now led to a large open space among the shelves, in which a crowd was already gathering.

It was certainly the *strangest* crowd Alice had ever seen. No two people in it were alike. A tall gentleman in an elegant dark suit, expertly tailored to accommodate his six arms, stood beside a smoke-belching clockwork spider. A young woman appeared to be melting, her form sagging and indistinct. Several variations on the basic theme of sprites—thin, gangly humanoids with colorful eyes and hair—stood in a group, glaring daggers at one another. In the back, a lion with a human face and a crocodile tail sat in a prim, Sphinx-like pose that reminded Alice of Ashes when he was being particularly difficult.

Ashes himself arrived just as she'd nerved herself to step out in front of this bizarre multitude, with Mr. Black, Mr. Wurms, and Emma on his heels. The cat dashed out in front of the crowd and over to Alice, and she scooped him up and set him on her shoulder.

"What did Mother say?" he whispered.

"She told me to *reassure* them," Alice said. "But something else is happening. I think she was talking to the other labyrinthine."

"This lot doesn't look happy," Ashes said.

That seemed to be the case, inasmuch as Alice could read their expressions. In the front row, an older woman wearing a dress made entirely out of bones and wire stood with her arms crossed and her jaw set. Beside her, a very old hunchbacked man leaned on a stick, while the glowing mushrooms that sprouted from his back flashed angry-looking colors. The girl beside him didn't look older than ten, sporting a red-and-white-spotted mushroom cap in place of hair, but she seemed equally worried.

"And I just . . . talk to them?" Alice whispered.

"You're the Reader's apprentice," Ashes said.

Not if the Reader has any say in the matter. Alice suppressed a hysterical giggle. She walked, stiff-legged, out to the front of the crowd and raised her hands for silence. The chattering creatures quieted down, more or less, except for the clockwork spider, who couldn't seem to help her clanking and steaming.

"Um," Alice said. "Hi. I'm Alice, Geryon's apprentice—"

"What in the name of Ushbar is going on?" said the bone woman. "Someone lit off enough power to wake the dead. Where's the Reader?"

"He's—" Alice's eyes found Mr. Black, who was staring at her suspiciously. A number of other creatures burst out with "Yeah!" and "What happened?" and Alice had to raise her voice.

"Geryon has vanished," she said. "He was investigating a book, and there was some kind of accident."

The spider-thing extended a small screen, composed of a grid of tiny spinning paddles, black on one side and white on the other. These whirled madly for a moment before settling down to form black text on white. ACCIDENT = FALSE. PROBABILITY: ENEMY ACTION.

"She's right," the melting woman said in a gloopy voice. "If Geryon's disappeared, it's probably some trick of one of the other Readers."

"It doesn't matter *why* he's gone," the bone woman said. "What are we going to do? The others will find out soon enough, and then it will be open season for anyone under Geryon's protection."

"I'm sure Geryon will be back soon—" Alice said.

"Really?" the bone woman snapped. "I'm not. If Anaxomander or someone has got him, he's in for a rough time."

"Regardless," Alice said, trying to regain some control over the situation. "The others can't *know* that he's gone, not for sure. They'll move cautiously. And I'll work to make sure they don't find out—"

"You?" sang the lion-crocodile-man in a beautiful bass baritone. "What are *you* going to do?"

PROBABILITY: APPRENTICE INADEQUATE, the spider's screen displayed. INFERENCE: SITUATION DESPERATE.

"We're doomed," one of the sprites said, turning wildly in a circle as though excited at the prospect. "Doomed! Doomed!"

Alice tried to say something, but the rising babble drowned her out. She waved her arms frantically, but no one was paying her any attention.

"*ENOUGH!*"

Ending roared the word, a feline growl that cut through the noise and echoed back from the distant ceiling. All the creatures went silent as the labyrinthine stalked out beside Alice, eschewing the shadows. Her coat was so black, it seemed to drink in the light. Muscles moved underneath like the rise and fall of mountains. Her teeth were long and white, ivory fangs the size of daggers. The paw that came down beside Alice's foot was as big as a catcher's mitt.

"The girl is all you have," Ending said with a snarl, "whether you like it or not. You can trust in her, or you can start running away now. But shouting at her isn't going to help."

There was a long silence, broken only by nervous exhalations of steam from the spider.

"I, for one, am running," said Mr. Black.

"I expect nothing better of you," Ending said.

"You're bound to serve Geryon," Alice said. A week ago, she would have been happy to see him disappear, but at the moment she felt like she could use all the familiar faces she could get.

"Geryon won't be back," Mr. Black said. "Even if he can eventually get free, the others will pick this place clean long before then. There's nothing keeping me here."

He turned his back on the gathering and stomped away, his footsteps ringing loud in the quiet that followed.

"That's all well and good for him," the bone woman said. "But some of us have family and friends on the other side of those portals."

"Then stay," Alice said. "Please. I'll figure something out, I promise."

PROBABILITY: LOW, said the spider. She paused, then added, ALTERNATIVES = {}.

"For now," Ending rumbled, "go back to your books and stop causing *more* trouble. Geryon may be gone, but *I* am still here."

With a general muttering and whispering, the gathering dissolved, slipping back into the aisles and corridors of the library.

Mr. Wurms came up to Alice as the others were leaving and ducked his head respectfully. "I will go back to my table and get on with my work," he said. "You have my full confidence."

"Thank you," Alice said, willing to take what she could get at this point.

"If any of the other Readers do take over, though, perhaps you could mention my record of sterling service?" He attempted a smile, which, given the state of his teeth, was a ghastly sight. "Just in case."

"If I get the chance," Alice muttered.

"Good," Mr. Wurms said, patting her on the shoulder. "Full confidence, though."

He wandered off, leaving only Emma, who waited blankly as always for someone to give her an order. Alice sighed.

"Emma, go to the kitchen, make up a basket with some sandwiches and bottles of water, and bring it back here. Then go back to the house and wait."

Emma nodded and hurried away.

"I get the feeling," Alice said, "that we might not get the chance to break for lunch any time soon."

"It seems unlikely," Ending agreed. "The first apprentice has already arrived."

"Already?"

"It's your little friend with the back door and the disreputable jacket."

Isaac.

Ending sent Alice to an intersection among the shelves where Isaac was waiting, hands in the pockets of his battered coat. When she stepped around the corner, he grabbed her in a fierce hug. This took Alice a bit by surprise, but not nearly so much as it did Ashes, who was dislodged from his perch on Alice's shoulder and jumped to the floor, clawing Isaac's ear as he went by.

"Ow," Isaac said.

"Serves you right." Ashes sniffed. "You should give some warning when you're going to engage in such gestures. Perhaps you could be equipped with an air horn."

"I . . ." Isaac turned his gaze from the cat to Alice. "I'm just glad you're all right. We felt the power surge, but we didn't know what happened." He caught Alice's expression. "You *are* all right, aren't you?"

"For now," Alice said. Her hands tightened. "Geryon is gone."

Isaac's eyes widened. "Gone? You mean he's dead?"

"I don't think so," Alice said. "But he's trapped."

"That's not good," Isaac said. "One of the others must have slipped something through his defenses. I hadn't heard anything from my master, but maybe the Eddicant or—"

"It wasn't any of the others," Alice interrupted. "It was me."

"What?" Isaac said.

"*What?*" Ashes said, from the floor.

"I set a trap for him," Alice said. She was surprised at how calm her voice was. "It worked. Except it wasn't supposed to let everybody in the world know what I'd done."

"Are you *crazy?*" Ashes said. "Where in all the worlds did you get the idea—"

"How did you do it?" Isaac said.

Alice explained, giving an abbreviated account of her journey to find *The Infinite Prison.* It felt good to finally tell all her secrets, especially to Ashes. Isaac knew some of them, but she'd been hiding the truth from the cat, since he wasn't particularly good at keeping secrets. He also didn't take the revelation particularly well.

"You're mad," he said. "You've gone mad. There's no two ways about it."

"Your mother was the one who helped me," Alice said.

"Then she's gone mad too. Do you have *any idea* what's going to happen?"

"The other Readers will move in on Geryon's territory," Alice said. "They'll tear the library apart."

"I mean, do you know what they'll do to *you*?!"

"Honestly, I don't," Alice said.

"*Neither do I,*" Ashes said. "Because it's the kind of thing that, when you do it to someone, they're *never heard from again.*"

"I'm hoping we have a little time," Alice said. "They won't know for sure that Geryon's gone, and they'll have to organize."

But Isaac was shaking his head. "After Esau's death, they're all on edge. My master was already talking to the others about sending their apprentices here. He was practically in a panic. I was hoping I'd be in time to warn you."

"*Warn* her?" Ashes said. "That's like running to warn someone who's set off a bomb that things are about to get a little hot!"

"You know, you could be a bit more constructive," Alice said.

"I'm still trying to wrap my head around the magnitude of your insanity," the cat muttered. "Once I've got that handled, I'll get started on the mind-numbing terror.

It's not just *your* neck on the block here, you know!"

"I know," Alice said. "I'm sorry! I thought we'd have more time!"

"Running isn't going to work," Isaac said. "Mr. Black might be able to get away if nobody goes looking for him, but the old Readers will follow Alice wherever she goes. A rogue Reader, even an apprentice, is too dangerous."

"And most of the creatures can't run," Alice said. Isaac shot her an odd look, then nodded slowly.

"As I see it," Isaac went on, "you've got two options when the apprentices turn up. You can tell them it was an accident, and surrender. If the Readers don't figure out that it was *you* who trapped Geryon, they'll probably assume one of them did it. I bet one of them would take you in. Apprentices are valuable. I could try to convince *my* master that you'd be useful."

"They'll still tear the library to pieces," Alice said. "All the creatures—"

"Not to mention Mother and me," Ashes said. "The Readers won't allow one of their own to control two labyrinthine. They'll imprison Mother and probably toss me to the wolves."

Isaac's face fell. "The other option is letting Geryon loose and begging for mercy. Tell him it was a mistake, or that one of the others had a spell on you. He might let you live."

Alice closed her eyes.

Revenge. She'd followed the snarling, red-eyed beast of her anger, all the way through the lava tunnels and the fortress of the ice giants to the Palace of Glass. She'd done what she intended to do, punished Geryon for everything he'd done to her and her father, but somehow it had all gone wrong. *Now Isaac wants me to let him out?* She couldn't bear the idea. *But without him, it's all going to fall apart. All the creatures he protects, Ending and Ashes, not to mention* me. She'd been ready to accept danger to herself—after all, going to the Palace of Glass had been dangerous enough as it was. But she hadn't realized how much else depended on Geryon.

But it doesn't depend *on him, not really. They pay him tribute so they won't have to pay it to someone else or get wiped out in a battle, like my father was. Geryon's just . . . sitting on top of the pile. They all are.*

Like Ashes had said, everyone bowed to someone.

Everyone . . .

She opened her eyes again.

"I'm not letting him out," she said. "And I'm not going to surrender."

"What, then?" Isaac said. "Don't tell me you want to *fight* the apprentices. You'd never win, and anyway, it isn't *their* fault."

"I'm not going to fight them," Alice said, thinking of Flicker. "I'm going to talk to them."

CHAPTER TWENTY-FOUR
ASSAULT

ALICE DIDN'T HAVE TIME to do more than explain the outline of her plan before Ending arrived through a gap in the shelves that hadn't been there a moment before. The great cat was breathing hard.

"My brothers and sisters are closing in."

"The other labyrinthine are coming *here*?" Alice said.

"They don't need to leave their own libraries," Ending said. "The Readers have ordered them to extend their power to bind me, to block me off from my own labyrinth, so the apprentices can enter undisturbed." She let out a long growl. "I do not understand. They cannot know for certain that Geryon is imprisoned, and yet they seemed to be in a panic. I will fight for as long as I can, but against all the labyrinthine at once I am outmatched. I will not be able to help you when the apprentices arrive."

"What about me?" Alice said. "The Dragon granted me some of its power—do you think that they know *I* can touch the labyrinth?"

"I doubt it," Ending said.

"Unless one of the other apprentices told their master about you," Isaac said.

Alice tested and found that she could still grip the fabric of the labyrinth easily. "So far, so good."

"That will be your only advantage," Ending said. "Use it carefully. If they find out, the other labyrinthine will bind you too. I am sorry, Alice." Ending's tail lashed. "I did not expect this."

"I knew there were risks," Alice said. "And we may get out of this yet." She turned to Isaac. "You should go back. If your master knows you've come here—"

"The hell with it," Isaac said. "There's no time. If you can convince the other apprentices to go along with your story—to tell their masters that Geryon is still in control—then it won't matter."

"And if I can't, Anaxomander will kill you," Alice said. "Isaac, please. You have to try to return before he notices you're gone."

"I'm not going to leave you alone." Isaac stepped forward and pulled her close against him. Alice's heart thump-bumped, and she could smell the ancient fabric of his battered coat. His voice was a whisper. "I lost Evander. I'm not going to lose you too."

"I . . ." Alice swallowed hard.

"The labyrinthine are here," Ending said. She let out a roar and slipped away, disappearing into the shadows.

Alice felt the fabric of the labyrinth give a little shiver as new minds took hold of it, closing in on Ending. The great cat could keep moving, but sooner or later they would box her in. In the meantime, the rest of the fabric went calm, quiet and undisturbed. Moments later, she felt the faint quiver that meant there were other humans in the library.

Alice pushed herself away from Isaac, blushing only a little. She looked down at Ashes, who was hunched miserably by her foot.

"What about you?" she said. "Do you want a safe corner to hide in until this is over?"

"No point," the cat mumbled. "If they lock Mother away, they'll come for me wherever I go." He extended his front paws and then stretched, tail curving over his back. "You may as well bring me with you. At least that way I'll get to see what happens."

Alice picked him up and set him on her shoulder. "Just get clear if it *does* come to a fight."

"Oh, I certainly intend to," Ashes said.

"You're not very loyal," Isaac said as Alice took his hand.

"Loyalty," Ashes sniffed, "is for *dogs*. Cats have better sense."

"Stay close," Alice said.

She twisted the fabric, connecting *here* to *there* for just long enough to step through. They emerged near an intersection of a narrow aisle and a wide one. There was a gap between two of the shelves, and from this vantage point Alice could spy on the broad aisle without being seen. She pressed her eye against it, and Isaac knelt to look as well.

Five people walked down the aisle, sticking together in a tight group. In the lead, Alice recognized Ellen, dressed in worn, cream-colored leather. She was tall and thin, with pale skin and close-cropped blond hair, and the bright light of her halo hovered a foot above her head. Behind her came Dexithea, her dark, frizzy hair tied up in a messy ponytail.

Then, side by side, were a boy and a girl Alice didn't recognize. The boy was black, with short hair and round metal glasses that gave him an owlish look. His prim impression was reinforced by his clothes, which were gray and sober, a bit like the suits Alice's father used to wear. The girl, in contrast, wore shorts and a floppy, oversized shirt, and her skinny white legs were grimy and covered in scabs. Her hair was such a bright red that it reminded Alice of Flicker. She guessed both of these newcomers were a little younger than she, perhaps ten or eleven.

Last of all was a taller figure, wearing a long, dark cloak. Isaac's breath hissed.

"Is that *Garret*?" he whispered.

"Garret's dead," Alice said. It *did* look a little like Garret, but it was hard to tell in the shifting shadows.

"Are you sure? I was too busy running away to be certain."

"That whale-thing ate him," Alice said. "Just before it smashed the bridge."

"Maybe his master fished him out again."

Ellen turned her head, and the light of her halo caught the tall figure's face. It was definitely Garret, with his long, animated features and theatrical silk cloak billowing out behind him. Shadows clung to his feet, boiling in the light like water on a hot skillet.

"Are you sure you want to do this?" Isaac said as the intruders approached.

"Garret doesn't change anything," Alice muttered. "We still have the same choices."

"I'll be right here," Isaac said. "In case something happens."

"Me too," Ashes said, from somewhere in the vicinity of the floor.

Alice straightened up, squared her shoulders, and

pulled on the devilfish thread. Her hands started to glow an eerie green, enough to light up her face. When Ellen was perhaps ten yards away, Alice stepped out from behind the shelves, hands raised.

The party of apprentices came to a halt at once. Ellen squinted, then dimmed the light from her halo.

"Alice?" she said. "Is that you?"

"Hello, Ellen," Alice said. "Hi, Dex."

"Sister Alice!" Dex said. "The auguries informed me we would be seeing one another again, although I must admit I did not anticipate the circumstances."

"I wondered when you'd show yourself," Garret drawled, pushing his way to the front of the group. Ellen, Alice noticed, stayed close by his side. "It's good to see you, Alice."

"You too," Alice said. "I'm a little surprised."

"That I'm not dead, you mean?" Garret grinned imp-ishly. "I surprise even myself sometimes."

Something crossed Ellen's face, a flicker of remem-bered pain. She and Garret had been close, and Alice wondered how long she'd believed he'd been killed in Esau's fortress.

"I don't think you've met Michael and Jennifer," Gar-ret said, waving at the two newcomers. "This is Alice,

Geryon's apprentice. She's going to give herself up like a good girl."

"Is that what you're here to do?" Alice said. "Take me prisoner?"

"Something Geryon did has gone very wrong," Ellen said. She looked nervous. "He released something that ought to have stayed imprisoned." She took a small green book from her pocket. "My master gave me a spell that can recapture it, if we set it in the right place."

"We're supposed to bring you in to explain exactly what happened," Garret said. "And to make sure you don't mess anything up once we activate the spell."

Released something? That didn't make any sense. Pyros and Helga had warned her about the Palace of Glass, but nothing could have followed her home without Ending seeing it. *All I came back with was the book.*

"You've got it wrong," she said aloud. "Geryon is busy with his own affairs, but he sent me to tell you to leave right away. You can tell your masters that he doesn't appreciate the intrusion."

"Is that so?" Garret said. "If he were that irritated, you'd think he'd come down here himself."

"Like I said, he's busy. And you're lucky he is. Do you really want to see an old Reader get angry?"

"You think we're lucky." Garret's grin widened. "I think you're bluffing."

"You don't have to do this, Alice," Ellen said. "Geryon won't blame you for not standing up to all of us. Just surrender and come along quietly, and everything will be fine."

"I must agree with Sister Ellen," Dex said. "I do not wish for us to quarrel. Stand aside, and we complete our mission and let our masters decide what happens next."

"It's a reasonable request," Garret said. "Unless the prisoner has already gotten to her."

Dex looked pained. "Garret—"

"My master warned me it might try something like that," Ellen said, staring hard at Alice. "There's no telling what it's capable of."

"I'm not under anyone's control," Alice said. "But I'm not going to surrender."

"And I don't plan to keep chatting all day," Garret said.

"Are you really going to try to hurt me?" Alice said. "Dex? Ellen?"

Dex opened her mouth but for once seemed to have nothing to say.

"Please don't make me," Ellen said.

"I'm not making you do anything," Alice said. "Can we

forget the mission, just for a minute, and talk about this?"

"I think we've had enough talking," Garret said.

"Garret—" Ellen began, but the boy had already raised his hand, shadows flowing along his arm like dark quicksilver.

"Get her," he said pleasantly. "Try not to kill her, if you can help it."

For a moment, Alice didn't think anyone was going to obey. Then Garret shot Ellen a sharp glance, and she swallowed and raised her hand. Beams of brilliant white light lanced out from her halo, reaching for Alice like spreading fingers. Alice ducked, wrapping herself in the Swarm thread. Where the blasts hit the shelves behind her, books exploded, burned pages fluttering down all around her.

Between blinks, Dex encased herself in the silver armor of her caryatid, and the young girl, Jennifer, raised her arms and summoned an enormous hawk. The bird rose above her with a screech, eyes trained on Alice as it flapped madly to gain height. In the center of the confusion, shadows roiled around Garret, but the blades of darkness Alice had been expecting didn't materialize. *Thank goodness for small favors.*

Even if she'd been willing to fight the other apprentices, she didn't think she'd be able to win against all five of them. She paused, ducked another beam from Ellen, and shouted to Isaac.

"Now!"

Isaac, still hidden around the corner, demonstrated his latest trick, calling on the powers of the iceling and the salamander at the same time. Frost whispered across the ground, painting it with a slick of feathery ice that flashed almost instantly into steam as the salamander's fiery breath rolled over it. Thick, white clouds billowed up, engulfing Alice and the other apprentices in fog.

Alice could still see Ellen's halo, shining through the murk like a lighthouse, and she sighted on that. She yanked hard on Spike's thread, pulling the dinosaur into the world, and then sent him charging toward the apprentices. His claws clattered like horseshoes on the stones as he built up speed, head lowered to bare his horns.

Anyone he hit would either be trampled or skewered, but Alice hoped none of the apprentices were *that* stupid. She watched Ellen's light move as the girl dodged, vanishing into an aisle. Spike crashed through where the rest of them had been standing, mist swirling in his wake, and let out a bellow.

Then Alice played her trump card. She took hold of the fabric of the labyrinth and twisted hard. Every one of the aisles that the apprentices had used was suddenly *there* instead of *here,* scattered across the vastness of the library. Alice could still feel them through the fabric, tiny movements, like beetles running across her dress. They'd been split up into at least three groups, though it was hard to tell exactly who was where.

"You can come out now," she called over her shoulder, waving at the fog. "And get rid of this stuff."

A moment later, a wave of frigid air rolled across her. The steam condensed, droplets forming all over Alice, on the shelves, and in little rivulets on the floor. Alice mouthed a silent apology to the books, which had first been blasted by Ellen's light and were now getting soaked.

"Once again," Ashes said, coming around the corner, "your plan involves me getting *wet.* You do this on purpose." He stepped carefully to a dry patch of floor and began licking himself clean of the droplets that had formed on his fur.

"They're gone?" Isaac said, his jacket shedding its own harvest of moisture.

Alice nodded. "I've got them split up and wandering."

"You *could* leave them to wander," Isaac said. "I'm just saying."

She shook her head. "Even if I was okay with doing that to Dex and the others, it won't work forever. Once the labyrinthine have Ending pinned down, they'll notice what I'm doing and block me off as well. We don't have a lot of time."

"What did they mean about something being released?" Isaac said.

"I have no idea," Alice said. "Maybe that's the story their masters told them? They may not want to admit an apprentice tricked an old Reader."

"If something *had* gotten loose in the library, Mother would have known about it long ago," Ashes said.

Isaac frowned. "You still think you can talk them into cooperating with you?"

"I don't have a choice," Alice said.

"Garret didn't seem terribly inclined to help," Isaac said.

Alice sighed. "I know."

Chapter Twenty-five
NEGOTIATIONS

ALICE FOLDED PEEPHOLES TO spy on the apprentices' progress. Dex was on her own, while Michael and Jennifer had stuck together, as had Ellen and Garret. Alice left the two pairs to wander, and made herself a passage to an aisle near Dex.

"Stay out of sight," she told Isaac. "I don't want anyone to know you're here yet."

He nodded. Ashes, who had taken up a position on Isaac's shoulder, was still too busy licking his paws to reply. Alice, holding the Swarm thread, went around the corner and found Dex sitting with her legs crossed at the base of a bookshelf. Her eyes were closed.

"What are you doing?" Alice said.

"Attempting to consult the auguries," Dex said. "With some difficulty, since I lack the proper equipment. When I discovered I was lost, it was easy to guess that you retained your control over the labyrinth."

"You're not wearing your armor."

Dex opened her eyes and tipped her head toward Alice. "I have decided to stop lying to myself. I will not fight you, Alice. Not after what we have been through."

"I don't want to fight you either." Alice's eyes stung with tears, and she blinked them away.

Dex rose gracefully and came closer. Alice held on to the Swarm thread until Dex hugged her tight; then she let the magic lapse with a sigh and hugged back.

"So," Dex said when they pulled apart again. "We have established that we are not going to do battle. What *are* we going to do?"

"How much did your master tell you about this prisoner that's supposedly escaped?"

"Very little," Dex said. "The Most Favored attempted to contact Geryon, and when that failed she guessed it had destroyed him. She told me only that we had to help Ellen set her spell, and that you and anyone else left here might have been influenced." Dex cocked her head.

"Have you been taken over by some monster, Alice?"

"Not that I know of." Alice gave a weak smile. "I haven't seen any escaped prisoners either."

"But Geryon *is* gone?"

Alice hesitated, then nodded. "At least temporarily. When the other Readers make certain of that, they'll tear the library to pieces."

"So what are you going to do?"

"I'm going to try to convince all the apprentices to say that he's still here. The old Readers will assume it's some kind of trick and be cautious. That should at least buy some time."

Dex frowned. "That . . . might work. The Most Favored would seek other ways to be certain of Geryon's presence, but that will take time, and she will be worried he might be concealing himself."

"And when she *does* find out, you can always say I tricked you somehow," Alice said. "She never needs to know we lied."

"I thought you would come up with a way to avoid fighting, if only I could get Brother Garret to quiet down." Dex grinned, but only for a moment. "I do not know that the others will agree."

"Ellen might, if we can get her away from Garret," Alice

said. "What do you know about the other two? Michael and Jennifer, was it?"

"Not a great deal. They are both apprenticed to Vin Einarson, but I have never worked with them before. I believe them to be relatively inexperienced."

"Okay. I might be able to talk some sense into them, then."

"That leaves Brother Garret," Dex said.

"That's a problem," Alice said, shaking her head. "Did you know he was alive?"

"Not until today. He joined us after we entered the library. I had thought him lost in Esau's fortress."

"Me too," Alice said. "You've known him longer than I have. What might convince him to lie to his master?"

"I am not certain. Sister Ellen, perhaps? The two of them are close, though they try to hide it. But . . ." Dex's lip twisted. "He is stubborn."

"We'll leave him for last," Alice said. "I'll take you and Isaac to a place where you can wait for the others while I see what I can do with Michael and Jennifer. Maybe the two of you can think of something in the meantime."

"Brother Isaac is here?" Dex said.

"He came to warn me," Alice said, a faint blush rising in her cheeks.

"I should have known he would not stand idle," Dex said, smiling.

Alice blushed a little further. She turned away to cover it, reaching out for the fabric again. A few deft twists connected them to Isaac and Ashes, and she led everyone to the clear square that surrounded Mr. Wurms' table. The scholar's books were still scattered about, but of Mr. Wurms himself, there was no sign.

"Hello, Brother Isaac!" Dex said.

"Hi, Dex." Isaac sat down on the bench beside the table, then started coughing at the cloud of dust he raised. Ashes jumped from his shoulder and picked his way delicately over the books to stand beside Alice.

"Aren't you going to introduce me?" he said.

"This is Dexithea," Alice said. "Dex, this is Ashes-Drifting-Through-the-Dead-Cities-of-the-World, or Ashes for short."

"Charmed," Dex said, not at all alarmed by the talking cat. The other apprentices, Alice reflected, had been better prepared by their upbringing for the library than she had been.

"You three try to come up with something we can say to Garret," she said. "I'm going to see the other two."

"Should I—" Isaac began.

"I don't plan to fight them," Alice said. "I'll be fine."

Alice rounded the corner, stepping out of the portal of folded space, and almost immediately had to throw herself to the floor to avoid having her eyes clawed out. The huge hawk swooped past her, pulling up with a flap of its wings that raised whirlwinds of dust on the floor, and circled around for another dive.

Michael, one hand on his glasses, stood a little farther down the aisle, with Jennifer protectively in front of him. Alice waved her hands.

"I just want to talk—" she began, then ducked again as the hawk swooped. This time its claws got hold of a twist of her hair, which tore free after a painful yank. Alice felt blood well on her scalp. "Would you *stop*?"

"Jen—" Michael began.

"She's trying to trick us!" Jen said. "Don't listen!"

The hawk came around for another pass. This time, Alice pulled hard on the Swarm thread, toughening her skin, and borrowed Spike's superhuman strength. She stood her ground, letting the bird's claws scrape at her neck and shoulders. They tore great rents in her shirt, but couldn't pierce her skin, and the moment of surprise this created gave her the opportunity to grab the creature by the throat and jam it against a bookshelf. Its talon flailed against Alice's arm, and its wings flapped madly, but it was no match for the dinosaur's strength.

"Avia!" Jen said.

"Let go of the bird's thread," Alice said. "And we can talk. I promise I won't hurt you."

Jen looked over her shoulder at Michael. "You're not going to help?"

The boy adjusted his glasses and frowned. "If she wants to talk, we should talk. I can't see the harm."

"Hmph."

The hawk vanished with a *pop*, and Alice let her own threads go. Jen stalked across the aisle from Michael and leaned against the shelf, crossing her arms. Alice approached, keeping one eye on the girl in case she showed a sudden desire to resume the fight.

"I'm Alice," she said, holding out her hand. "You're Michael, I hear?"

Michael shook hands cautiously and nodded. "And this is Jennifer."

"We know who you are," Jen said. "Master told us you'd been corrupted by the prisoner."

"Your master has gotten something wrong," Alice said.

"I don't think there *is* a prisoner. Did he give you anything to do here, specifically?"

"To stay with the others, mostly," Michael said.

"And to make sure they didn't try to take anything," Jen said sulkily. "Ellen had the real responsibility."

The same mission, more or less, that Alice had been given in the group that went to find Jacob in Esau's fortress. *That makes things easier.*

"I don't want to fight," Alice said. "Not against other apprentices. You know as well as I do that none of us chose to be here."

"But you said you wouldn't surrender," Jen said uncertainly. "So what are you going to do?"

"I have a few ideas," Alice said. "But all I really want is to get everyone to sit down and *talk* about this. Do you think we could do that?"

"What's the point?" Jen said. "Either you're going to give up, or you're going to fight us. Why drag it out?"

"Jen," Michael said. "Remember what Master Vin told you?"

Jen pursed her lips and flushed, looking at the floor. "That I should listen to you," she muttered, "instead of letting my temper run away with me."

"I think you're missing something important," Michael

said. "Garret told us the labyrinth here would be under control, but we still got separated from the others." He looked up at Alice, who kept her face blank. "She's got something up her sleeve that even Garret didn't know about."

"So, what?" Jen said. "Are you saying we can't take her?"

"I'm saying it might be better to at least *listen* to what she has to say," Michael said. "She's right about the apprentices not having a choice. Would you fight *me* if Master Vin told you to?"

"He wouldn't—" Jen bit her lip. "I mean—" She rounded on Michael. "Why are you on *her* side, anyway?"

"Because it's logical," Michael said.

"Hmph," Jen said. "Logic." She glared at Alice for a moment, then looked away. "I guess we could talk about it. But no tricks."

"No tricks," Alice agreed. "Come on. I'll take you to the others."

"Brother Michael, Sister Jennifer," said Dex. "I'm glad to see you decided to join us."

"Hmph," Jen said again. She stalked across the clear space to Mr. Wurms' table and flopped on the bench, raising an impressive cloud of dust. Ashes, who was sitting on the table, coughed.

"What's the matter?" he said. "You look like something sour crawled into your mouth and died."

"It's none of your—" Jen began, then seemed to realize who she was speaking to. "You're a cat."

"A half-cat, actually," Ashes said, delicately licking one paw. "But I'll forgive you the mistake—hey!"

Jen had grabbed him in both arms and pulled him to her chest, rubbing her face in his fur. "You're adorable! Look how cute you are!"

"Young lady," Ashes said, squirming desperately, "if you do not release me *at once* you're not going to get away with only a flesh wound."

"Master Vin won't let me have a cat," she said, letting Ashes go. "What's your name? I was going to name my cat Precious."

"Ashes. And I'm not a cat, I'm a half-cat."

Aggrieved, he walked in circles a few times, then sat down in front of Jen to indicate that he'd suffer being petted, but only on his own terms. He closed his eyes and sighed as she scratched him behind the ears. Alice turned away from the pair of them and went to the other end of the table, where Michael sat opposite Dex and Isaac.

"Brother Isaac is an old friend of Sister Alice's," Dex was saying. "He's here to help us work things out."

"Did your master send you to negotiate?" Michael said.

"That's not important right now," Isaac said. "What matters is that we can all fight each other, the way the masters want us to, or we can work something out like reasonable people."

Michael glanced at Alice. He spoke quietly enough that Jen wouldn't hear. "Speaking as the ones who would probably *lose* a fight, we can hardly object to that. But I notice Ellen and Garret aren't here yet."

He has a way of getting right to the heart of things, doesn't he? "I've left them for last," Alice said. "If the rest of us all agree, it might make things easier."

Michael nodded. "Well, you've got my support, for what it's worth. And I think your cat has distracted Jen."

Ashes, Alice noted, had consented to receiving a belly rub.

"All right," Alice said. "I'll bring Ellen and Garret through."

CHAPTER TWENTY-SIX
REVELATION

A QUICK PINCH OF THE fabric brought Ellen and Garret to Mr. Wurms' table. Ellen was pressed tight against Garret's side, their fingers interlocked. When they saw the others waiting for them, they stopped.

"Garret," Alice said. "Ellen."

"What's this?" Garret said. He stepped forward, away from Ellen. "A tea party?"

"We've decided we'd rather talk about things than fight amongst ourselves," Alice said. "We were hoping you would join us."

"What's there to talk about?" Garret said.

"That's what I'm hoping to find out," Alice said. "But you have to sit at the table."

"Listen to Sister Alice," Dex said. "We should not have to hurt one another just because our masters disagree."

"Talking can't hurt," said Michael.

"Hmph," Jen said again. It seemed to be her favorite expression. She tickled Ashes' belly. "I mean. We can always start the fight afterward."

"It's too bad we're not putting it to a *vote*," Garret said. "In case you've forgotten, our masters sent us here to do a job, and we were specifically told that Alice might be under the influence of the monster. What makes the rest of you think this is a good idea?"

"Garret, maybe we should—" Ellen began.

"Don't *you* start." Garret looked at the assembled apprentices. "Is this what happened in Esau's fortress after I was . . . inconvenienced? This girl just took over?"

"Sister Alice saved us," Dex said. "None of us would have escaped alive if not for her."

"She's right," Isaac said.

"What are you doing here, anyway?" Garret said. "I don't recall anyone inviting you."

"Alice needed my help," Isaac said.

"Very touching. You know, I have had about enough of this. Ellen, let's get things started."

Ellen stepped closer to Garret's side, her halo dim and

flickering. "Dex is right, she *did* save us back in the labyrinth. I owe her."

"*You* owe her," Garret said. His face grew dark with
rage. "She didn't do anything to save *me*."

"I would have," Alice said, "if I could."

"Just sit down," Ellen said. "What can it hurt to try?"

"Shut *up!*" Garret said. "I said that's *enough!*" He put
his hand between Ellen's shoulders and pushed, sending
her stumbling toward Alice. "Destroy her already, Ellen."

There was something in his voice that sounded familiar. A faint static buzz.

*Dex said Garret joined them in the library, not before
they arrived . . .*

"I . . ." Ellen raised one hand, then looked back over her
shoulder. "Garret?"

"No," Alice said, stepping around the table to face him
directly. "You're not really Garret, are you?"

"What are you talking about?" Garret said.

"The real Garret could be a jerk, but he wasn't a bad
person," Alice said. "And he cared about Ellen."

Garret narrowed his eyes. "How would *you* know?"

"I have to say I think Sister Alice is correct." Dex got to

her feet. "The Brother Garret who retrieved my arm from the crocodile would not be so callous."

"The Garret *I* knew," Isaac said, "wouldn't shout at someone else to fight for him. He'd do it himself."

"That can't be right," Ellen said. "It's him, I know it is. None of you understand him—"

"I'm sorry," Alice said. "But I think Garret is dead. This is . . . something else."

She tugged on her threads, calling a swarmer into her and pulling on Spike's power. Winding up like a major league pitcher, she winged the little creature snout-first, right at Garret's shoulder.

A human would have at least flinched—the swarmer's beaks were sharp, and getting impaled by one was like having a nail hammered into you. But when the little creature hit, it stuck and hung there quivering, like an arrow shot into a target. Garret didn't move a muscle, as though he were carved from stone.

"Well," he said, after a moment. "Enough *is* enough."

Garret reached up and grabbed the swarmer. It *melted* in his hand, vanishing as though it had been sucked into his palm. Alice gasped. Whenever one of her creatures died, she felt it as a physical pain, like a needle in her chest, but this was ten times worse. It felt like a fraction of her energy, of her *life*, had been torn away.

Garret grinned. His eyes were black from edge to edge.

"Stay away!" Alice shouted as the Garret-thing advanced on her. She backpedaled, moving to put the table between her and whatever creature was wearing Garret's skin. The other apprentices followed suit, spreading out around the clear space. Ashes was a gray streak, vanishing among the shelves.

Only Ellen didn't move. She stood directly in the thing's path, halo flickering.

"It's not true," she said. "It's not true, is it? I thought you were dead, and you came back." Her eyes were full of tears, and her voice cracked. "You wouldn't lie about that, would you?"

"Ellen!" Alice shouted, frantically wrapping herself in her threads.

Garret came forward another step, until he and Ellen were face-to-face.

"You wouldn't hurt me, would you?" Ellen said.

She leaned in, standing on tiptoe, to kiss him. The Garret-thing's hand came up, fast as a snake, and grabbed her by the front of her shirt. Ellen's eyes went wide as he lifted her without apparent effort.

"Please," she said, eyes streaming with tears. "Please."

He tilted his head, his movements suddenly utterly inhuman. Ellen tried to scream but couldn't find the breath. Something began to flow between them, a stream of brilliant light bursting from Ellen's eyes and mouth, crossing the few inches to flow into the dark void that lurked under the Garret-thing's eyes. It was *life*, swirling away like water down a bathtub drain.

The stream lasted only a few moments, and then Ellen slumped. Garret tossed her aside like a rag, and she landed on her back on the dusty floor. Thick white smoke rose from her eyes and mouth, as though something inside her had burned to a crisp.

"Like I said." The Garret-thing's voice had a strange buzz to it now, like radio static. He reached into Ellen's pocket and pulled out the green book she'd shown Alice. His grip tightened, and he ripped it in half, leather cover and all. "Let's get things started."

Dex was the first to react. Her caryatid armor flashed into being around her, and silver swords dropped into her hands. Isaac, standing beside her, raised one arm and sent out a stream of fire. Garret made no effort to avoid it, and Alice could see his hair burning, the fire spreading to his cloak. But when Dex came at him, sword swinging at his neck, he moved as though the flames didn't bother him at all. His hand closed around her blade. The bright silver warped and vanished, sucked away inside him. His other hand grabbed her wrist, wrenching her close to him.

"Dex!" Alice shouted.

Dex's second sword bit into his waist, but that bothered him no more than the swarmer had. He grabbed Dex by the chin, and her silver mask melted away. Before the deadly streams of energy could form, though, Spike slammed into Garret at full tilt, knocking the two of them apart. One of his horns sank six inches into Garret's chest, and the dinosaur's momentum picked the boy up and carried him into a nearby shelf, which toppled in a thunder of dust and falling books.

"Are you all right?" Alice said, falling to her knees. Dex nodded, coughing, the rest of her silver armor fading away.

"I am, Sister Alice," she managed, "but—what's wrong?"

Alice doubled over, as though she'd been kicked in the stomach, and slapped one hand over her mouth to keep from throwing up. Spike had died—not just died, been snuffed out like a candle, all at once—and the same weird suction had taken a chunk of her energy. Her fingers and toes prickled, as though she'd dunked them in ice water, and her vision went gray at the edges.

"Sister Alice!" Dex struggled to her feet, pulling Alice with her. "Get up!"

Isaac had his eyes closed, and Alice could hear just the edge of the Siren's melody, the hypnotic song directed into the cloud of dust. Jen had her bird hovering over her head, and Michael stood at the center of a swarm of tiny metal shards, buzzing around him like silver bees.

"It's not working," Isaac muttered. "It feels like there's nothing there at all."

Garret was up, his cape shredded and burning, hair askew, bloodless cuts and tears all over from Spike's horns and Dex's sword. His grin was still there, but his eyes were just empty holes.

"Now!" Jen shouted. Her hawk dove, tearing its claws into Garret's face. Michael pointed, and the silver shards zipped toward Garret in a single stream, slashing at him and impaling him like the spines of a porcupine. Isaac, giving up on the Siren, sent a blizzard of sharp-edged ice fragments blasting into the creature's face.

The hawk snapped its beak at him, coming away with a flapping, torn piece of *something*, like a ripped cloth.

Garret's hand shot up, grabbing the bird by the throat, and it screeched in protest. Then it melted, losing focus and flowing into Garret's hand like colored smoke. Jen gave a choking cry; her eyes rolled up and she collapsed, Michael only just catching her before her head hit the flagstones. Isaac backed away, letting the icy wind fade for a moment, and Alice gasped.

Half of Garret's face was gone, torn away by the hawk, and the rest dangled in strips and flaps. There was no blood—it was as though he'd been wearing a rubber mask, and beneath it was only blank, black nothingness. His clothes were falling away, revealing more of the same, as though inside the outer shell that looked like Garret was a hole in the world, a void in the shape of a man.

"If at first you don't succeed," the creature said, the half of its mouth that was left twisting horribly, "then you die."

"Alice?" Isaac said. "Any ideas?"

"Run," Alice said. "Back into the aisles. Isaac, help Michael with Jen."

"But—"

"I'll be right behind you, don't worry," Alice said. "Go!"

They did as they were told. Between them, Isaac and Michael lifted Jen, her head lolling, and hustled her away, with Dex following behind. Alice backed up to the table as the creature advanced.

Think. Think! Magic doesn't seem to work; it swallowed the fire and the ice without a problem. It sucks up our creatures. Spike had at least *stunned* it, though. *So maybe...*

Alice grabbed for Spike's thread again, but it was as though the creature's touch had coated the thread in oil. She had to bear down in order to wrap it around herself, strength flowing into her limbs. As the Garret-thing got closer, she bent and picked up one of Mr. Wurms' benches, a solid length of wood a good eight feet long. She stepped clear of the table, wound up, and swung the bench at his head.

Without Spike, she couldn't even have lifted it, but with him, the wood whistled through the air like a baseball bat. Garret put his hand up to block, but as strong and fast as he was, he didn't have the weight, and Alice's impromptu club slammed him off his feet. He skidded along the floor in another cloud of dust, and before he'd come to a stop, Alice brought the bench down vertically, like a lumberjack splitting a log. The far end broke with a mighty *crack*, the blow tearing away most of Garret's scalp. Alice tried another swing, but this time Garret grabbed the splintered end of the bench and twisted, ripping it from her hands.

"A good effort," the creature buzzed. "I knew you were smarter than the others."

The thing got to its feet. More than that, Alice realized as she backed up toward the table and the second bench. It was *growing*. Soon it was close to Mr. Black's size, limbs thickening, chest widening. What was left of its disguise split and fell away, leaving only darkness.

No, Alice thought, *not* just *darkness*. There was something else there, a web of silver threaded through the black, very fine and very faint. It caught the light as the thing moved, gleaming now and then like stars twinkling in an overcast sky.

"But not smart enough to know better," the thing said. "Not smart enough to realize that when you open a door to put something *in* a prison, you might let something *out*."

She grabbed the second bench and swung it in a roundhouse arc. The creature held out one arm to block, and the wood shattered against it. There was a horrible static buzz that might have been laughter.

Alice dropped the amputated stump of the bench, turned, and ran after the others.

CHAPTER TWENTY-SEVEN
THE OUROBOREAN

She TUGGED ON THE fabric of the labyrinth to catch up with the others, then pulled all five of them across the library, leaving the Garret-thing behind. Something was wrong with the labyrinth itself, though—it was flattening, growing still wherever the creature walked, as though it were being stapled to a board. The effect was spreading fast. *Ending said the labyrinth was being damaged by something.*

"What *is* that thing?" Isaac said as they came to a halt at an intersection. Up ahead was the wild part of the library, with its random clusters of bookshelves and portal-books.

"I have never heard of its like," Dex said. She was

breathing hard. "The caryatid armor can be broken, but I have never seen it . . . *melt.*"

A prison, Alice thought. *The Infinite Prison.* That *thing* had been inside all along. Someone had trapped it, and hidden it away in the Palace of Glass. *And I let it out.*

"I've never seen a creature disappear that way," Isaac said. "As if it was *absorbing* them."

"It was." Ashes hopped down from a shelf in a puff of dust. "Alice, are you all right?"

She blinked. "I think so. I feel a little drained."

"Jen won't wake up," Michael said. His voice was calm, but Alice could hear the urgency underneath.

"Drained is about right," Ashes said. "If it got one of her creatures, it took a lot of her energy along the link. She'll wake up okay, if we get out of here."

"How do *you* suddenly know so much about it?" Isaac said.

"I talked to Mother," Ashes said. "At no small personal risk, let me tell you, because the fur is flying over there. But that thing . . ." He huddled in on himself, ears flattened, tail sweeping back and forth in the dust. "It's called the Ouroborean."

"*The* Ouroborean?" Alice said. "Like there's only one of it?"

"Exactly. It's not a creature, not like you or me or anything on the other side of a portal. It's more like a living spell, or a walking book. The Readers *made* it, a long time ago, in the time before the libraries and the labyrinthine. It's a weapon. And then they had the good sense never to use it, which if you know anything about Readers should already be terrifying."

"Why *wouldn't* they use it?" Michael said. He'd sat down with Jen's head in his lap.

"Because once it gets started, it can't be stopped," the cat said. "It *eats* magic, uses it to make itself stronger. It'll devour anything you can throw at it, and anything it finds in the library. It just keeps going and going until there's nothing left. What's the point of a weapon that devours all the treasure you were hoping to steal?"

"What's it doing *here*?" Isaac said.

"I brought it here," Alice said, her voice flat and dead. "I went looking for something I shouldn't have, and I brought it back with me and let it out. This is my fault."

"No wonder the Readers are so scared," Isaac said.

"The Most Favored must have known what happened," Dex said. "She sent us here to lock it back up again."

"No," Ashes said. "Even the old Readers couldn't manage that, not on a few hours' notice. Mother thinks the spell they gave you was a *shield*, something that would block off the library entirely when you activated it, cut off all the portals. The Ouroborean would be trapped here."

"Along with all of us?" Isaac said.

Ashes nodded.

"Of course," Alice said. "You—we—are expendable."

"I . . ." Dex's unflappable cheer cracked, just for a moment, and there was something lost and scared behind it. "I don't know. The Most Favored . . . she wouldn't . . ."

"Master Vin wouldn't just send us to die," Michael said.

"My master would," Isaac snapped. "And yours would too. That's what apprentices are *for*. You don't get to be an old Reader by taking risks."

"Ashes, what do we *do*?" Alice asked. "How do we stop that thing?"

"You don't," Ashes said. "I'm sorry. Once it's activated, the Ouroborean will keep going until it runs out of magic to absorb. You can slash it, crush it, smash it, whatever you want, but it won't stop. It's a spell that *feeds itself*."

Guilt tightened her chest. "There has to be *something*! If it devours all the books in the library—all the portals—" *Flicker told me it was locking the portals in books that started his world's decline. What would happen if they were destroyed entirely?* "It's not just the library that's at stake. Every world connected to it is in danger."

"The Readers will stop it eventually, but not soon enough for anyone here. Mother said the only thing you can do is get out of the way. Take the first portal you can find, and keep running until you get to another one." Ashes lowered his head miserably. "I'm sorry."

"But—what about Ending?" Alice said. "She's trapped here, isn't she?"

The cat looked at the floor and said nothing. Everyone was silent.

Pyros told me to stay away from the prison. So did Helga. But I had to have revenge, and now everyone else is going to suffer for it. Guilt and anger warred inside her. *The Readers collect "tribute" and say they provide protection, but they don't dare risk themselves. They'll sacrifice their apprentices without a second thought just to protect themselves. They made the Ouroborean.* She had a sudden image of the old Readers as vast monsters, squatting over the landscape of a thousand worlds, devouring them to feed their appetite for power and their paranoia. *"His magic is based on cruelty and death." Ending told me that, but I never really understood it.*

Revenge on Geryon wasn't enough. It would never have

been enough. *Because it's not just about Geryon. He hurt me, but the old Readers are hurting everyone. Someone has to stop them. Someone has to take responsibility.*

Starting now.

"I have to fix this. I'm not running," Alice said.

"I know," Isaac said.

"What?" Alice blinked. "What do you mean, you know?"

"You wouldn't give up in Esau's fortress," he said. "I can't imagine you doing it here."

"But this is all my fault," Alice said. "I let the Ouroborean loose. None of you would be in danger if it wasn't for me!"

"We have all made mistakes," Dex said, her cheery smile restored. "What's important is how we deal with them. I will of course be at your side, Sister Alice."

"So will I," Isaac said.

"I'll help," Michael said nervously. "If I can. But I have to take care of Jen."

"But—" Alice stopped. In Esau's fortress, she'd tried to argue with them when they'd chosen to stay with her. It hadn't worked then, and she couldn't see it working now.

"Okay," she said. "I've got . . . *kind* of a plan."

"I still think I should be the bait instead of the messenger," Isaac muttered.

"You haven't got any protection like Spike," Alice said. "We'll be careful, don't worry. Ashes, you'll show him the way?"

The cat's tail swished nervously. "This doesn't strike me as the best idea. What if nobody's there?"

Then at least one of us will be safe. "They'll be there. Just hurry."

"I should be doing more," Michael said. His glasses were slightly askew, and his neat hair was ruffled. "I could stay here with you."

"You get Jen somewhere safe first," Alice said. "We'll need you in the end."

She straightened up and looked at Dex, who gave a broad grin and nodded. "Sister Alice is correct," she said. "We will need everyone to do their part, if this is going to work."

Reluctantly, Isaac and Michael took up the still-unconscious Jen and lifted her between them. Ashes led the way toward the rear of the library, in among the portal-books.

Alice could feel the Ouroborean draining the power out of the fabric of the labyrinth. It seemed to be able to sense them too, because it was coming toward them as straight as an arrow.

"Okay," Alice said. "We need to buy as much time as we can. Just don't let it get close to you."

"I understand." Dex held out a long silver spear, featureless as a giant toothpick. "I will make as many as I am able."

Alice took the spear. She'd last used Dex's moon-stuff when she'd confronted Torment. It was fantastically light, hard, and wickedly sharp. The Ouroborean absorbed summoned creatures and shrugged off magical effects, but physical impacts seemed to slow it down. Between Spike's strength and Dex's weapons, she hoped they could keep it away for long enough for Isaac to return.

"Here it comes," Alice said. The labyrinth fabric seized up around her.

The Ouroborean ambled around the corner. It had its arms out, running its fingers along the shelves on either side, and Alice could see tiny sparks of magic flowing out of the books and into the creature's black-and-silver body.

"Hello, Alice," it called, voice mocking beneath the static.

She hefted the spear, drew back, and threw, pulling

Spike's thread as tight as it would go. The weapon sang through the air, fast as a bullet, and hit the Ouroborean in the chest. It sank deep, and the creature staggered backward.

Dex was already handing Alice another spear, and she threw again, before the creature could recover. This time she hit the Ouroborean in the shoulder, spinning it into a bookshelf, which wobbled dangerously at the impact. The third spear sank into its stomach, and the fourth caught it in the arm and continued on to embed itself in the wood, pinning the thing in place.

Alice hurled the fifth spear, but the creature had recovered from its surprise. The Ouroborean raised its hand, the spear impaling it through the palm, point stopping bare inches from its blank, eyeless face. Then, all five spears dissolved, liquefying and flowing into the creature's black skin. They left no wounds behind. Dex grunted.

"Continue to struggle, by all means," the Ouroborean said. "It is in your nature, clearly."

"How do you know what's in my nature?" Alice said as Dex panted for breath.

"Time and distance mean nothing on the other side of the mirror," the Ouroborean said. "I learned a great deal about you when you visited the Palace of Glass, Alice Creighton."

"You all right?" Alice said to Dex, taking a step backward.

"I believe so." Dex's first step was a little unsteady, but she recovered quickly.

"Then run!"

They ran. The Ouroborean pushed itself off of the bookshelf and followed, its loping stride closing the gap between them with terrifying speed. Alice stopped at the next intersection to grab the shelf on one side and pull it down in an avalanche of books and dust. The Ouroborean stumbled as the heavy shelf slammed into its shoulder, and it brought one massive fist around in a blow that cracked the shelf in half and sent splinters of wood flying. Dex handed Alice a pair of dagger-length spears, and Alice sent them zipping over the wreckage just as the thing got up, snapping its head back as they sank in where its eyes ought to be.

"Keep going!" Alice said as the creature climbed over the wrecked shelf. "Left! Around that corner!"

Dex was panting, and the dust-choked air burned Alice's throat. They were in the back of the library now, dodging between clusters of bookshelves, each its own tiny world with a portal- or prison-book in the center. Alice pointed to one.

"In here!" Alice shouted. "Squeeze between the shelves!"

She hit the gap at a run, scraping her shoulder on the wood, feeling the familiar queasy stretching as she went from the library to the strange space where the book's world had leaked through. From the inside, the bookshelves were enormous stone monoliths, so tall, they blocked out the sky, ringing a clearing and a small pond, surrounded by dense jungle. This was where Alice left her acorns to charge with energy, in the raging torrent of raw living power that leaked from the book sitting by the side of the pond.

"Head that way," Alice said. "Over toward the waterfall."

Dex nodded. Alice paused in the center of the clearing, listening to the distant hooting of strange birds, the crash of water, and the buzz of insects. She waited.

It didn't take long. One of the stone monoliths shook, shifted, and began to fall outward, making a sound like a collapsing mountain. The Ouroborean stood in the gap, where it had pulled a bookshelf over, and now the place where the two worlds met was a raw, eye-twisting wound that made Alice look away.

"You think you can hide from me?"

The tree-sprite popped into being at her call, a slim, green-skinned creature only half her size. At her mental direction, it scampered into the jungle, growing a thick layer of bark over itself like armor as it scrambled up one of the swaying trees. Moments later, branches twisted like living things and lashed out at the Ouroborean as it came on through the underbrush. They wrapped around it, squeezing hard enough to crack granite, pulling its limbs in opposite directions in an effort to tear it apart.

But wherever it touched the monster, the vegetation started to wither. All around, death spread, first through the grass and then into the foliage. Tree trunks toppled, pitted and rotten, and the Ouroborean easily ripped free of the dying husks. The tree-sprite fell back, sending more trees into the fray, but it was obviously a losing battle.

Keep it here as long as you can, Alice told the tree-sprite. She grabbed the portal-book—she couldn't bear to leave it to be devoured—and squeezed past the great stones to emerge between shelves in the library. Dex grabbed her hand and they ran together, while behind them the jungle *snapped* and *cracked* as it died.

CHAPTER TWENTY-EIGHT
ROLLING THE DICE

ALICE FELT THE TREE-SPRITE get sucked into the Ouroborean's bottomless maw. She stumbled, and only Dex's grip kept her on her feet as a wave of light-headedness swept over her.

Nearly there. Michael was waiting by the shelves, guarding the portal to the fire-sprite's world. To Alice's surprise, so was Jen. The girl looked a little wobbly, but she was on her feet. There was no sign of Isaac.

"He's not back yet?" Alice said.

"Not yet," Michael said, fumbling for his glasses. "How far behind is it?"

"Not far, I fear," said Dex, letting go of Alice and turning to face the direction they'd come. Her caryatid armor flashed into existence again.

"We can't keep running forever," Alice said, setting the book down. She felt like she was about to drop, and her legs had turned to jelly. "We'll have to make a stand." She looked at Jen. "Isaac was supposed to take you through with him."

"That's what he told me," she said, setting her jaw stubbornly. "I told him he could shove it."

Alice hesitated for a moment, then shrugged. "Don't use magic directly on the Ouroborean. And don't let your creatures get caught; they'll just get sucked in."

"That's what Michael told me." Jen grinned shakily and raised her hands. Her fingers lengthened, hooking into hard, pointed claws.

"It's coming," Dex said.

Alice looked one more time at the shelves where Isaac had gone, then turned back to the shadows of the library. The Ouroborean emerged from them, a deeper darkness threaded with a web of silver. It was still changing shape, growing even taller and longer-limbed, slowly losing the last vestiges of a human form. Its head was a mere lump on its shoulders, and its hands no longer had fingers. The static buzz of its voice rang in her ears.

"I will not be stopped," it roared. "Not this time."

Fighting Torment, Alice had been terrified and in pain, but looking at the Ouroborean she felt something worse, something close to despair. Torment, for all his size and power, had been a living, breathing creature. He'd bled when she'd wounded him. The Ouroborean was like a machine, an engine woven of magic, a trip-hammer that would pound away, over and over, until something broke.

Or until it *does.*

She looked over her shoulder again. *Come on, Isaac.*

"We are not so different, Alice Creighton. I will eat my fill." The Ouroborean stalked closer. "And then I will have my revenge on those cowards who locked me away. You know how it feels to want revenge."

I'm not like you. And I'm not a coward. There was no time left. *We have to try.* Which meant, probably, that they would all be killed. She thought of Ellen's dead face, smoke pouring from her eyes and mouth, and swallowed hard.

"Dex," she said. "Go on the right. Jen and Michael, the left. Just try to keep it from grabbing me—"

The light reflecting off the flagstones took on an

orange-yellow tone. A voice like a crackling fire said, "And where do you want me?"

"Flicker!" Alice turned to see the fire-sprite emerging from the narrow crack between the bookshelves. Actinia was just behind him, his blue-tinted hair flaring to white at the tips. They both carried long black spears. "Pyros sent you to help?"

"Pyros said it was too dangerous," Actinia said. "But we came anyway."

"And when *I* heard there was a fight to be had," another voice said, "I followed."

From between two other shelves, Helga emerged, with Erdrodr on her heels. The older ice giant was just as Alice had last seen her, but Erdrodr had donned battle gear similar to her mother's, and carried a two-handed ax.

"We were at the fire-sprite village," Erdrodr said, "talking about trade. Then Isaac turned up."

Isaac squeezed through last of all, the edges of his coat scorched from his passage through the heat of the portal chamber. He sighed with relief at the sight of Alice. "I wasn't sure we'd made it in time."

"*Just* in time." Alice turned back to face the Ouroborean, who had paused to assess these new arrivals. "You told them the plan?"

"Keep it off of you," Flicker said.

"It doesn't *look* so dangerous," Helga said, unshipping first one massive ax, then another. She gave them a twirl between her fingers.

"It doesn't look like much of anything," Erdrodr said. "Not even worth sketching."

"You think this gives you a chance?" The Ouroborean's laugh was like a screech of radio noise. It approached, and Alice and her friends sprang forward to meet it.

Helga took the lead, shouting a war cry, her enormous strides outdistancing the others. She skidded to a halt just in front of the Ouroborean, planting her heel and letting her momentum pull her into a spin, putting all the force behind the swing of one of her massive axes. It caught the Ouroborean just below the shoulder, slicing entirely through its arm and biting deep into its torso. The severed limb fell away, evaporating like black mist before it hit the ground.

The Ouroborean brought its other arm around, a roundhouse blow aimed at Helga, only to find Erdrodr intercepting it with an overhead swing of her own ax. This one cut the creature's other arm off at the elbow, leaving it to flail hopelessly with the stump. Flicker and

Actinia circled behind her, spears at the ready, while Michael and Jen went around in the other direction.

"Are you sure you know what you're doing, Sister Alice?" Dex said.

"No," Alice said, and darted forward, dodging Helga's oversized feet.

Dex stayed by her side as she closed in, their heads only reaching the Ouroborean's waist. She put her arms around one of its legs, holding her own wrist, squeezing with all of Spike's strength to keep herself in place. Then she closed her eyes, and looked at it the way she'd looked at her own spells while Writing.

Down, down, down—

She felt the Ouroborean moving underneath her, a mesh of magical filaments in the crude shape of a living thing. She could feel what it felt, and she understood why it shrugged off blows and weapons. The shape was just a shape, a physical incarnation *of* the spell, but *not* the spell. It could be whatever it needed to be.

"Watch and learn, Reader." The buzzing voice resonated through Alice's skull.

The creature's severed shoulders rippled, and two new limbs emerged from each, as long and flexible as tentacles. A pair of them reached for Erdrodr; she chopped one

331

of them out of the way, but the other wrapped around her waist. The two fire-sprites rushed forward, skewering the tentacle with their spears, and the ice giant girl wriggled free. Two more tentacles reached for Helga, but her flashing ax blades cut them in half.

In the shadow-world of Writing, Alice tore at the structure of the Ouroborean, ripping the spell to pieces. It shredded in her mental grasp, no more substantial than cobweb, and it took her a moment to realize that she wasn't making any progress. The Ouroborean was intricate, interlaced with itself a thousand times over, and the pieces she ripped away were drawn back into alignment as though they'd never been torn.

"A fine effort," the Ouroborean buzzed. "But if the Readers could have destroyed me, don't you think they would have, long ago?"

Ripples spread from the creature's shoulders to its back, and more tentacles burst forth. Five, ten, twenty ribbons of darkness curving through the air, trying to get at Alice.

Her friends stood in their way, hacking and slashing and stabbing. Black mist flew around Helga, and Erdrodr severed tentacle after tentacle while Flicker and Actinia watched Alice's back. Michael's silver darts and Isaac's slashing blades of ice harried the twisting limbs, and Jen leaped onto the creature's back to slash the tentacles off at their roots with her claws. Dex stood directly in front of Alice, her swords intercepting anything that got too close.

"Your friends are persistent," the creature said. Alice felt its structure twist and shift. "But you have led them to their deaths."

Alice wanted to shout a warning, but that would mean returning her attention to the real world, and she didn't dare. She ripped at the structure of the spell, searching desperately for a way to hurt the Ouroborean faster than it rebuilt itself, bits of wrecked magic floating all around her.

More tentacles sprouted, and their tips were as sharp and hard as spears.

The Ouroborean redoubled its attack, slashing and stabbing instead of trying to grab. Helga's axes rang, ice blade against solid darkness. Erdrodr grunted and went to her knees, thick white blood flowing from a slash on her thigh, and Flicker and Actinia fought side by side with whirling spears, knocking back the creature's attacks as she limped away. Jen jumped clear of the thing's hide just before two tentacles skewered her, and she landed in front of Michael, deflecting another pair of attacks with her claws. Isaac ducked and dodged, and spear points glanced off Dex's armor with a metallic shriek as she slashed the tentacles away with her swords.

"Erdrodr!" Helga struggled to fight free and reach her daughter, but the Ouroborean's onslaught wouldn't let up. Ever more tentacles sprouted, hundreds of them, looping over and around until they blotted out the rest of the library in twisting, weaving darkness. They were all coming for Alice, to stab her, slice her, tear her apart for the temerity of what she was trying to do.

"I will drink all your lives," the creature buzzed, "and I will save you for last, Alice Creighton, so that you can watch all the others—"

Come on, come on. Alice felt tears leak from between her eyelids. *There has to be* something! *If you can make a spell, you have to be able to un-make it.* But it was so *complicated.* Just trying to trace the flows of power made her head throb, one branch twisting and looping around the next, complex and interwoven, like—

—a labyrinth.

She let her tight grip on the spell go, letting her mind roam over its complex framework. Power flowed, and she flowed with it, from one junction to the next, through corridors and rooms. Something tingled, an echo of what she felt when she touched the fabric of the library. *There has to be somewhere that it all comes together. Even the most complicated maze has—*

Someone screamed, and then choked off abruptly. Alice's heart double-thumped.

—a center.

She had it. A single junction, no different from any of the others. But all the flows united there. *This has to be it.* Alice reached down and tore it away.

"What?" the Ouroborean roared.

This time, the damage didn't repair itself. It spread, blocks tumbling, dominoes falling, a house of cards coming down. The intricate network collapsed, slowly at first but building speed as it went. Alice pulled herself back to reality, opened her eyes, and released her grip.

"Not possible!" The creature's voice rose to a frantic, buzzing shriek. "No *Reader* can destroy *me*! You—"

The Ouroborean had frozen in place, the silver thread woven through its black body flaring bright white. One of its tentacles had impaled Helga through the midsection, her hands gripping it where it punched into her stomach and came out her back. Erdrodr was screaming.

"Alice Creighton!" the Ouroborean wailed. "What *are* you?"

Slowly, the tip of each tentacle began to fade, coming apart into black mist. The disintegration sped up as it went, racing along the limbs to the hulking main body of the thing, no longer even vaguely human. With a final blast of static, the Ouroborean came apart, exploding into a dark fog that quickly faded altogether.

Helga smiled, wheezing, one hand pressed to a dark stain on her stomach.

"Ha," Helga said. "A good fight."

Then she collapsed, and Erdrodr went back to screaming.

CHAPTER TWENTY-NINE
DECLARATION OF WAR

SHE IS A GOOD girl, but over-inclined to worry,"
Helga said. "It will take a great deal more than this to slay
Helga the Ice Flower!"

"She wasn't the only one who was worried," Alice said.

She was sitting cross-legged beside the makeshift bed
they'd made for Helga in an alcove of the library, out of
several sets of bed linens and pillows from the house.
Erdrodr lay curled up and asleep by her mother's side.
Helga's wounds, and everyone else's, had been sealed by
the same numbing ice they'd once used to treat Alice.
The stuff went on like a thick plaster, and it apparently
worked wonders, since Helga was already sitting up in
bed.

I'll have to get her to leave some of it here. Having something better for first aid than a bandage would be welcome.

"I'll admit it was a hotter battle than I'd anticipated," Helga said. "Had I the time, I'd have brought a few more of my warriors along."

"We're just lucky you were in the fire-sprite village when Isaac got there," Alice said.

She'd sent Isaac running for the portal-book, looking for anything that might help stop the Ouroborean. Since summoned creatures and magic were useless, she'd reasoned that regular spears and axes might help. *But if Helga hadn't been there . . .* Flicker and Actinia had defied their elder's order and come to her aid, but on their own, Alice wasn't sure they'd have been enough.

"Lucky for both of us. I got to repay my debt to you, for keeping my willful daughter safe." Helga stroked Erdrodr's hair fondly. "She is a warrior after all."

Looking at the two of them, mother and daughter, made something in Alice's chest ache. She did her best to smile. "She's a warrior *and* an artist."

"True enough."

"Thank you," Alice said. "For everything. This was all my fault."

"And you took responsibility for it." Helga waved a hand. "I understood only a little of what your Isaac said, but this creature would have threatened our world too. Better to fight it here, with you at our side."

"He's not really *my* Isaac," Alice muttered.

"No? I hear his voice when he speaks of you, and I think . . ." Helga gave a crafty smile. "Well. You are young. You will learn, in time."

Alice, blushing, wondered exactly how much Helga could know about it. She'd yet to work up the courage to ask if there *were* male ice giants and, if so, what role they played. Fortunately, she was saved from further discussion on the subject by a faint scrape of claws on stone. Alice looked around and found Ending's yellow eyes gleaming from the shadows of the nearest library aisle.

"Ah," Helga said, her own eyes narrowing. "You had better go."

Alice nodded and got to her feet. Ending's tail whipped back and forth, slashing the air like a metronome.

"Alice," she rumbled. "Will you walk with me?"

Alice fell into step beside the huge cat. "Is everything all right?" she said. "With your siblings, I mean."

"For now," Ending said. "The other labyrinthine have retreated, and we can expect a breathing space. The old

Readers cannot be certain what happened, but fear of the Ouroborean will keep them away for a time."

"How long do we have?"

"I cannot say with certainty. Weeks, perhaps a month. Even if they dare not use the portals, they can send creatures to spy on us across the physical world."

A month. Compared to the frantic pace of the last twenty-four hours, it seemed like an eternity, but also like no time at all. *How much can we possibly accomplish in a month?*

Into the silence that followed, Ending said, "I am sorry."

"For what?"

"I told you to find *The Infinite Prison.* I knew using it on Geryon would free whatever was inside, but I assumed it would be something I could easily deal with. I never expected the Ouroborean. Its very presence tore up the labyrinth and blinded me to what had happened. I was ... too confident." She paused. "I asked Ashes to tell you to run."

"He did," Alice said. "Did you really expect me to?"

"No," the big cat said. "I expected you to die."

Another pointed silence.

"I'm sorry to have disappointed you," Alice said.

Ending turned her head toward Alice and gave her a toothy smile. "I should have known better. You have a habit of doing the impossible." The labyrinthine stopped just ahead of another intersection. "What will you do now?"

"I thought about that, a little," Alice said.

"And?"

Alice laid out her plan, trying hard not to stammer. When she was finished, Ending blinked slowly, and then gave a deep, rumbling chuckle.

"You don't think it will work?" Alice said.

"I'm not in a position to say," Ending said. "I believe you are the one I have been looking for all these years."

"Someone you can work with," Alice said. "A partner, instead of a master."

"A rare thing. A Reader who does not think like a Reader," Ending said. "Who turns against abusing her power. Why?"

"Because it's wrong. It's cruel."

"Rare indeed," Ending murmured.

"You'll help?" Alice hesitated. "I don't think I can do it without you. I never would have gotten *this* far without you."

"At this point, I have little choice," Ending said. "My lot is cast. But for what it is worth, I think you are right. I will help as best I can."

"Thank you."

On impulse, Alice reached out to touch the fur on Ending's shoulder. Her hand sank into it, the downy black softer than the softest of pillows. Ending's tail lashed again.

"They are waiting for you, by Mr. Wurms' table," Ending said. "The library creatures and the apprentices. I asked Ashes to bring them together. You had better speak to them."

Alice nodded, then thought of something and swallowed hard. "What about . . . Ellen? Is she . . ."

"I have put her body somewhere safe," Ending said gently. "When we are finished, I will show you a place where she can be buried."

"Thank you." Alice straightened up. "I guess it's time to face the crowd, then."

"It is."

She gave a weak chuckle. "I think the Ouroborean was less terrifying."

"Was it?" Ending said.

Alice shook her head. "No."

She took a deep breath and stepped around the corner, from *here* to *there*.

They were all gathered, all the creatures who'd come to her looking for reassurance after Geryon had disappeared—the clockwork spider, the sprites, the woman in bones, the bent-backed old man with his mushrooms. There was no sign of Mr. Black, but Mr. Wurms was there, having crawled out of who-knew-what hidey-hole. Helga was still in bed, of course, but Erdrodr stood at the edge of the crowd, her slate out, sketching frantically. Flicker and Actinia were in the front row, long black spears at their sides.

The other apprentices were there too. Isaac, Dex, Michael, and Jen stood together, a little separate from the rest. They were covered in patches of healing ice, and looked worried and exhausted. *And no wonder. I was fighting to defend my home. They may have lost theirs. They can't go back to their masters, not now.*

Ashes walked back and forth on the now bench-less table, stepping lightly over the scattered books.

"Thank goodness," he said, when Alice arrived. "This lot is getting fractious. I—hey!"

Alice scooped the cat into her arms and planted a kiss on his fuzzy forehead.

"What was that for?" Ashes sputtered. "What have I ever done to deserve that?"

"I wanted to say thank you," Alice said, putting him on the ground. "For everything."

"Yes, well. Far be it from me to dispute my own heroism," Ashes muttered. "But proper thanks should involve tuna."

Alice laughed. "I'll keep that in mind."

She clambered onto the table and raised her hands for silence. This time, the murmuring died away easily, and she felt every eye fixed on her. Alice looked out over the crowd and suddenly felt the weight of her exhaustion. *It's been a very long day.*

"My name is Alice Creighton," she said. "I am a Reader."

Near the back, someone coughed. The clockwork spider hummed and clanked.

"Master Geryon took me as his apprentice when he found out I had the Reader talent. He didn't give me a choice, or"—Alice found Emma's blank face in the crowd, beside Mr. Wurms—"not *much* of a choice. The same is true of all the other apprentices I've met. I imagine it's not too different for most of you." She nodded at Flicker. "The fire-sprites, say, didn't ask to be part of Geryon's . . .

empire, his domain, whatever you want to call it. But it was that, or be prey for one of the other Readers."

"Everybody knows all of that," the bone woman called out.

"I know." Alice took another deep breath. "I went to Esau's fortress hoping to find out what happened to my father. I had thought he might be alive somewhere. I was wrong. He's dead, and Geryon and Esau killed him."

She heard a gasp from Dex and pushed on in spite of the pain in her chest.

"I wanted revenge. I went looking for a way to get it, and I found one. I trapped Geryon in a place where he'll never be able to hurt anyone ever again."

That brought a mutter from the crowd. The clockwork spider raised a sign that said, QUERY: HOW? Others shouted or shook their fists, at her or at one another.

"What's important," Alice said, raising her voice, "is that I didn't think about what would happen afterward. To me, and to all of you. I want to apologize for that."

"Fat lot of good that does us," the bone woman said. "It's too late!"

"It is too late," Alice agreed over a number of similar shouts. "All I can tell you is what I'm going to do now."

"You're going to take his place!" said one of the sprites.

"No. I won't. I won't because no one *should* have that kind of power. All of this"—she spread her hands to encompass the library with its millions of books, the estate, the whole world—"is a system the old Readers created for their own benefit. They'll do anything to defend it. When they realized that the Ouroborean was loose, they sent a spell here that would have walled off the library, leaving everyone in it to die. It would have killed their own apprentices, but that didn't stop them.

"If they were scared before, now they'll be terrified. We've *beaten* the Ouroborean. We're a threat to them. They may wait for a while, but they'll be back."

Silence had returned. Even the spider had quieted herself. Alice hesitated, just for a moment.

"I'm going to fight them," she said. "I'm going to tear it all down, the whole thing. The libraries, the prison-books, the tribute. Everything. I'm going to take away every bit of power they've ever used to hurt anyone, in any world. They've controlled us for long enough.

"I don't know if I'll win. But I do know I'm going to need help. Ending asked me to be a different kind of Reader, a partner instead of a master. So that's what I'm going to do. You're all welcome to join me."

In the deepest recesses of her heart, she'd expected

cheers. Applause, at least. *Something.* But the crowd of strange creatures simply stood, silent, as though they'd all been hypnotized. Then the spider's sign clicked and whirred.

HYPOTHESIS:, she said. SUICIDAL INSANITY.

That broke the spell. Everyone was suddenly talking at once, arguments rising in a dozen places, a babble of voices that threatened to overwhelm her. Alice hopped down from the table and went to her fellow apprentices, who stood in a tight group off to one side.

"That could have gone better," said Ashes, who'd joined them.

"They're just scared," Isaac said.

"Of course they are scared," Dex said. "No one stands up to the old Readers. No one ever has."

"Is it true, what you said about your father?" Jen said.

Alice nodded. Dex hugged her.

"Oh, Alice," she said. "I'm so sorry."

"You know I'm with you," Isaac said. "I can't go back to my master, not now. He probably thinks I'm dead."

"The Most Favored . . ." Dex hesitated, her ever-present smile flickering. "I wish to say that she would never sacrifice me to the Ouroborean. But I am not certain. I have realized . . . how little I am certain of."

"I'm staying with you," Michael said. They all looked at him, including Jen.

"Why?" Jen said. "You barely know her!"

"Because she's right," the boy said simply. He pushed his glasses up his nose and ventured a smile. "Shouldn't that be enough?"

Jen let out an exaggerated sigh. "Then I guess I have to stay as well. Someone has to take care of you."

"Thank you," Alice said. "All of you."

"Girl!" said someone behind her.

Alice turned to find the woman dressed in bones looking down at her. She cut a large, impressive figure, with long dark hair bound back in a no-nonsense bun.

"I'm sorry," Alice said again. "I know it's not enough, but—"

"Never mind that. You're really going to stand up to the old Readers?"

"I'm going to try," Alice said.

"It's about damn time *someone* did," the woman said. "They're a pack of nasty cowards, if you ask me. If there's anything I can do, just ask."

"Oh!" Alice shook her head. "Thank you. I didn't think—"

"Goes for me too," said the old mushroom man, edging

around the bone woman. "Never heard a Reader talk like you do."

A half-dozen sprites yammered excited agreement, until the bone woman shushed them.

"I think most of the others will come around too," she said. "If they don't, I'll tan their hides."

"I don't want anyone to help if it's not of their own free will," Alice said hastily.

"Right," the woman said. "They'll decide to do it of their own free will, or I'll tan their hides."

"And I'm going to talk to Pyros," Flicker said, cutting in before Alice could pursue that argument. "Once he hears what happened, I think he'll agree it's safer for us to help you than do nothing."

"Please don't think too badly of him," Actinia said anxiously. "He just has to do what's best for our people."

"I know," Alice said. "And thank you." She raised her voice. "Thank all of you!"

"Well," Ashes said, from somewhere by her ankles. "It's a start."

CHAPTER THIRTY

THE CIRCLE IS NOW COMPLETE

THERE WAS ONE MORE thing she had to do.

Sitting at Mr. Wurms' table, after sending all the others away, Alice put one hand on the cover of *The Infinite Prison*. Ending had fetched it from its hiding place, deep in the library. Alice closed her eyes and let her awareness brush the edge of the spell, just lightly.

She found herself in a dark place, with no floor or walls or ceiling. Geryon stood in front of her, and beside her, and behind her, mirrored and replicated over and over. All the Geryons looked surprised to see her, the same brief moment of shock copied a million-fold. Then their whiskered faces smoothed to the usual calm.

"Alice," he said. "Have you come to get me out of here?"

"No," Alice said, biting back the "sir."

His eyes narrowed. "Then it *was* you. A clever trick, I have to admit. Where did you find it?"

"It's not important. I want you to answer a question."

"What?" Geryon frowned. "Don't presume to dictate to me—"

"I'll presume whatever I like," Alice snapped. "You're in no position to argue. Now answer the question. *Did you kill my father?*"

He crossed his arms, glaring daggers. Alice shrugged.

"Have it your way," she said. "I'll be back. Eventually."

She paused a few heartbeats, and the old Reader cracked.

"Wait!" he said. "Wait. Please."

"Well?" she said.

"Yes," Geryon said, a fragment of his composure returning. "You obviously know this already. I was there the night the *Gideon* sank, though it wasn't until afterward that I realized the importance of what had happened."

"You didn't even *know*," Alice said. "You killed him and you didn't even *know* what you were doing."

"He was a human," Geryon said. "Humans die."

"We're human too."

"No, we're not," Geryon said. "We're different from them. You know that. If you left here, went back to one of their cities, would you be able to feel like you were a part of it? The same as the rest of them?"

"I . . ." Alice paused.

"You have power that no king or president ever dreamed of," Geryon said. "You're confused, I understand. But—"

"Enough," Alice said.

"Who put you up to this?" Geryon said. "Anaxomander? The Eddicant? Or—" He caught her eye and his face went pale. "No. It wasn't any of them, was it? It was *Ending*."

"What if it was?" Alice said. "You've treated her just like your other slaves."

"Oh, child. You have no idea what you've done, what powers you are dealing with." Geryon shook his head. "She is a *labyrinthine*. You have to let me out of here. I will swear any oath that you care to name that I will take no retribution against you, I'll give you whatever you wish, but you have to let me out."

"I don't have to do anything of the sort," Alice said. "I

will let you out, eventually. But there are some things I need to do first."

Geryon was getting frantic. "You can't trust Ending. You can't trust *any* of them. The labyrinthine lie as naturally as breathing—it's what they *are*. You think we've kept them bound all this time just to be cruel? If she gets what she wants, it won't just be the Readers who pay the price."

"I don't know if I can trust Ending," Alice said, shaking her head. "But I *know* I can't trust you."

"Alice! You don't understand! Please—"

Alice opened her eyes and took her hand off the book, Geryon's pleading scream ringing in her ears.

She went back up to the house after saying good night to the others. It was actually only mid-afternoon, and the sun and snow of the outside world came as a shock after so long in the gloom of the library. The invisible servants made her roast beef and vegetable soup, and she had three helpings, along with a big mug of hot chocolate. Then she had a bath, soaking away the dirt and sweat and prodding her bruises.

When she was clean, she dressed in her nightshirt and brushed her hair. She patted the ancient, threadbare rabbits in the window, pulled back the covers, and got into bed. Enough sun leaked past the window shade that it wasn't truly dark, but she could feel sleep tugging at her already.

"I'm going to tear it all down," she whispered.

She dreamed of her father, smiling at her as he had so often in life, the smile that meant he loved her more than anything in the world. And she dreamed of a huge, cat-slitted silver eye, vast and alien, that somehow felt like home.

END

ACKNOWLEDGMENTS

I have run out of pets for the dedication, unless you count parakeets and goldfish. Instead, this time I thank all the hardworking cats of the world, who spend countless hours every day carefully training their humans.

First, I need to thank everyone who read my early drafts: Robyn Murphy, who met up with me at Phoenix Comic-Con to assure me I was on the right track; Cat Rambo, whose reading speed and critical eye practically count as superpowers; and Casey Blair, who managed to find time to help me in spite of her own insane schedule. All three are excellent writers, and my work is always better for their assistance.

Second, as always, my agent Seth Fishman (who doubles as a draft reader in his own right!) and everyone else at the Gernert Company: Will Roberts, Rebecca Gardner, and Andy Kifer. Also as usual, Caspian Dennis at Abner Stein keeps everything going on the UK side.

Third, my editor, Kathy Dawson, and her assistant, Claire Evans, who are insightful and endlessly patient with me.

Fourth, Alexander Jansson, whose covers and artwork continue to be one of the highlights of writing this series.

Fifth, all the excellent people at Penguin and publishers around the world who bring these words to physical (or digital) reality. In particular, this time I'd like to thank the people at Penguin Young Readers who set up visits and Skype sessions with classrooms and libraries across the country. (If you're a teacher or librarian, check them out: www.penguinclassroom.com.)

Finally, of course, my thanks to readers everywhere. I hope you're all having as much fun with Alice's adventures as I am.

DJANGO WEXLER

is a self-proclaimed computer/fantasy/sci-fi geek. He graduated from Carnegie Mellon University with degrees in creative writing and computer science, worked in artificial intelligence research and as a programmer/writer for Microsoft, and is now a full-time fantasy writer. Django is the author of The Shadow Campaigns, an epic fantasy series for adults published by Roc (an imprint of Penguin), and The Forbidden Library, a classic fantasy series for young readers published by Kathy Dawson Books (an imprint of Penguin Young Readers Group).

Learn more at www.DjangoWexler.com, and follow Django on Facebook and Twitter (@DjangoWexler).